GIVE UP THE GHOST

A VIOLA VALENTINE MYSTERY

CHERIE CLAIRE

CONTENTS

CHAPTER 1

*I*t's well below freezing and the wind that's biting my face in anger blows in above the sparkling *blue* waters of Green Bay.

"You can see Michigan from here," our guide announces.

No one disputes this piece of information while I stand there shivering from my lack of winter protection, trying to imagine how Michigan got on top of Wisconsin. And you can bet that question isn't coming out of this Southerner's mouth.

We're in Door County, a peninsula that stretches up from the mainland of Wisconsin like the thumb on a left-handed mitten. Lake Michigan flows on the eastern side of the peninsula but today we're visiting Peninsula State Park on the west side, which faces Green Bay with its namesake city further south where the mitten's thumb and hand meet.

I sneak a glance at Winnie Calder, another travel writer who has turned into one of my best buds since our first press trip almost three years ago in Eureka Springs. Winnie's from my neighboring state of Mississippi and she's looking as lost as last year's Easter egg. I lean in and ask the dreaded question, hoping her quizzical look isn't the result of it being butt-numbing cold.

"Michigan?" I ask sheepishly.

Winnie shrugs. "I thought it was on the other side."

Thank you, Winnie. Stupidity loves company.

She leans in close so no one hears. "We'll check the map when we get in the car."

I nod because I've already been chastised for bringing a lightweight coat on this trip. I thought my Dillard's special with its faux fur collar was sufficient since it has kept me warm during the past few winters in South Louisiana—although most winters are mere weeks with above-average temperatures, thanks to Global Warming that has sent us six hurricanes in three years. I did remember to bring my mittens, so I should get some pie, but I expect my toes to crack off any minute now. Who needs Botox with this frigid wind?

I look around and all the travel writers born above the Mason-Dixon Line appear cozy in their down jackets, scarves wrapped tightly around their cheeks. Some have even braved photographs but my hands are never leaving my pockets until the temperature rises above forty.

"When's lunch?" I ask Winnie.

I don't eat breakfast, just a milked-down coffee and a cracker these days. It's all I can manage until the sun's high in the sky. Right now, it's nearing its zenith and I'm starving.

Winnie sends me a look as if she can read my secret. I'm closing in on my second trimester but haven't told a soul, not even my husband. TB hasn't suspected, even though my clothes have been shrinking and I'm barely eating. But then, bless his heart, TB isn't the sharpest tool in the shed.

"What?" I ask, feeling my blood pressure rise and almost hearing cartoon birds chirping around my head. I don't wait for Winnie to respond, don't ask for permission from our PR professionals leading this trip, simply head back to the van before I fall face down into the Bay of Green.

Unfortunately, Winnie's hot on my heels.

"Vi," I hear her say to my back, but I'm too focused on getting into a warm car and placing my head between my legs. I've fainted once before, thankfully without doing myself harm. I rose from the couch too fast while watching *Jeopardy*—I had nailed the final question and was jumping up to reward myself with a chocolate Yoo-hoo—and whatever blood existed in my face fell immediately to my toes and I was out cold. I woke up with my cat Stinky licking my face, grateful the couch took my fall and not my houseboat's hard wooden floors.

Of course, I told no one.

I pull the van's side door open and slip inside, grateful to be sitting and out of that horrid wind. I leave the side door open, allowing the fresh air to relieve the nausea rising in me.

And to abate the stink of rotting fish.

I turn toward the bane of my press trip existence, a scrappy thirty-something man covered in ruddy hair, his face almost completely hidden by the thickest beard I've ever seen, reminding me of the man on the cover of the Gorton's fish sticks box. He's dressed in a heavy yellow waterproof coat that my friend from Boston calls a "slicker," a thick corded sweater underneath, and matching yellow work boots up to his shins, ones we call Cajun Reeboks back home.

He's not alive, of course, but that's not why he stinks.

"What do you want?" I ask again, even though I know this ghost doesn't talk. Many of them don't.

I see ghosts on a regular basis, but only ones who have died by water. I saw all manner of apparitions when I was young but repressed the ability when people didn't believe me or deemed me crazy. When Hurricane Katrina came barreling through my hometown of New Orleans in 2005, four years ago, the trauma pushed that psychic door wide open. Only now, I'm limited to ghosts who have perished in a watery death, like this fellow who no doubt fell off a fishing vessel.

I'm called a SCANC, a ridiculous anachronism I did not

invent, one that stands for a person who has Specific Communication with Apparitions, Non-entities and the Comatose. My specialty is water. I'm not alone; apparently, the world is full of SCANCs. I even attended a SCANC convention last fall with my other travel writing bud, Carmine Kelsey, who wears this title as well. Carmine's also a descendant of angels—apparently way back when angels ignored God and did a little hanky panky with humans—and I'm carrying witchy DNA from a long line of mediums and witches thanks to my crazy Alabama ancestors. But, front and center are the ghosts who never stop reaching out.

The fish smell is getting the best of me and I know I'm going to retch if this ghost doesn't move on.

"Dude, I can't help you if you don't talk," I say. "Plus, I'm pregnant so if you don't speak or get out of here, I'm going to hurl what little breakfast I managed to eat."

The man stares at me, looking confused, and I wonder if the newly dead — those vinyl boots with the L.L. Bean logo make me think this was recent — haven't learned to communicate with the living yet. I don't have time to wait for whatever reaction he will offer me because that tiny cracker is making itself know. I'm about to head out of the van, back into the frozen north wind when Winnie appears, her hand holding the sliding door open, her face sending me a mom look.

"Vi, what's going on?"

I look back at Mr. Gorton and he's disappeared. So, is the fish smell. I take a deep breath of the fresh air and my stomach calms down.

"Not feeling too hot."

"No kidding. You're a puke shade of green."

I offer up my best fake smile. I'm not ready to discuss my current disposition, not until I tell TB. My husband started school at Smoky Mountain University in southeastern Tennessee a few weeks ago and I've been waiting for the school health insurance to kick in before I visit a doctor and find out what's what. Only problem, the school doesn't offer its students full healthcare. My husband agreed to work with his uncle's construction company one weekend a month in exchange for our healthcare coverage. Once I get back to Tennessee and get checked out I'll spill the beans. For now, though, it feels wrong to discuss my situation with anyone else before I tell my husband.

Especially considering all we've been through.

"I'll be okay. When's lunch?"

Winnie's not having it. She's a mom of three, raises goats on a farm outside Oxford, Mississippi, and writes travel for several freelance outlets, including the popular blog, *Might as Well be Talkin' to a Fence Post*. She sends me the stink eye, letting me know she sees right through me.

Just then the rest of the group arrives, huddling around the van but not yet climbing inside, even though the brutal temperatures and wind must be getting to them as well. This dance around the van happens often on press trips. We're all journalists, whether on staff at publications or freelance, like me. Destinations around the country charge hotel and motel taxes and share that money with local economic development offices or tourism, who then invite press to their towns, putting us up at lovely accommodations, feeding us well, and showing us sites like the beautiful, but cold, Door County Peninsula Park. They almost always pick us up at the airport and drive us around in vans and buses.

Here's the rub. No one likes to sit in the back of the van. You must climb over seats, stumble over seatbelts that get tangled in your feet, squeeze into tight spaces. Which is why everyone's milling about, some checking their phones, others looking at photos they captured on digital cameras. If you wait long enough, other writers will climb into the back and then the van's second aisle is free and so is the passenger side in the front. Usually on every press trip, there's one or two people who hang back while others pile inside. Sometimes, there's even a person or two who claims car sickness and immediately climbs in front.

I'm a Southern girl taught to give up seats to my elders and most of the time I'm one of the younger journalists on the trip, unless the destination brings in bloggers. I'm also not one to stand around while others are pretending work so they can nab a choice seat. I just huff and climb in the back.

This morning, I'm not in the mood.

"Okay, everyone," says our guide Nellie Peters, hoping to get everyone on board. "We're off to lunch."

Two or three people glance up but they're not moving.

"Pa-leese," says Winnie under her breath in her thick Mississippi accent and climbs in the back. She hasn't left the van's rear since arriving two nights before.

I usually follow her but today I'm feeling aggressive. Funny, how pregnancy does that to you, taking over your body and mind and giving you superhuman strength. I won't be picking up this van like Wonder Woman but I will stand up for the disagreeable creature inside of me who's demanding sustenance. I open the front door and climb into the passenger seat, pull the door close before the editor of a Wisconsin cheese magazine will object. She's been complaining about headaches since day one — only during van rides, of course. I must admit, picking the front also keeps me from having to explain more to Winnie.

We travel to a quaint town located on the Lake Michigan side—thankfully not too far away—and pile out, Miss Cheddar complaining about her head the whole time. I find a seat inside the café next to my favorite couple, Stephanie and Joe Pennington, who produce an award-winning newsletter, a radio show, and webinars on travel. I've traveled with them before and still feel guilty for doubting Joe's photography skills. Sometimes husbands join wives (and vice versa) and pose as photographers to get a free trip but Joe's the top in his field, producing stunning photographs and videos. The Penningtons are also from Wisconsin so I pick their brain every chance I can.

I lean in close. "Why is Michigan on that side of Door County?"

Stephanie doesn't judge, simply takes out a pen and draws how Michigan rises north toward Canada, but there's a piece to the left that hangs over Wisconsin. I smile my thanks, all the while shoving crackers into my mouth.

"Slow down," Joe says with a laugh. "You know they're going to feed us well."

Another thing about press trips. You never go hungry. Even if they didn't feed you enormous meals to showcase the destination's culinary prowess, they leave you snacks in the hotel room. Every time I go on a press trip I swear I will watch my intake and not eat the Hershey Kisses and local food products the PR people have left in the room, usually in a fancy shopping bag with coffee cups, brochures, and other remembrances of the visit. Of course, I eat the snacks. I'm a freelance writer so money is scarce and I never know when I'll eat as well. At least that's how I'm spinning it.

Right now, I'm starving but as soon as I down several crackers I'm reminded why I'm hungry. The green monster has returned.

Or maybe it's that fish smell again.

I look up to see Gorton staring at me through the front glass of the restaurant, his gaze painfully pleading. A few expletives leave my lips, along with some cracker spittle. I wipe my mouth and apologize. Another thing I hate about being pregnant, I turn into a slob.

Just as that thought hits my brain, guilt pours through me. For not the first time in my thirty-year life, I wonder if my lack of being happy the first time I was with child brought on what happened to Lillye. In all honesty, it's the main reason I haven't told TB. I know it's crazy to think my daughter died because I didn't want a child fresh out of college, but my emotions are raw these days.

I push that horrid feeling aside and rise, placing my napkin in my chair. "Excuse me," I tell the group.

I grab my jacket and enter the parking lot. I don't care if anyone sees me talking to air, I just want this man and his nasty odor gone.

"What do you want?" I say too harshly.

He doesn't answer but this time his lips move slightly.

"I can't help you if you don't tell me." I pull my jacket tight around my chest. "And I'm freezing out here. I was born in New Orleans fish man."

He stares at me with those vacant eyes and, although I feel sorry for the man, I just want him to tell me the message and let me ease the grumbling in my innards.

"Last chance?" I say when nothing happens. "I'm leaving in the morning and I really don't want you around tonight. We're going to a fish boil, whatever that is, and I'm exhausted from not sleeping well and throwing up every morning so I need a break."

Still nada.

"Okay, then."

I turn around and head back inside when I feel a small earthquake. I look back at my fisherman who I swear is the guy on the Gorton's box and he's stomping his feet on the asphalt, looking as if he's happy the movement entered my physical plane.

"Okay, cool." I don't know what else to say. "Well done, ghost Jedi."

His confidence is rising and he looks around, hoping to find a way to communicate. He spots the restaurant sign and points, first to an M and then to a B.

"MB?"

The smile he delivers is almost blinding.

"What's an MB?" I ask and his smile fades.

He glances at the sign again, but this time in frustration. I'm about to think this is hopeless when he sees an advertisement for a lawyer on the back of a bench. He points to the word, "Accident."

Now we're getting somewhere. "You had an accident at sea?"

He frowns, frustrated.

Then I think of why most ghosts reach out to me. "It wasn't an accident?"

He nods, thrilled I got the message.

"Out there?" I point to Lake Michigan.

That aggravated look returns and he shakes his head.

"Some other place that involves water."

He puts a finger to his nose like a contestant in Charades.

I pull my jacket tight across my chest, feeling peevish and ready to be warm again. "Is that it? I'm freezing here."

The sadness in those eyes makes my pity come, as my Aunt Mimi likes to say. He seems like a nice guy and I'm sorry I was so abrupt. I'm about to tell him as much when he evaporates. Poof, he's gone. But the smell lingers for some reason. And in that moment I revisit those crackers I hurriedly ate only moments before.

As I'm barfing in the shrubs, guess who shows up? I feel Winnie's soothing hand on my back. "How far along are you?"

I straighten, feel so much better, and once again I'm ravished. I'd kill for a sweet tea right now.

"Ten to twelve weeks maybe," I say. "It happened on November eighteenth."

We're into February in the great year of 2009 so I'm pretty accurate, although the way my clothes are filling out it feels like I'm further along.

"When's your due date?"

I accept the handkerchief Winnie's offering and wipe my face. "There's the rub. I don't know yet. Sometime in August probably."

"What did the doctor say and why the big secret?"

I look over and see the group watching us through the window. "Later. Okay?"

We head toward the restaurant and retake our seats, me ordering a club sandwich with potato salad, plus an iced tea that I saturate with sugar while everyone stares. Nothing I hate more than having to *add* sugar to tea, but it is Wisconsin. Someone comments about my four empty sugar packets and I look at Winnie who's fighting back a laugh. In the South, sugar is a food group.

"You sure you're okay to eat all that?" Stephanie asks when our meal arrives.

Now that the clock hands are moving on the right side of noon, I'm going to be fine.

After lunch, we have an afternoon filled with activities — museums, shopping, and a trip to a cherry company. Door County is known for its tart Montmorency cherries and boy are these delicious and yes, I eat my fill. I bypassed snowshoeing due to my condition and good thing, considering the lack of winter garments I possess. But even without attending the sports track of the trip, I'm pooped by the time we return to the hotel. I'm heading toward my room and a nap but Winnie will hear none of it. She grabs my fur collar and pulls me toward the lobby, pushing me into one of their oversized chairs by the fireplace.

"'Fess up."

I shrug. "I'm pregnant."

That stink eye returns.

I exhale loudly and she plops into the chair beside me, throwing down her bags of souvenirs she purchased from the cherry store.

"TB and I are back together."

Again, that look. "Uh, know that, girlfriend."

"And the last time we...." I raise my eyebrows and smile.

"Uh huh."

"...we weren't so careful. And here I am, a twosome."

She pats down her jeans as if they need patting down. "Why the big secret?"

So many reasons. My chest tightens thinking of the child I may be bringing into this world.

"TB was studying at LSU and it was taking forever, especially since working full-time with his uncle in New Orleans. Baton Rouge is a good hour away."

"That's why you moved to Tennessee."

I nod. "Smoky Mountain University offered him a chance to finish his degree in two semesters. It meant TB going full-time so we sold our house in New Orleans and bought a small houseboat in a town near the school."

Winnie knows all this, because I explained as much last month when I called and gave her my new address. She crosses her arms about her chest, waiting for more.

I lean forward, recalling the conversation I had with TB at Thanksgiving after we had been careless with our lovemaking. He had insisted that if I got pregnant he would give up his dream of being a research librarian and continue his construction job, a position he no longer enjoyed. Ever since Hurricane Katrina, when my newspaper job floated away and I became a travel writer, TB has assisted me in various ways, and learned how much he loved research. Like Joe Pennington, TB has become my partner in other ways.

Funny, how life screws with your head. In 1997, TB and I married after I became pregnant at LSU, his parents gifted us a house back in New Orleans, and I gave up a plum Washington internship to work the cops beat with *The New Orleans Post*. In all honesty, marrying TB and giving up *my* dream was devastating, but Lillye entering the world made it all right. The three of us were so happy for those fleeting five years. When leukemia took her away, TB and I entered Zombieland and I knew it was time to move on when Katrina stole the rest of our lives. I moved to Lafayette, two hours outside of New Orleans, and followed my dream job as travel writer while TB restored our water-damaged house. And somehow, we both grew and realized we belonged together anyway.

But having another child scares the crap out of me.

"I've been waiting for the health insurance to kick in," I explain to Winnie. "But, really, I don't know how I'm going to tell TB. And I don't know how to feel about this."

The tears pour down my face without warning and Winnie pulls me into her arms. She knows about Lillye and the tumultuous years following the Storm from Hell in 2005 when I learned I was a SCANC and then later, a witch.

Talk about a crazy three years!

And then there's Dwayne.

"I've been having nightmares about Natchez," I whisper.

Winnie shivers as if a skunk crawls on her grave, as my grandmother loved to say. "Understandable. You nearly got killed."

The fire crackles and pops and my heart jumps. I'm seriously worried about my blood pressure because my chest tightens again. As if she feels my anxiety, Winnie takes my hand and squeezes. "That man's lingering in some dank hole somewhere."

If only.

"Something's not right, Winnie. It's like Dwayne's in my head lately. Every night."

She leans in close and squeezes my hand. "That's also understandable. You, of all people should know how trauma messes with your head."

True dat. I had water dreams for months after Katrina.

Now, *I* lean in, whisper loud enough to be heard over the

popping of the fireplace. "You don't think he's messing with my mind, do you? Like sneaking in there in the night?"

Winnie stares at me for a few moments, no doubt wondering if I'm serious. Winnie was with me last fall on a press trip up the Natchez Trace in Mississippi so she's in on the angel thing, but I doubt she knows Dwayne's predilection. He carries angelic markers, too, only his ancestor was Lucifer.

She shakes her head. "I don't know anything about that woo woo stuff you and Carmine mess with…."

Mess with? More like born with, saddled with, cursed with?

"…but it's more than likely your mind trying to make sense of things, or fears bubbling through. I never stop dreaming of that time I slept late and raced to my biology class across campus and missed the whole final."

I cringe at the thought. I've had those dreams too. And there's the one where I stand naked on stage forgetting my lines to *Steel Magnolias*. Man, I hate that one.

I lean back in my chair and relax. Perhaps Winnie's right.

She leans back too. "It's the pregnancy. With my last child, I dreamed I was birthing a goat."

It's just what I need to relieve the tension and get my mind away from that horrid man. I snort with laughter and Winnie joins me. It doesn't take long for us to be roaring.

"And we're not even drinking," Winnie says, wiping her eyes.

We talk more, basically Winnie assuring me all will be well, that I'll give birth to a healthy child, TB will be thrilled, and we'll finally move on with our lives. I hope for the first two and doubt the last, but I smile and offer hugs which makes her feel like she's done her job.

The sun's disappearing and our last night will be outside—help me Jesus—so I head up to the room to change into something warmer, namely piling on lightweight long-sleeved shirts on top of each other, covered by that unsubstantial jacket.

We head to a fish boil dinner at the White Gull Inn, where a "boilmaster" grows an enormous fire, then places a massive pot of whitefish inside the fire's center. When he dramatically flings kerosene on the pile of wood a giant flame burns off the fish oil that has risen to the pot's top and cooks the fish nicely. The tradition hails back years, its origins in a community feeding plenty, but tonight it's drama at its best. When the fish is fully cooked, we all enjoy the lightly salted fish with extras, such as potatoes and onions, then Door County cherry pie for dessert. And now that the sun's fully set, I'm enjoying every last bite, laughing with Stephanie and Joe.

"How's that cute husband of yours?" Stephanie asks.

"In New Orleans," I say between bites of cherry pie. "Helping with the family business."

"Good man," Joe mumbles with his own mouth full of buttery crust.

The bonfire's toasting my back but I feel a warmth spread through my cheeks and tingle the roots of my hair. I can't wait to see my adorable husband, have those angelic arms about me. Can't wait to finally see a doctor and tell TB the good news.

The euphoria fades fast. As happy as another child will make us, the future's uncertain and scary as hell. I'm sure it's that way for all parents, but once you lose a child….

"You okay?" Joe asks me.

I nod and smile and try to focus on the wonderful evening. The fire's sending sparks into the universe and the crisp night air appears to make the stars that much brighter. It's been a fabulous trip with good friends, so I close my eyes and remind myself that most children born into the world are healthy and remain so, that what happened with Lillye won't happen again. But my chest feels heavy, like an invisible hand squeezing it tight.

I take a deep breath to steady myself, then rise with my empty plate.

"Can I take those?" I ask my friends, gather up their plates, and head to the restaurant cart full of dirty dishes that's waiting beyond the warmth and light of the fire.

It's there where Gorton awaits.

"Well, dang," I say to my now familiar ghost. "I thought I saw the last of you."

I'm kidding—sort of. I do want to help apparitions cross over but I'm tired, had a long day involving barfing and there's an early plane to catch in the morning. He appears frustrated, doing that foot stomping thing again. I place the dishes in the cart and wipe my hands on my jacket.

"Look, I don't know what it's like to be a ghost but the ones that talk say you have to relax, have to focus on communicating."

Gorton takes this in, appears as if he's breathing deeply—can ghosts do that?—and then swallows, if that's possible as well. His shoulders drop and he closes his eyes and it's then I notice a lone earring of three silver fish dangling from his right ear, glistening in the firelight. I stand there, staring off into the darkness to my friends at my back, waiting. Freezing too. Away from the fire it's frickin' cold.

Finally, when teeth start chattering and I'm about to hightail it back to the warmth of the fire, Gorton opens his eyes. And speaks.

"He's looking for you."

A rash of shivers run through me so violently I clamp my teeth together to keep from biting my tongue. I lift my collar tightly about my neck and wrap my arms about my body, then ask the one question of which answer I dread the most.

"Who?"

Gorton's fading fast. Whatever strength he managed to muster has gotten the best of him.

"Who?" I ask again.

Just before he slips away and the blackness descends he mutters, "Talk to MB."

We head back to the hotel since most of us must catch early flights after an hour or so drive into Green Bay. I attempt two calls to TB but they both go to voice mail. It's Monday night of the Martin Luther King Jr. weekend so he's likely on the interstate, driving from New Orleans back to our new home in Tennessee. He's easily distracted so he turns off his phone while he drives—not to mention plays seventies music too loud and sings so having the phone on would be senseless. I need to hear his voice tonight but I assure myself Gorton's dire message doesn't involve Dwayne. But it likely does. Who else would be looking for me?

I had become entranced with Dwayne on our trip to Natchez because he insisted I could develop my SCANCy abilities, evolve my talents to enable me to see my baby girl who did not die by water and therefore out of my reach. His solution, however, involved stealing the souls of the ghosts I helped move on. I didn't know this at first, and in my desperation to see Lillye, I almost followed him. Dwayne forced me to call forth a ghost whose mystery I had solved so he could steal her soul as she ascended into what we call the "God Light." I refused and he decided to kill me and take my soul instead. TB arrived in the nick of time, my cat Stinky gave Dwayne the scar of a lifetime, but Dwayne Garrett escaped police and is out there somewhere.

And apparently looking for me.

Sleep comes fitfully and I keep dreaming of Natchez. I wake before the sunrise, of course not feeling well, dress and head out the door. There's several of us in the van for this trip to the airport but our wonderful PR people have loaded us down with coffee and kolaches, a pastry with fruit in the center. I skip the latter, naturally, and we're silent for the ride, some writers grabbing the chance for a snooze. Once at the airport, we say our goodbyes and head to separate airlines. It's the Tuesday after a long weekend so it's surprisingly busy. I'm thankful because the crowds take my mind off my stomach and Dwayne.

I manage to sleep on the way to Atlanta—I live in the South so almost all my flights go through the Georgia capital—and then emerge like a zombie into the world's busiest airport. I'm hungry now, so I stop and pick up a biscuit at Sweet Georgia's Juke Joint, my favorite airport restaurant. I shove half in my mouth and keep the rest for later, then head toward my gate through the crowds.

And that's when I see him.

Dwayne's one hundred yards away, a bag over one shoulder and a Braves baseball cap on his head. He's staring at me through the throngs of humanity but it feels like the world has disappeared and he's the only face I see, that horrid scar down the side of his face and that cold steel gaze feeling as if he's reaching inside my heart.

I shake so hard my purse slips off my shoulder and something warm slides down my leg. I swear my heart has stopped beating and I gasp for breath. This is the end and I'm melting on the spot, I think to myself, like the wicked witch in The Wizard of Oz. Tears pour down my face and my knees buckle and I know I'm heading down.

And then, suddenly, two strong hands slip beneath my arms and hold me upright.

"I've got you," the angelic voice behind me says.

CHAPTER 2

$\mathcal{A}$ tall blonde woman in a military uniform arrives at my side, pulling one of my arms around her shoulder and grabbing my purse and suitcase with the other. She effortlessly leads me toward the women's bathroom and I stumble along without question. I gaze in the direction where I saw Dwayne but he's disappeared. Did I imagine the whole thing?

When we enter the women's room, my legs turn from Jell-O into working muscles and I remove my arm from my heroine's shoulder. She owns a lovely smile and a chest full of medals, no surprise. Despite my fear and the fact that I'm still crying, I think how lucky I am to have this woman serving our country.

"How did you know?" I ask, but she's busy scoping out the room. When a woman exits the handicapped stall, she leads me there, rolling my suitcase inside and placing my purse on the table.

"Can I get you anything?" she asks. "Paper towels?"

I look down and realize I've peed on myself. Thankfully, not too much, but there's a nice stain on the front of my jeans.

"I'm pregnant," I mutter.

"And you had quite a scare."

I take a deep breath and wipe my eyes. Did I imagine Dwayne standing there? Is the pregnancy getting the best of me?

"You're safe now," my angel in uniform tells me.

I grab her arm lightly. "I'm so sorry. I didn't mean to…."

She shakes her head, pats my hand, and that warm smile returns. "Don't be silly. Do you need…?"

I rally. "I'm fine. Have a change of clothes. Lots of hand wipes. I'll be fine."

"Okay then."

She exits the stall she discreetly closes the door, which I lock behind her.

I sit on the toilet and attempt a steady breath, try to recall what I saw and make sense of it. It must have been Dwayne. My cat had delivered a long nasty scratch on his face when he tried to cut my throat back in Mississippi; I haven't seen him since but that scar was there, stretching from his right eye all the way to his chin. And those eyes. He was staring at me with a gaze full of venom and hatred, enough to frighten me to the core.

Still, I could have imagined the whole scenario. How would Dwayne know where I was? Even if he had followed us to Tennessee he had no way of knowing I would be coming home from a Wisconsin press trip, changing planes in Atlanta at that very moment.

I try to clear my mind, take another deep breath and remove my clothes, thankful my mom stuck those hand wipes — and Band-Aids and Tylenol and a wide variety of first aid items — inside my bag when I wasn't paying attention. I clean myself up and use the plastic bag from the Wisconsin hotel to place the soiled items back into my suitcase. Now nothing I'm wearing matches, but I don't care.

I stand and feel dizzy but I'm okay. I don't want Ms. Military to wait for me, so I hurriedly pull myself together. But when I open the door, she's long gone. I didn't even get her name.

After washing up, I exit the women's room, peeking hesitantly down the aisles to make sure the coast is clear. Dwayne is nowhere to be found. My gate's only a few hundred yards away so I hightail it there and plop down next to the counter where two flight attendants busily work on computers. If I could sit on their laps, I would. When they call my flight, I'm the first in line, even though my ticket says zone four. The attendants send me quizzical looks while I wait at the front of the line, but I don't care. I have a full view of everyone getting on my plane as well as the crowds wandering up and down Terminal C.

Again, no Dwayne. And once more, I doubt my sanity.

The flight's only an hour to Chattanooga so I have time to resume a steady heartbeat. While I settle into my seat and eat the rest of my biscuit, I wonder where Ms. Military came from and why she knew I had been scared. Had a ghost sent her? Most of the time I solve the mysteries of my ethereal friends and send them heavenward but occasionally apparitions help me in my troubles. Like Gorton and his cryptic message. And this crazy woman in the New Orleans airport who likes to sing in the terminal aisles. I wonder if I'll see my Louisiana opera singer now that I live elsewhere.

And then there's Lillye. Soft, sweet laughter I swear is my daughter's sometimes filters through the ether. Occasionally, I think she's telling me something. I can't be sure of what I'm hearing and doubt the message, even though so many people insist she's always with me. I need to have faith and leave it at that but I want to see her, smell her hair, hold her tight, which is how I got into this mess with Dwayne to begin with.

When I heard Dwayne speak at the SCANC convention last fall, he had tapped his hand to his heart, looked straight at me, and said, "She's right here." But unlike everyone else who insisted Lillye was with me in spirit, Dwayne assured me I could have more.

"You can reach your precious daughter. You must learn how.

We can reach those who have left us but who are not in our," and he used his fingers to signify air-quotes, "'specific communication.'"

I can't help it. I still wonder if that's true, even though I've I learned who Dwayne Garrett really is.

We touch down into Chattanooga and I exhale, more loudly than I mean to; the guy to my right gives me a funny look. I'm okay, will face my fears without trepidation, but when I exit the security area and spot TB's blonde head above the crowd, I rush into his arms and hold him as if the world's about to end. He returns the affection, happy to see me as well, but when I linger, my head listing on his shoulder, I feel him tense. Finally, he pulls me away and studies me hard.

"What's wrong?"

My sweet husband may be clueless at times but he always knows when I'm troubled.

I swallow hard, try to keep the tears from creeping through. "I think I saw Dwayne in the Atlanta Airport."

TB's gaze intensifies and he says nothing. My husband's usually all laughs and giggles, unconditional love and happiness, but right now he's clearly worried. He nods silently, then wraps an arm about my shoulders and we turn toward the exit.

"Let's talk about it in the car."

My first thought is how odd for TB to be so stoic, but then he's likely taking it in. We knew the man might come for us, but we figured we'd be safe living on a houseboat in the middle of rural middle Tennessee. And yes, that's rather naïve of us, although I do share a bed with a man who can make heavenly light fly out of his fingertips.

TB carries DNA from ancient times when angels assumed God wouldn't mind if they co-mingled with humans. God took offense and put a stop to their fun, but there are people who walk the earth carrying angelic genetics. Called "descendants" and resembling angel ancestors, people like my husband have special powers. Ones they keep adamantly secret. If I hadn't met Dwayne and discovered he was a descendant of Lucifer, I'd never have known that my dear sweet TB carried on the line of Archangel Michael. Or that anyone did, for that matter.

I slip my arm through his elbow. "Glad I have a dragon slayer in my corner," I whisper, making a reference to Michael fighting the evils of Hell.

TB cringes, hates when I make comments like that. Yes, he carries some seriously strong angel DNA—from both his parents,—enough to save my butt when it needed saving, but he doesn't like using his powers. Or letting anyone know. And it's some serious shit. My sweet husband prefers sensing and then saving kids from falling off playground slides or telling runaways to avoid the bus station. He's a gentle soul so those bursts of protective white light or whatever he's capable of doing come only in extreme situations. Like last November when he stopped an armed robbery in a Texas convenience store when we had an *envie*—that's Cajun for desire—for late-night ice cream.

We climb into TB's pickup that's at least fifteen years old and I notice a bag on my seat.

"My class starts at one-thirty so I hope you don't mind, picked up fast food on the way here."

My heart drops because I really wanted to spend the day with him. He looks over and senses my disappointment.

"I can skip class."

I smile and try to look sincere. "Don't be silly. It's archival research, your favorite class."

His face lights up and it warms my heart. "Yeah, we're discussing the Library of Congress today."

When I met TB at LSU all he cared about was football games and imbibing jungle juice. As a journalism student with my head deeply entrenched in facts, TB was the last man I imagined myself marrying, although the sex and crazy dance contests we entered kept me dating the man. We made the best of things when Lillye arrived, then parted ways after Katrina. In those three years since, we've experienced a planetary shift. Now, he's excited about the Dewey Decimal System and I'm madly in love.

"I'll be fine," I tell him, but his smile fades and I know he doesn't believe me.

As I enjoy my spicy chicken sandwich from Wendy's, I explain seeing Gorton in Wisconsin and his grave message, then spotting Dwayne among the crowds in Atlanta and the mystery military woman who saved me. TB digests the news and nods. Finally, he says, "We need to call Clayton."

We met FBI Agent Clayton Ginsburg last fall in Galveston when TB and I, along with my Aunt Mimi and my sister Portia, discovered a mystery while searching for my father who had disappeared years ago. After the mystery was solved, Clayton had given me his card and told me he was available, should I need him.

He's also open to the paranormal, another plus, although explaining the angel thing might be a hard sell.

"I'll call him when we get home," I say between shoveling French fries into my mouth. It's closing in on noon, after all.

"Anything else you want to tell me?"

The fry gets stuck in my throat. A "no" comes out hollow and weak. Maybe today I can find a GYN.

I'm not sure TB believes me for he sends me a furrowed brow. I quickly look back to the meal in my lap.

It's a good hour to Emma's Cove, the tiny community where our houseboat is moored on an equally small lake that empties into the Tennessee River. We ended up here when searching for accommodations in nearby Lightning Bug, a town with a funny name where the university is located. It was a sports weekend when we moved to Tennessee and all the hotels were full, including the small motel in Emma's Cove. The nice motel owner — I say nice because she was then — offered us a night on the houseboat next door, one that was for sale, fully furnished, and available for rent. We ended up buying the boat.

Speak of the devil; I see Maribelle raking leaves in front of the motel as we drive up, talking animatedly to someone on her cell. Like a good Southerner, I wave. And like everyone else in this town, she ignores me, bending her head as if she hadn't seen my hospitality. But, I know she did.

"Weird."

"What?"

I've explained to TB how all the women in Emma's Cove—I have yet to meet a male resident—have been cold and unfriendly. My journalist's curiosity made me ask a lot of questions about the history of the town, who Emma was and that kind of thing, but I'm also used to knowing the life stories of my postal worker, the grocery store clerk and the person standing next to me at the bus stop. In South Louisiana, everyone talks to everyone and after a while they invite you home to dinner. Not here.

Lightning Bug remains the exception. The town's postal clerk hails from Knoxville but she went to LSU because her mother was from Baton Rouge, the grocery clerk laughs at my choice of pumpernickel bread, and I met the nicest woman at the bus stop who referred me to the perfect hair dresser.

Remember how I said TB is clueless sometimes? He hasn't noticed a thing about Emma's Cove. I guess that's how we'll become the perfect travel writing slash ghost-solving team. I'm highly perceptive and he's great in a library.

TB grabs my bags and we head inside but while I fall on the couch TB stands in the middle of the living room looking uncomfortable.

"Go," I tell him. "Class starts in thirty."

He keeps looking around as if expecting to find Dwayne lurking in some dark corner. "I don't want to leave you."

I stand and give him a giant hug, rising on my toes to make

sure my chin clears his shoulder. I adore this tall lean man with strong arms developed from years in construction. When he holds me tight, the world disappears. Finally, I let him go, feeling the cold air of the unheated houseboat drift between us. I fold my arms across my chest and try to appear confident.

"I'll be fine. Now, go."

TB kisses me soundly and I imagine good things to come later that night.

"Call Clayton," he says and heads out the door. "And lock everything behind me."

He pauses at the threshold, considering something. Finally, he turns and he's as serious as a preacher on Sunday.

"Don't go anywhere."

"What?"

"You heard me, stay put until I get home."

I sigh. Heavily. I'm a travel writer so you know staying put is not in my vocabulary.

"TB, I'm not going to avoid life because that man may or may not be in the world."

"You saw him, Vi."

"I *think* I did."

Now that time has passed, I'm not certain. The airport was so crowded and there's that pregnancy thing. Or maybe I'm just kidding myself so TB won't worry and I can get to the grocery store. Usually, when I'm on a press trip TB eats everything in the house and for some reason—ahem—fails to find time to visit the grocery.

He's standing sentinel at the door, hands firmly planted on his hips, gazing at me like a puppy who might lose his ball. I love this man so much and I tell him so, rise up on my toes once more to kiss him, then turn him around and push him outside. He pivots on the boat's deck, takes one last look at me.

"Go," I tell him. "I'll be fine."

Yeah, right, I think to myself. Since Katrina I have been

threatened by city mayors afraid of scandal, oil executives polluting a Louisiana lake, and a relative of Lucifer pursuing me, not to mention the cops who aren't too keen on female ghost sleuths investigating old murders. But I smile as if I have no cares in the world and TB sighs and heads off.

Once back inside—and you know I double lock that door—I do as I'm told, call my favorite FBI agent (only one I know) but Clayton's on the road. The man answering the phone assures me he will pass on the message.

I shower and change clothes, feel immensely better for it. My confidence returns and I refuse to let fear keep me holed up in my houseboat. Besides, it's the middle of the day and I have pepper spray in my purse.

Stinky, my orange and white cat who I swear has psychic powers, sends out a pleading meow, so I pause, plop on the sofa beside him, and offer a quick massage. The sun's starting to move toward the winter horizon, sending droplets of light upon the lake. Everything outside my living room window sparkles with hope.

It's so beautiful here, so peaceful and quiet. I wake up every morning and enjoy coffee on the deck, listen to the loons and other waterfowl calling out to each other. So far, the winter's been much colder than Louisiana, so I'm fairly certain summer will be milder and delightful, something I've never had back home in humid swampland.

"I love it here," I whisper to Stinky who winks. "You too?"

He closes his eyes and tilts his head, telling me to stop talking and scratch the ears. I do as I'm instructed but I need to think about getting answers.

"I'll be right back," I tell him. "Mommy needs to find a doctor."

We sold my Honda when we moved to Tennessee and because I've been traveling extensively since arriving at our new home, we haven't had a chance to purchase a new car. Everything in Emma's Cove is walkable and there's a bus heading into Lightning Bug three times a day, so if I need to visit the grocery store in town I either grab the bus or ride in with TB.

Today, I head to the library, a small building that used to be a store of some sort when the town experienced better days — at least that's what my intuition tells me; my Internet research into the history of the town revealed nothing. The library sits next to a roadside diner that serves up the best biscuits and gravy. Then there's a small auxiliary post office and a couple of abandoned buildings, one with enormous charm that I would love to renovate, if that was my thing (It's not but I imagine it is while watching the home shows on HGTV). The motel and my houseboat round out the town. I know other residents live somewhere surrounding the hamlet but since no one talks to me I've yet to be invited close enough to spot them through the thick woods.

There's an empty field behind the library, a stretch of green space that rolls down to the water's edge. I say green space but it's more like brown. Nothing grows on a large swath of land, not even kudzu, trees, and all forms of shrubbery exploding on the periphery. I pause at the library's front door, taking it in, when Maribelle nearly knocks me over exiting the library.

"Sorry," she mumbles, her head down.

"Wait!" I grab her elbow to keep her from fleeing. "Can I ask you something?" She looks at my hand on her elbow so I pull it away. "I need a reference to a female doctor."

Her gaze meets mine in a look that says, "Are you kidding me?" She frowns and waltzes away, angrily answering a call on her cell.

"Thanks a lot," I say to her back.

I sigh and head inside, hoping the librarian might be more helpful. She's not.

"We don't offer referrals, try the Internet," she says and heads toward the back.

At this point, I give up. The two o'clock bus is expected so I catch it and head towards friendly town. As always, the nice bus driver welcomes me onboard and off we go. Just for kicks, I ask her if she can recommend an OB-GYN.

"I can but my doctor's over in Cleveland, my home town, and that's in Tennessee, not Ohio." The bus driver sends me a bright smile. She knows I'm from Louisiana and clueless about my new state. "I've been going to her for years so I drive over when I need to."

"I'm from Jackson," a woman two rows back says with a heavy Southern accent. "And that's in Tennessee, not Mississippi."

There's only three of us on the bus and we're smiling at each other like old friends. This is what I'm talking about!

"I'm from New Orleans," I add, "but I lived in Lafayette for the past three years, evacuated there after Hurricane Katrina. Lafayette, like the American Revolutionary patriot, not La Fay-ette like y'all say here."

We all laugh, me more than these Tennessee natives, because I still think it's hilarious that the honorable French Marquis de Lafayette, aide de camp to President George Washington and hero of both the American and French Revolutions, is relegated to some Southern bastardization of his name.

Two women on the bus scoot over to where I'm sitting.

"I've heard that Doctor Morton Touché in Lightning Bug is really good," one says.

Speaking of Frenchmen.

"He's won a lot of doctor awards," the other says.

"Touché?" I ask. "Like sword fighting in French?"

They stare at me as if they don't understand. I forget that when you leave Louisiana the rest of America doesn't get French, hence La Fay-ette. I try for humor, instead.

"Kinda funny, though, for a female doctor. If you look at it written, it's touch-ee."

Again, *pas compris.*

"Never mind." I burn his name to memory. "Thank you so much."

The smiles return and we chat all the way to Lightning Bug. The driver even pulls up alongside Touch-ee's office instead of the bus stop, bless her heart. I thank them all and they wave me on.

When I enter Touch-ee's office—I really must stop calling him that or it will pop out of my mouth,—the lobby's full of pregnant patients. Good sign. I ask the woman at the counter for an appointment and she shakes her head.

"He's booked up for weeks," she says.

I can't wait that long, I think, not after stalling almost three months.

"I do have a cancellation for this afternoon, but it's iffy going forward. He's very popular and hesitant about taking on new patients."

I consider this. I need a doctor to see me through the birth but I also want to interrogate, I mean interview, doctors before deciding. And I really prefer a woman OB. On the other hand, I need to be seen. Like now.

"That's fine," I tell the woman. "I think...," I almost laugh at this, "...that I'm pregnant so I really need an examination. I'll take it from there, can always find another doctor."

She sends me a puzzled expression. "Dr. Touché is the best in the business. You won't find anyone better."

"Okay." Not sure what to make of that.

I fill out some forms, hand over my insurance card—thank you Uncle Boudreaux—and sit down with a pile of celebrity magazines after my search for good journalism comes up short. It's difficult to concentrate on Brad Pitt and Angelina Jolie's hoard of children because a dozen eyes are watching me carefully; the room's full of taxidermy fish hanging from every spare space. There's even a threesome—three fish on one board—filling a long narrow wall.

"I don't know, you think the good doctor's a fisherman?" I tell the woman next to me, who smiles politely as if she doesn't get my sarcasm. It's okay, not many people do.

I head back to reading about the Amazon losing its rain forest and how Prince Charles calls for a focus on the problem —thank you Prince Charles—but those fish are creeping me out.

"Shouldn't you eat these and not stuff them for the wall?" I ask again. "I know I love a good trout with a meunière sauce."

"I don't know," my neighbor says with that smile again, shrugging her shoulders and going back to her People magazine.

Sometimes I really miss the newsroom. Call us what you will, but my journalism friends have a wicked sense of humor. I don't miss chasing police, sitting through boring municipal meetings, and crushing deadlines in a rush but I long for my buds.

After about thirty minutes of fish and Amazon, my name is called and I'm ushered into a room and quickly dressed in paper. A nurse asks a million questions, including why haven't I seen a doctor all this time.

"I hadn't realized I might be pregnant," I lie. "My periods are so erratic."

She buys it, but when Doctor Touché arrives, he doesn't.

"You can't not go to a doctor," he says with a patronizing tone and I immediately dislike this man. He's large and sports a head full of black hair that doesn't look real, piercing blue eyes, and super large hands that scare me because I know where they'll go. He fills up the small room with his presence and if I could crawfish back from him on the patient table, I would.

He appears aggravated looking over my chart, shaking his head.

"Three months? You really didn't think you were pregnant until now? Or did you think you could deliver this baby on your own?"

Now, it's getting strange. I lean forward, not caring that he's way into my personal space. "What are you talking about?"

He shakes his head, asks me to lean back and put my feet into those damn stirrups. If I didn't want answers so badly, I would have said never mind and left this place, but I do as I'm told. He gives me an examination and it's not the most pleasant experience. They never are, but this man isn't even trying to be gentle. I'm glad he's not accepting patients because he's last on my list.

He then pulls out a fetal Doppler, rolls it around the bottom of my belly. I stop breathing and close my eyes, dreading what comes next. I know I couldn't have gotten this far into the pregnancy without the baby being somewhat healthy but still, once you lose a child, the fear remains.

Suddenly, a strong heartbeat emerges and I light up like a lightbulb.

"Good strong heartbeat," the doctor says. "Sounds like a very healthy baby. You're lucky."

My happiness fades. "Lucky?"

He straightens, pulling off the Playtex gloves. "You took a big chance waiting three months. I'll never understand how women can play with their health like that."

I'm now fuming inside, but I bite the inside of my lip. "How far along am I?"

"Guessing from what you *thought* was your last period...."

"I'm certain of the date."

His gaze narrows and he crosses his arms over his chest. "If you're certain of the date, then why did you wait this long?"

I'm sure the inside of my mouth is bleeding from my grinding me teeth. "Due date?"

"I suspect you are twenty-three weeks along and your due

date will be the first week of August. You'll need an ultrasound, though, to confirm that."

At least I got that much information.

"First time?" he asks.

Did he even look at my medical history? He appeared to do so.

"Second," I whisper.

"Second? And you didn't know you were pregnant until now?"

I sit up, pulling my paper gown around my chest. He's getting on my very last nerve. "You don't need to talk to me like this. My body is my own business."

"You're one of those crazy liberals, then? Is that why your name is different from your husband's?"

I shake my head. "What?"

"You have him listed as next of kin."

"I'm a journalist and I kept my last name for business reasons."

He smirks. "Figures."

I'm done. "I'm ready to leave, thanks. I'll be finding another person to birth my child."

He throws his gloves into the trash and stands. "Fine. Have one of those insane women in Emma's Cove help you, then."

And with those final words, Doctor Touch-ee leaves the room.

I look at the nurse who stares in disbelief as he closes the door behind him. She, no doubt, is as surprised as I am at his rude behavior.

"He doesn't approve of them," she finally says.

"Who?"

She leans in close and whispers, "Those women."

I want to ask more but another nurse comes in to take a blood sample. Now, it's my turn to stand and be abrupt.

"No, thank you," I tell her. "I'm going to dress, pay my copayment, and get the hell out of here."

The two nurses look at each other, say nothing and leave. I hurriedly dress, pay at the window, and hit the sidewalk. When I emerge into the sunlight, however, I'm mad as hell and equally confused.

It's then I spot Maribelle on the other side of the street, hauling plants and potting soil into the bed of her pickup. It's February and too early for spring planting but I've noticed the endless greenery in her kitchen window. She's *really* into plants.

She notices me but turns away, continues with her duties. I check for traffic and march across the street.

"I need to talk to you," I say and I'm not too nice about it.

My tone causes her to turn and examine me.

"I need to know what the hell is going on in Emma's Cove."

She smiles sarcastically and nods toward Doctor Touch-ee's office. "So now Doctor Know-it-all is enlisting spies."

I shake my head because this song-and-dance routine is driving me nuttier than a blind dog in a meat factory. I stomp my foot because between the Dwayne episode and this weird town mystery — not to mention being hormonal and grumpy — I'm about to pop a blood vessel.

Just then the counter woman at Doctor Touch-ee's office emerges and runs over to my side of the street, handing me my insurance card.

"You forgot this," she says. "And you forgot to make another appointment. He says you need an ultrasound."

I laugh. "There's no way in hell I'm ever going back to that rude, insulting man. Tell him I'm going to do my own ultrasound."

The woman's taken aback, glances over at Maribelle nervously, and leaves. I look heavenward and sigh. Loudly. I still need an ultrasound to make sure my baby's okay, not to mention a doctor to help bring my child into the world. Maybe I need to drive to Cleveland—Tennessee, not Ohio—to find one.

When I glance back at Maribelle, she's softened. She throws the last bag of mulch into the back of the pickup, takes my elbow, and leads me to the passenger side.

"Coffee?" is all she says.

CHAPTER 3

We enter the Lightning Latte Coffee Shop and I stop to allow my eyes to adjust. It's barely lit inside but the walls are filled with painted lightning bugs drinking giant cups of caffeine, their tails glowing tiny sparks of light.

"Cool," I mutter as Maribelle leads us to the back.

We pass students in tattered jeans and T-shirts, their heads deep in laptops. A group of Tennisians—what Winnie calls women in tennis garb who don't work and spend hours at lunch —pause in their animated conversation and healthy salads to look our way.

"Ignore them," Maribelle mumbles.

The back is even darker and no lightning bugs.

"Did someone forget to pay the light bill?" I ask.

As we sit in two comfy chairs, a girl sporting one long braid down her back and an enormous collection of freckles arrives.

"Hey Linsey," Maribelle says to the petite girl. "Two of your ginger scones, one dark roast and the chamomile blend, you know the kind."

She nods and I can't stop staring at her freckles. It's as if a supernovae exploded on her face and sent tiny drops of brown everywhere. With her enormous chocolate eyes and that braid, she's quite fanciful looking.

"And I'll have…." I raise my hand.

"The chamomile."

Freckles takes off and I send Maribelle a look. "I thought only arrogant men order for women. And for the record, I hate chamomile."

Maribelle leans in close. "It's my special blend that I've developed. Only special people—and me, of course—know to order it. It'll help with the morning sickness. Tomorrow morning you'll feel much better."

"How did you know about the morning sickness?"

Maribelle leans back, gets comfortable in her chair. "What did Doctor Perfect say?"

I exhale because I'm still wound up from the encounter. "That if I want to take my baby's life in my own hands, to ask the women of Emma's Cove."

"Asshole," Maribelle mutters.

"Big question is why did he say that?"

Now it's Maribelle's turn to exhale. "He doesn't like us."

"Really?"

She sends me a stink eye. "We have history."

My sarcasm's feeling spry. "Let me guess, could it have something to do with the fact that y'all are cold, unfriendly, and sometimes rude?"

"I'm sorry about this morning," she says, looking away. "I had to talk to someone I'm not too happy with."

"I'd say you and the other women in town aren't happy with anyone, anytime."

She looks back and her gaze has grown cold. "We have our reasons."

"And they are?"

Caroline arrives with our drinks and places both on the

table between us. Maribelle's smells like heaven, that intoxicating freshly roast coffee aroma. Mine smells like dirt.

"Sugar?" I ask her.

"She'll have it plain."

Now, it's my turn to send Maribelle the stink eye.

"Drink it," she instructs me. "You'll thank me tomorrow."

I sip the giant cup of herbal medicine, tiny tea bits floating inside, and surprisingly, it's not bad. I bite my scone and send my companion a look as if it's the scone that tastes good and not her weird-smelling tea.

"So, what's the big issue with Emma's Cove?" I ask. "And who was Emma, anyway. I can't find much on her."

"Why would you want to know?"

Again, that ridiculous suspicious nature. "Uh, because I live there, it's the name of the town, and I'm curious. Why the big deal?"

She sighs and relaxes a bit. A bit.

"Have you looked in the library here in town?"

"I don't know if you know what I do...."

"You're a travel writer."

I'm impressed. Didn't think she spent a moment thinking about me and TB.

"Well, I haven't had much time to look into it and the librarian in Emma's Cove wasn't much help," I explain.

Maribelle looks around the room. "Lightning Bug and Emma's Cove have a history. They don't like us and we don't trust them. Go to the library here and they'll talk your ear off about our town. We won't."

With an afterthought, she adds, "How's the tea?"

I push the cup forward between us. "Want me to answer that and finish the cup? Explain."

Maribelle slips the last bite of scone into her mouth, chews it thoughtfully, and follows with a swig of coffee. She looks around the room again but we're the only ones in the dark back corner. Finally, she leans forward.

"Emma's Cove has a reputation for being a haven for women looking to get out of bad situations."

"Like what?"

"Abusive marriages, family troubles." She shrugs. "Sometimes a crime."

I sip my tea that's beginning to grow on me. "Go on."

"I came here because I was looking to start over." She leans back, gets comfortable again in her chair. "My husband was a good man but I didn't love him, married him to get away from my insane parents and an abusive brother. After a few years, I desperately needed a change. He was sweet but the possessive type, always wanting to know where I was, who I was with, didn't want me to work. I felt suffocated."

"So, you came to Emma's Cove?"

"The motel was on the market, I had some money, and I had a skill, thought I could work and renovate it on the side until it was up and running. Today, it is."

I don't see conflict or reasons for distrust in any of this. Maribelle suspects my thoughts, places her elbows on the table and leans forward.

"I worked as a midwife."

"Ah," I say, because now I'm beginning to catch Touch-ee's disapproval.

"Doctor Best-in-the-Business over there never approved, talked trash about me all the time."

"Are you still practicing? I've always been curious about midwives and I would love to...."

"No, I'm not."

There's a deep sadness in that last remark and I don't know why, but something tells me to reach out and take her hand. Surprisingly, she doesn't recoil.

"My husband showed up, didn't cause trouble but he

wouldn't leave, said he was there to protect me, like I needed protection. He hung around the motel, living in one of the rooms, and was here so long he lost his job back in Rhode Island."

"That explains your accent," I say. "I've been trying to place it ever since I met you."

"What accent?"

She attempts a smile but her heart's not in it.

"What happened to the husband?"

Her half-hearted smile fades and she rubs her forehead nervously. "They found his body behind the motel. Autopsy said he drowned, which is weird because he spent his life on the water. The police had no clues but Touché convinced them I had killed my husband."

My immediate thought is "Did you?" One thing I've learned in this ghost-solving business is that the most obvious person to kill the victim is usually the perpetrator. My witchy Aunt Mimi says use your intuition, and I don't know if it's my warm chamomile-enhanced gut talking but I don't sense Maribelle capable of killing anyone.

"They arrested me but had to let me go because they had no evidence." Maribelle stares into her empty coffee cup. "But Touché convinced the board to have my license revoked and that was the end of my midwifery career."

"That's awful." I understand what it's like to not follow your dream job.

Maribelle shrugs but the darkness in her eyes remains. I'm still confused, however.

"So, I'm assuming Doctor Touché was rude to me today because he spotted my address on my chart. And that's bad enough, of course, but why are the women in Emma's Cove so unfriendly?"

"There's history between the two towns."

"But…."

Suddenly, Maribelle's standing, throwing money down on the table. "I have to go. Come by the diner at eight tomorrow morning and I'll explain more."

I shake my head, thinking about what morning brings. "Sure, but I don't eat breakfast these days."

She pulls on her coat. "You will tomorrow." And with those final words, heads out the coffee shop.

The last bus leaves in thirty minutes but I pull out my cell and call TB, hoping he's available to give me a ride home.

"Vi?"

"I'm at Lightning Latte. Ride home?"

In the silence that follows, I remember him insisting I stay home. "It's fine. There are tons of people around." Not true, the Tennisians have left, but I am in the middle of town. "And we needed groceries." True, but I failed to get there. "Pick me up at the Piggly Wiggly in ten?" At least, I can get milk.

"I'll be right there," he says softly and hangs up, both of which are unusual. He never ends a call without saying he loves me at least twice.

I try not to think about it, head to the grocery and grab a few items as fast as I can. He's waiting by his pickup truck as I exit the store, grabs my one bag and opens the passenger door. He's not smiling. We don't say anything as we slip into the car and are silent halfway to home. Finally, I can't stand it anymore.

"You're mad at me because I left the house?"

His hands flex on the steering wheel and I see the muscles in his jaw tighten. This is so not like TB. I can count on one hand the times I've seen him mad.

"Seriously, TB, I was careful. I told you I wasn't about to stay…."

"Is there something you want to tell me?"

My heart pauses beating. There's no way he could know. "Uh, what do you mean?"

"Some doctor's office called and said you needed an ultra-sound for the baby."

My mind whirls. I had listed TB's cell phone number on my chart as an emergency contact. How dare them call him and not me?

"I can't believe this," I say with more force than I should. "They called *you*?"

TB's hands grip the wheel. Hard. "You're three month's pregnant and you haven't told me and you're mad at the doctor?"

He's practically shouting, which also isn't like my demure husband. "*Almost* three months."

He glances at me with a look that says I've lost my mind. And maybe I have.

"I suspected but I was waiting for the insurance to kick in."

We're so close to home I spot Maribelle's motel, but TB pulls off to the side of the road and shoves the truck into park.

"You suspected? How long have you suspected, Vi?"

I swallow hard. "A little while."

He's staring at me, hard, with so many emotions seeping through that gaze. He's angry, but he's also scared, worried. We're bringing another child into the world after losing the first. What happens now we have no idea.

I reach for him but he pulls away. Then in a quick motion, wipes his eyes with the back of his sleeve, pulls the truck into drive and we head toward our houseboat. We pull into our parking spot so fast dust flies and I spot Maribelle in her kitchen looking out her window with a curious gaze.

"Please, let's talk," I whisper.

TB turns off the truck, slamming the door as he leaves and heads into the woods beside our home. From the stomp of his gait, he doesn't want to be followed. I grab my one bag of groceries and head inside, greeted by Stinky at the threshold, who immediately dashes into the woods.

"Thanks, y'all."

It's more than an hour with darkness descending over our pristine lake when the men return. Stinky heads for the food bowl, which I refilled thanks to my Piggly Wiggly visit. TB heads to the kitchen and pulls out a beer. I sit on the couch watching those HGTV shows—I keep thinking I'll use their advice to renovate our floating home—while I wait for one of my roommates to resurface into the living room.

Finally, TB turns the corner and, without looking at me, joins me on the couch.

"How long have you known?"

I hate admitting my lie but now's the time to lay out the truth. I turn off the TV.

"Since Thanksgiving."

TB closes his eyes and winces.

"You said then that if I were to get pregnant, you would stay in New Orleans and work for your uncle. I didn't want that to happen."

"Three months, Vi?"

"Not quite three months."

He sends me that incredulous look again.

"Okay, I'm sorry. But we didn't know about the insurance until right before my Wisconsin trip. And with our history I didn't want to tell you until I saw a doctor."

He pulls a hand through his thick blond hair and leans back on the couch. "What did the doctor say?"

"First of all, he's a jerk and I'm not going back there."

"What?"

"It's a long story but he was rude and calling you first, what doctor does that? It's a privacy infraction at least."

TB thinks on this, finally asking, "Would you have told me otherwise?

I turn to face him, take both his hands. "Of course, I was going to tell you tonight."

He looks at me for a long time, his eyes welling up. "Is everything okay?"

The only person more scared of birthing this child is my husband. He feared for everything when I was pregnant with Lillye and now, with her history behind us, I can tell he's frightened to his bones. That painful gaze he sends makes my tears fall but I nod my head.

"She's fine. Healthy heartbeat."

He finally smiles, too, but his tears are falling. "She?"

I shrug. "We won't know until the ultrasound and maybe not even then."

TB straightens. "Call them right away and make an appointment."

"No way. I have to find another doctor."

I explain to TB what happened this afternoon and Maribelle's explanation for Touché acting as he did. I assure him I will find a new OB in the morning and get my ultrasound and we agree that we'll tell family after the test. TB's still reeling from the news but from the gleam in his eyes I know he's starting to imagine children again. After dinner we lie in bed discussing logistics. We'll have to convert half of the second bedroom, now my office, into a nursery and baby-proof the houseboat. We consider buying a small house or renting an apartment near TB's school but we've grown to love our little cove, so we vow to make necessary adjustments.

"We'll make it work," TB says, and I know his carpenter skills will do just that.

"Or we'll cross that bridge later."

It's a perfectly appropriate remark but underneath there's the fear that our child may become sick like Lillye and we'll have to move to a larger city with hospitals. Neither one of us talks for a long time, both of us staring out the bedroom door, down the hallway to the giant picture window overlooking the lake.

"And hopefully Clayton calls in the morning," TB whispers.

For not the first time, I wonder how I will bring a child into the world with so much violence and disease.

"Vi, do you ever consider...?"

"Yes."

I don't have to explain. I've done it before and I can do it again. Simply turn off the ability to see ghosts.

THE PHONE JOLTS me awake at seven and I sit up in bed, trying to bring my heartbeat back to normal. I dreamt of Dwayne again, this time the horrid man was watching TB and I sleep from the living room's window. The bedroom door's closed now so I can't see the window down the hall and am thankful for it. But, I wonder if I must keep the door closed and give up my lake view in the morning, must alter my life now to fear.

The phone rings again so I gingerly rise, since the faster I've gotten up from sleeping, the worst my morning sickness. I carefully open the bedroom door and gaze down the hallway but outside the window there's nothing but water. I head in that direction because it's the only phone outlet on the boat.

"Vi," Clayton says from the other end when I pick up. "I wasn't sure if you were on Central or Eastern time so I hope I'm not waking you."

"Not at all, I'm awake," I lie, since the answer is Central. I walk around the living room peeking behind doors and glancing outside to the nearby woods. From what I gather, it's just me here. While I make myself comfortable on the couch I gaze around and notice TB gone; on Wednesdays, he has an early biology class. Stinky, on the other hand, lies across the floor along the back of the front door and sends me a confident gaze. Anyone else would never assume the cat's being protective —what cat does that? But they don't know Stinky.

"What's going on?" Clayton asks.

I explain Dwayne and how he almost killed me in Natchez, but unbeknownst to me Clayton's on top of it, having looked up my file when we parted ways in Galveston last fall. I relate my recent experience in the Atlanta airport and, because Clayton insisted he's a Fox Mulder *X-Files* type of FBI agent, add the part about Gorton and his cryptic message.

"I could have imagined the whole thing. Maybe the ghost put the idea into my head."

"That would have been a pretty big hallucination, Vi."

I exhale and close my eyes, thinking of the discussion the night before. "Well, I am pregnant, so there's that."

"*Mazel tov*," Clayton says with enthusiasm. "How wonderful."

I find myself smiling broadly. Now that I've seen a doctor and TB knows, I'm having a baby!

"Thank you."

"But you're not imagining things. You just gave me incredible details about the man's scar and it's right on."

My happiness fades.

"We've been searching for Dwayne Garrett for a long time, even before he escaped police custody in Natchez. Fraud, tax evasion, among other things. He was spotted not long ago in a small town called Lithia Springs outside Atlanta."

My heart sinks. "I know the place. It's about three hours away."

"He's been recently traveling under the name of Robert Johnson."

"The blues singer?"

"You know the story?"

I laugh, because I know Dwayne. He'll be creative in disguises, even if it gets him caught. Intelligent criminals worry more about how they *perform* the crime, as if they're playing for an audience.

"Robert Johnson sold his soul to the devil on the crossroads in Mississippi," I say. "Or so the story goes. Of course, I know the tale. I almost sold my soul to the Devil—Dwayne—myself, on a crossroads along the Natchez Trace. He's quite the charmer. He's likely chosen it for me, connecting the dots between Johnson's story and our meeting last fall."

"He's been moving around and just when we think we have him, he disappears," Clayton continues. "But lately he's slowed down. We suspect he's feeling confident. Which is good news. When criminals get to this point, they get sloppy."

I pull my hand through my sleep hair. "I hope he doesn't get sloppy killing me."

"Where are you now?"

I explain how TB and I moved to Emma's Cove after Christmas and give Clayton my address. He's stationed in Birmingham so he promises to drive up this afternoon when TB's free and we can discuss this more.

"I doubt you have anything to worry about," he says. "He must know that we're watching you."

"Wait, what?"

"Vi," he says like a father, "you were almost killed by a man who's now on the loose, then you helped solve a murder last fall in Galveston involving an international drug cartel. You're on our radar."

I can't decide if that's a good thing or not.

"Dwayne's not going to chance getting caught visiting you."

"I wish I could believe you."

"Just take precautions."

After more catching up and my FBI hero (at least I hope) offering me safety tips, we say our goodbyes. It's then I realize it's quarter to eight.

I rush into the bathroom and jump in the shower, throw on jeans and my favorite LSU sweatshirt and hit the front door with two minutes to spare. I think about what Clayton said, so I pull my pepper spray out of my purse's zippered sleeve and place it in my jean pocket where I can retrieve it easily. He insisted I get a gun and learn how to use it but I'm not a fan of firearms.

I pause at the door because Stinky's refusing to move. The moment allows me to consider, once again, leaving my SCANCness behind, which may, in turn, be the reason Dwayne's searching for me. All I have to do is tell the ghosts to go away, stop tapping into that plane of existence, let someone else carry them over to heaven or wherever death takes us.

Stinky cocks his head and sends me a funny look.

"It's just a thought," I say, then gently move him aside with my foot.

Maribelle's waiting in the back of the diner but thankfully it's well lighted and I can see my way. Plus, there's this gorgeous bay window stretching along the back offering a wide view of Emma's Cove. In all the town, which isn't saying much considering its size, this remains my favorite spot.

"I can't believe this sweet little town never got developed into a resort of some kind," I say sitting down.

Maribelle grimaces.

"Not that I want it to," I quickly add.

"How're you feeling?" she asks.

Now, that I think about it, I feel great. No morning sickness, no dizziness, no revisits of dinner.

"Wow, pretty darn good."

She slides a bag of herbs my way and I feel like a stoner getting a bag of weed. "Smoke this or brew?"

She doesn't react so I sit across from her and grab my menu. Naturally, there's a cup of chamomile waiting, no doubt with other ingredients because it smells weird.

"This isn't a *Rosemary's Baby* kind of thing, is it?"

Maribelle looks up clueless so I don't bother explaining the horror movie involving a pregnant woman forced to give birth to a devil. Too close to home anyway.

We do small talk for a while, mainly how cold the mornings

have been lately and the inauguration of the nation's first African American president. When breakfast arrives, I hungrily down scrambled eggs, stone ground grits with butter and salt, and a biscuit smothered in brown gravy — and yes, I groaned.

"Town history?" I mumble.

Maribelle butters her wheat toast and gets comfortable. "Emma came here at the turn of the twentieth century when her husband was hired to clear the land for a timber company."

"But the area's full of old growth trees," I say with a mouth full.

"It was too rocky and hilly so the company moved the men and their families west toward Chattanooga."

I wipe my mouth. "Let me guess, Emma wanted to stay."

"They lived in an employee cabin that the company was going to abandon and she was an expert seamstress. She had a loveless marriage and the husband wanted to keep moving with the company so they came to an agreement. She would stay here and work to support herself and he'd move on. They agreed that neither would remarry so they didn't bother with a divorce." Maribelle takes a long drink from her coffee, cupping it to enjoy its warmth. "They both thought it was for the best and Emma Harrington knew how to take care of herself."

"I suspect she did since the cove's named after her."

Maribelle motions for the waitress to bring her more coffee and I stare longingly as Patrice—it's on her name badge—pours Maribelle another cup.

"She worked as a seamstress in Lightning Bug when she needed cash," Maribelle continues, "but mostly made money creating gorgeous quilts and fabric pieces that she sold in big cities like Chattanooga, Nashville, New Orleans. She was an artist, really, hailed from the mountains near Gatlinburg. She garnered some fame, had some big shots from New York come visit over the years, and she was in an issue of Look magazine once. She deposited much of her earnings in the bank in Lightning Bug so folks there knew all about her."

I finish the bowl of grits and practically lick it clean. "Let me guess, people in town weren't too happy with a self-made woman."

Maribelle smiles, but it's a sad one. "She was the Martha Stewart of her day."

I save for last the biscuit swimming in thick gravy with pieces of ham. "Is that the bad blood between the towns?"

Maribelle looks outside toward the lake and that ugly patch of brown. "No. Well, sort of."

I wait to hear more but Maribelle's focus moves elsewhere. Patrice returns to pick up our plates and I almost ask for a cup of coffee to get my neighbor's attention.

Finally, Maribelle sighs and checks her watch. "I have to run, have a couple arriving at nine for the RV slot."

"Wait, what about the rest of the story?"

She slides me a piece of paper with a phone number. "Doctor Mary Mahoney. She's a bit of a drive, on the other side of Lightning Bug, and she's not taking on new patients. But I called her and she said she would take you on as a favor to me. Call her right away, though, so you can get your ultrasound."

"Thanks."

"She's good." She stands there wavering as if I might doubt her reference.

"I believe you."

She nods, grabs her jacket, and heads toward the counter where she hands the waitress a twenty. "It's on me," she says and looks back. "We'll continue this later."

"You paid for the coffee yesterday...," I say, protesting to the fleeting image heading out the door. Despite her generosity, I feel cheated, like I was watching The History Channel and the lights went out.

Suddenly everyone in the diner is looking at me. Where

once I garnered a quick look and then complete avoidance, now I'm the town's curiosity. I attempt a smile but receive none in return.

"Okay, then," I say to myself and head out the door toward the library. I doubt the library will have what I'm looking for but it's worth a trip. When I arrive next door, I pause and gaze down at the brown patch by the water's edge. On a lark, I bypass the library and walk down the bank and stand dead center in its middle. The lake waters stretch smooth with barely a ripple but there's a cold front expected soon and gray clouds line the horizon. No birds are chirping, likely headed to a safe place, which is where I'll be next. But the silence is unnerving, as if I'm standing in a holy place.

But it's not holy. There's no peace here.

I don't know how thoughts pop into my head, but my Aunt Mimi says they are messages from beyond and to not discount them. And if a person's present, spit them out.

"These are divine messages," she told me. "Always pass them on."

She believes I'm a witch, from a long line of witches, including her. Since last November Aunt Mimi has tried to teach me the "Craft," and I've been successful on some accounts and grossly a failure on others. I'm a work in progress.

I gaze around and there's no one to recount this message to so I close my eyes, trying to discern what happened here, if anything did.

My first sense is I'm cold, which almost makes me laugh. And then I do the ADHA meditation thing, where I tell myself to stop thinking, but then that's thinking and then a voice says I'm thinking that I'm still thinking. Finally, I yell, "Will you both shut up!" I take a deep breath and try to forget the morning chill, but that cold permeates like it did in Wisconsin.

And something black.

People died here and it was sudden. There was nothing

anyone could do, but others were blamed. I don't sense ghosts so I'm assuming whomever it was has passed on. Still, there's an unsettled darkness that hugs the area and it feels angry.

Suddenly, I'm *very* cold and I want out of this place. I forgo the library and head for home, but that darkness clouds my mind, making me feel jittery, and I almost forget to gather the mail TB and I missed the day before. I head inside, lock the door, and check all the windows. I realize I'm being silly because my husband has the place battened down like a hurricane's coming but that fear I discovered at the brown patch has taken hold of my senses.

I fall on to the couch and call the doctor and make an appointment for the following day, then watch an hour of HGTV with Stinky in my lap. I'm about to move into another episode of *House Hunters* since the mindless TV helps get my mind off the fear but it's a couple of twenty-somethings with "only" a six thousand dollar budget and picky as hell. When they complain about the historic Craftsman house and how they want to pull out the gorgeous built-ins I yell at their stupidity and turn off the set.

I need to do something and I'm not in the mood to write my travel piece on Wisconsin. The weather's about to turn nasty, so I gather up my dirty clothes and tell myself it's okay to step outside. Our watery haven contains a floorplan much like a house—two bedrooms, a master bathroom and a tiny half-bath in the hall, a nice-sized kitchen (for a houseboat), small dining area and a living room spanning the width of the boat along the front. Or back, however you see it. We call that side facing the lake the boat's front since the other side sports the engine and the boat's name, which in our case is *The Lillye Bea*.

It's why we bought the boat. We left New Orleans with a handful of items, having sold our house and what little furniture we still had after Katrina. The house sold quickly so we decided to head to Tennessee and figure out living arrangements once we got here. But, our hearts were heavy. Even though I hated that house in New Orleans, was glad to see it go, it was the home where we shared our lives with Lillye Beatrice Boudreaux.

We arrived at Emma's Cove well into the evening and found the hotels booked, including Maribelle's motel, so she offered to rent us her neighbor's houseboat for the night. When we saw the name, we purchased it instead. We considered it a sign, that our little angel approved.

The only problem is the dang washer and dryer. I must exit the side door and walk along the deck that surrounds the boat to access both appliances in a lean-to that's attached to the rear of the house. I suspect the designer wanted to provide more living space inside but it's a pain braving the cold when I want to do laundry.

Not to mention anyone lurking in the woods. I'm still thinking about that dream and the feeling I got at the brown patch, so I bring my pepper spray just in case. As I'm loading the washer, I catch movement in my peripheral vision. I pretend I don't notice, pull out the pepper spray and have it at the ready but head back inside, locking the door behind me. Then I move to the master bathroom which faces the woods and peer through the tiny window gracing the top of my shower.

Gorton waves from beneath a towering pine.

"What the fudge," I exclaim but I don't say fudge.

I leave out the front door—the one on the lake side facing the woods,—still gripping my pepper spray, and head toward my Wisconsin ghost. He's waiting for me on the lake's edge, glancing around nervously.

"What on earth are you doing here?"

He swallows hard, no doubt still trying to master the art of verbal communication.

"Did you follow me here?"

I've heard that ghosts will attach themselves to you or antiques and you may unwittingly bring them home.

"I want to help," he says so quietly, I'm not sure I hear him.

"Excuse me?"

"Y'all," he says with a funny smile that takes me aback, "need me."

I'm so confused I don't know where to start.

"Dude, usually I'm the one helping apparitions get to the other side."

He shakes his head. "We help too."

I know this, and he did warn me about Dwayne. And there's

that opera singer in the New Orleans airport who sends me messages as I'm coming and going. Still, this one's following me.

He senses my apprehension. "Talk to MB."

That last sentence takes all his strength and he fades.

"I don't know who MB is," I yell to the woods.

"Talking to yourself?"

I jump at the sound, turn and find a giant of a man standing at the end of my dock.

"You're early."

Clayton checks his watch. "It's five after noon, so technically I'm not."

I head his way, and even though it's not appropriate, give the tree of a man a hug, my face landing in the middle of his chest. I'm used to tall men since my husband's six feet two to my five foot seven. But Clayton's NBA tall. And thick. And wide. And solid as a brick. If this man has my back I have nothing to worry about.

I try not to linger but boy does he smell good. Like a forest on a spring morning. Earthy and manly at the same time. I try not to blush as I invite him in.

He follows me down the dock and on to the deck surrounding my floating home. Stinky greets him upon arrival, sniffing his ankles intently.

"Who's this?" Clayton asks, leaning down to give Stinky a proper scratch behind the ears. My cat eats it up, rolls on his back, and immediately starts purring.

"He doesn't like most people but boy he likes you."

"Is this the one you brought on your trip across Texas when I first met you?"

"Have cat, will travel. He's more like a dog, really, but don't tell him that."

Stinky winks at Clayton.

"Amazing."

I offer coffee and pull out some Oreo's I nabbed at the Piggly

Wiggly yesterday. I'm embarrassed to expose my affinity to the cookies everyone's saying has trans fat and are horrible for you, but I'm pregnant and I'm playing that card as long as I can. Clayton lights up at the sight so I'm relieved to find a cohort in my trans fat crime. I know I'm supposed to avoid caffeine, too, but when the French Press is ready I pour us both a cup and add a ton of milk to mine. One cup of coffee full of milk can't hurt, right? I'll sip it slowly.

"When is your husband getting home?"

I sit on the couch across from Clayton and grin slyly. "What are you insinuating?"

He takes a sip of his coffee and I spot a smile behind the rim. "Aren't you peppy today."

I place mine in my lap and sigh. "Actually, I'm quite discombobulated."

"I love writers. Such big words."

I explain my trip to the doctor, how Touché violated my privacy by calling my husband. I relate how the town's been unfriendly and Maribelle's reasoning for their coldness, although I only know half the story. I top it off with Gorton in the woods.

Clayton shakes his head. "Wow, girlfriend, you've had a week."

"No, I've had a weird three-and-a-half years. Ever since that bitch of a hurricane blew into New Orleans in 2005."

"So, you never had psychic experiences before the storm?"

"Yes, but I repressed them."

"Is that difficult to do?"

I'm not sure why he's asking but it feels weird since it's been on my mind lately.

"A bit, but it can be done. If I hadn't repressed them, however…."

"You wouldn't be a SCANC now."

"Exactly."

Clayton thinks about this. "So, you're sure Gorton died by drowning. And he said it wasn't an accident."

"Appears so."

He pulls out a notebook and writes something down. "How old do you think he was when he died?"

I describe his outfit and the L.L. Bean boots, the three-fish earring on his right ear that seemed more modern for a man. The heavy beard, yellow slicker, and the fact that he resembles a grocery store product.

Clayton takes it all in. "I'll see what I can find."

I hear heavy boots on the dock and Stinky rushes to the door.

"Told you, my cat's like a dog."

My *cat* sends me a stink eye but turns his attention to TB when my husband waltzes across the threshold. TB effortlessly pulls Stinky into his arms while greeting Clayton and shaking his hand. Two oversized, handsome men in our small living room. I'm thinking—at least, in this moment—that life is pretty darn good.

I retrieve an extra cup and pour TB some coffee while he and Clayton get comfortable and make small talk. I watch from the periphery, absorbing it all, noticing TB's body language change as he studies Clayton. For one, TB hasn't released Stinky from his lap and the cat's giving both he and I a strange look as if to say, "What's up with Dad?" Second, he moved the living room chair further away from the couch, sitting a distance apart from Clayton. And to top it off, he's not smiling.

I hand TB his cup. "School okay?"

He doesn't look up. "Just dandy."

I return to my seat next to Clayton and feel strange sitting next to this gorgeous sequoia of a man while my husband looms way over there, balancing a cat and a cup of coffee. Clayton senses that something's amiss and leans forward toward TB, elbows on his thighs.

"Dwayne's on the move. He was staying in a short-term rental in Lithia Springs, Georgia, but when we caught up to him, the place was empty. All except for a pile of clothes in the corner of a room."

"If you knew where he was, how'd you miss him?"

There's almost an accusatory tone from TB but Clayton ignores it. I send him a frown, but TB ignores me.

"It was the morning Vi spotted him at the airport. We checked flight records, to see why he would have been in Atlanta the day she was there, but found nothing."

"How could you find nothing?" TB asks, that tone again. "You can get inside the Atlanta airport without a plane ticket."

Clayton takes a sip of his coffee. "The man has an elaborate underground network. People love him and he has many followers. He's been using fake passports and IDs, no doubt derived from his fan base."

TB shakes his head. "We're in post-9-11 America with tough security at airports and y'all can't find this man?"

I'm a bit uncomfortable but Clayton takes it in stride. After all, it is an appropriate question.

"We're on his trail." Clayton turns his cup around and around in his hands, finally looking up and giving us both a steady look. "I assure you, this man will be caught."

If only he was just a man, I think.

TB and I go silent. As if Clayton reads our minds, he asks, "Is there anything either of you can tell me about Dwayne Garrett?"

I look at TB and wonder if we should divulge Dwayne's angelic background but he's not talking, so I don't swing at that pitch.

Clayton brings TB and me up to date about the places Clayton's been, some of the people involved with Dwayne that the Bureau *did* catch, and where they think Dwayne might head next.

"We've got men watching the area, both outside Atlanta and in this vicinity."

My husband takes it in, nods his head.

"I tried to get your wife to get a gun but she won't hear of it," our Fed adds.

"I have one," TB answers.

The comment flies out of left field so fast I literally shake my head. "What?"

TB doesn't look my way, continues staring at Clayton. "I have one. And I know how to use it."

Shivers run up my back because if I'm not mistaken, TB's letting Clayton know that he's armed and prepared. What is happening here?

Clayton senses it too. His eyes narrow looking at TB and there's tension in the air for several seconds. Finally, Clayton pats his tree trunk thighs and stands, turns to me.

"Thank you, Vi, for the lovely coffee and Oreo's."

"You're not leaving, are you?" I'm not ready to be left loose in the world without his giant safety net.

He pulls a card from his wallet. "I'm in Birmingham so I'm not far away. This has my direct line so call if you see or hear anything."

I nod staring at the card, but he places a finger at my chin and raises my gaze to his. "Anything, Vi."

TB rises and Stinky takes off, no doubt happy to be let loose. "I've got her back."

Clayton glances at TB but doesn't refute his protectiveness, simply nods and says, "Great. I feel much better for it."

The two glare at each other while I study the weird scene before me but Clayton ends up smiling, holds out his hand and TB takes it. Clayton makes his goodbyes and off he goes, his footsteps sounding loudly on the houseboat's deck.

I close the door behind Clayton and look back at my husband. "What the hell was that about?"

TB shrugs. "What?"

"You were practically rude."

TB stares at the door as if Clayton's still on the other side. "He smells weird."

I shake my head. "What?"

"There's something not right. I don't trust him." And with that remark, he heads to the bedroom.

I look down at Stinky. "Smells weird? Clayton smells wonderful."

"You would say that," I hear from the bedroom.

I follow TB and he's exchanging his shirt for a thick sweatshirt. I feel it too. The oncoming cold front's dropping temperatures.

"What's going on?" I ask. "Something happen at school?"

He throws his shirt in the hamper a little too hard.

"Sure, Vi. I failed a paper I wrote for English class. We have little money in the bank and my second round of tuition is due. And my wife's pregnant with a due date around the time I graduate. Likely without a job, I might add."

I sigh, sit on the edge of the bed. "I have checks coming in, TB. Did you forget that I work too? Don't worry about tuition."

He throws his hands up. "And taking care of a child? On a library science degree?"

In addition to rarely seeing my husband mad, he hardly worries. But these are not ordinary days. I take his hand and urge him down on the bed next to me.

"First of all, we're fine. Tuition will be paid. We still have the house sale in savings."

"That's for emergencies."

"And if we don't have enough for tuition and the baby, that's an emergency."

"But...."

"What happened with the English paper."

TB sighs, then rises and heads to the living room. He's so

nervous the air feels electric, or maybe it's the oncoming storm. I secured my nappy hair in a ponytail but if I let the curls loose right now they may stretch out like Buckwheat's afro.

I follow TB and find him rustling through his backpack, pulling out a paper with red ink scratched everywhere. He sighs looking at the mess.

"I don't know what I was thinking, Vi. I'm not a college student."

While he starts pacing the living room, I grab the paper and check it out. Yes, it's poorly written and TB's made freshman-style mistakes. Short, simple sentences. Lots of grammatical and spelling errors. Even the punctuation screams failure. The paper reads like he rushed through the process. At the top is a big fat F.

"Why didn't you ask me to help you?"

He pauses in his pacing. "You were in Wisconsin. And if I can't do this on my own, how am I going to be a librarian? Or whatever the hell you do with a library science degree."

"That's your family talking."

"My family's right."

I throw his paper down on the coffee table, grab my husband by the shoulders and force him to look me in the eyes.

"The only thing that's right is following your dream. And then showing your children how it's done."

He pauses because even though he's wallowing in pity and fear right now, he knows I'm right. But then he shakes his head.

"I'm thinking of dropping out."

"What? Why?"

He pulls his fingers through his hair and rattles off a list as he paces the room again. "I'm not cut out for this. I'm not smart enough. I'm spending all our money on a degree that's not going to pay. I could make more money in construction. Plus, we need the health insurance."

I land a flat hand on his chest and force him to stop.

"When did you talk to your parents?"

He frowns like a kid caught with his hand in the cookie jar, avoids my eyes. "It's more than that."

"TB?"

He shrugs. "Monday. A conference call with my uncle."

"Uh huh. And they put those ideas into your head."

The Boudreauxs are good people but they haven't supported our move to Tennessee or TB leaving the family business. I say good people but right now I want to throttle them. For the first time in his life, my husband has a dream and is happy. At least he was until this week.

He still won't look at me, no doubt thinking of their words and the new life we're expecting in August. Guilt will do that to a person.

At this point, my mommy voice comes out. I forgot I had one.

"You listen to me Thibault Boudreaux, we came here to start a new life and for you to do what you love. You are going to get in your car, head back to campus, and talk to your teacher. You tell her that your wife is having a baby and your head wasn't clear and ask for a rewrite."

He's balking — and yes, I'm full of baseball puns today — but he's also considering what I'm telling him.

"Do they do that?"

"The good ones do."

"I like this teacher. She's helpful."

"Then ask her."

He takes a deep breath and exhales. "Okay."

The wind's picking up outside and we both glance at the horizon, which has become dark with clouds. "Maybe do it tomorrow," I add.

He grabs his jacket from the back of the chair. "No, I want to get this over with. I won't be long."

I give him a bear hug and he rests his chin on my shoulder.

"Love you BooBoo," I say.

He finally smiles as he gazes into my face, then places both hands on my cheeks and plants a hot kiss there.

"Hurry back," I whisper when we finally break apart.

That adorable dimple emerges. "I won't be long."

He grabs his paper and backpack and heads out the door, turning back with that old serious face. "Lock it behind me."

"Yes, Dad."

"I mean it, Vi. Lock everything."

I nod, because I realize that on top of the financial fears and the failed paper, there's Dwayne on our minds.

After TB leaves, I remember the laundry. The clouds linger on top of me now, low and menacing as if they're trying to commune with the lake. I grab my pepper spray and exit the side door, finish throwing the clothes and laundry detergent into the washer and pushing the on button.

As I turn to head inside, I spot Maribelle on the back side of her motel, placing lawn equipment inside the tool shed, no doubt due to the coming inclement weather. When she finishes her chore, she turns and sees me. I wave but she doesn't smile and her back straightens as if her hairs have risen to attention. There's an intense look in her eyes as if I'm Dwayne come to steal her soul. Then she starts marching away.

I rush down the dock and head over to her place, meet her just as she's about to go inside her apartment.

"What's happened?" I ask.

She stops abruptly, still fuming. "What happened is I trusted you."

I scour my brain trying to think what might have occurred since breakfast. "I don't understand. Of course, you can trust me."

She plants hands on her hips, shakes her head menacingly. That old saying about if looks could kill? Seriously, I feel like I'm disintegrating on the spot.

"What are you doing here, Vi? First, Touché. Now, the Feds."

I relax. A little. Attempt a smile. "Clayton? He's here for me. Has nothing to do with you or the town."

She's not buying it. "Really?" she says sarcastically.

"How did you know he was with the FBI?"

She looks heavenward as if she's talking to a moron. "I can smell the Feds a mile away."

Again, with the man's aroma.

"Seriously Maribelle, he was here for me. I have a crazy person stalking me and Clayton came to give me an update."

Nothing.

"I was attacked in Natchez, Mississippi, last fall and the man's still on the run."

Again, she remains silent, staring at me accusingly so I exhale loudly, because I'm tired of this game.

"I'm a medium and this man tried to use me for some nefarious purpose and failed, but he's still looking for me. Clayton's helping."

She crosses her hands across her chest and her gaze remains cold as steel.

"You have to believe me," I insist.

"I don't have to do anything." She brushes past me, opens her door, and slams it shut.

And that's when the sky decides to fall. The rain pelts down so hard it burns my face. I rush back inside, soaking wet, and lock the door behind me. I'm dripping on the welcome mat we keep on the inside of our houseboat to clean off our shoes and I think how apropos that is. Folks are welcome inside our little home, but not in Emma's Cove.

CHAPTER 5

$\mathcal{I}$ woke to a brilliant morning, cool and breezy, sun sending sparkles across the water as if the lake winked at me in rapid succession. I'm back to feeling nauseated, credit it to the horrid dream I had the night before and not my fall from grace in imbibing Oreos and coffee. I was doing the laundry at the rear of the houseboat and suddenly noticed movement in the woods. Instead of Gorton waiting for me there, it was Dwayne, head back, hands on his hips, laughing for all the world.

I bolted awake, sweat pouring down my cheeks, then quickly retrieved my dream book by the side of the bed. Experts say you dream of people who represent aspects of your personality, not the actual people. But Dwayne was so real, so menacing. It felt as if the man crept into my brain in the night and invaded my sleep.

TB emerges from the shower looking as if he, too, has been plagued by bad dreams, but says nothing. I keep quiet as well. He's worried about so many things these days, I didn't want to add one more.

After breakfast, we grab our things and head out, TB to his

early morning class and me to the Lightning Bug library to see what the *friendly folks* think of my cove. Afterward, it's off to the new doctor for my ultrasound.

TB pulls up in front of the two-story library, something modern and new compared to the run-down mini version in Emma's Cove. TB runs a nervous hand through his hair.

"Don't worry," I tell him. "It'll be fine. Remember, the heartbeat was strong."

He nods and exhales but he's tightly wound inside. I know this because I feel the same.

"Call me as soon as you're done," he says with a catch in his throat.

I give him a super long, super passionate kiss and send him on his way, then head inside. The librarian at the central desk immediately welcomes me.

"What can I help you with?" she asks with a warm smile.

Night and day.

"I'm looking for the history of Emma's Cove."

I wait for some form of rebuttal, a snarky remark, a suspicious look or maybe a dozen questions, considering how Maribelle painted this picture. Instead, the librarian asks nicely how I want to proceed.

"We have a series of folders on the town, each containing paper resources such as articles, brochures…."

"Brochures?"

"The logging company printed one to attract workers and their families."

"Didn't last, though, right? The land wasn't conducive to logging?"

The librarian with a slight accent that makes me think South of the Border leans her elbows on the counter, gets comfortable. Still so affable.

"They logged quite a bit in the area, so they were selling the whole region. If you visit you'll see some sections of land with new growth."

I'm thinking of that brown swath by the lake and the actual town. That must have been the first attempt to deforest the area before they gave up.

"In fact," this nice librarian continues, "Emma's Cove did prove to be difficult, but not all of it. I can imagine some developers right now would love to get their hands on some of that lakefront property."

I think back to the woods on the other side of Maribelle's motel, a lovely plot stretching down from the road to the lake with only a gradual slope, wonder who owns it.

"We also have a local historian who wrote a book about the town, and primarily Emma Harrington," the librarian adds.

"I'd like to see it all," I say.

She smiles, which takes me aback even more. So nice. "There's a lot."

My ultrasound's at one p.m. so I have time. "Bring it on."

Camille Smith—her name's on her lanyard—leads me to a room that's self-contained and brings me books and folders that pile up on the table. She tells me to be sure and ask for more assistance should I need it, then closes the door discreetly behind her.

I sigh and start with the first pile, working in chronological order. On the top in the first folder marked 1905-1919 I find the company brochure. Clark-Everhart Timber Company made it look like heaven, old-growth trees fresh for the taking, pristine streams that lead to a small cove eventually emptying into the Tennessee River, and comfortable company cabins. Inside the brochure are photos of happy families living the good life.

On the back, however, are men standing proudly on top of massive downed trees, looking arrogant as if they had bagged a lion on an African safari. My witchy heart aches viewing the deforestation of such beauties and my environmental righteousness—these trees must have been at least a hundred years old—makes me want to yell at the photo.

I quickly push the brochure aside and pull out articles from the early *Lightning Bug Chronicle* about Clark-Everhart Timber heading west and south toward Chattanooga, where land is "easier to tame" and the railroad rolls through. Again, I grit my teeth. Why must nature always be "tamed?"

And yes, I'm a tree hugger. I hail from South Louisiana where sleepy live oaks dripping with Spanish moss stretch their arms as if to embrace and protect us—and many times they do. Nothing spells peace more to me than a good book beneath a shady, welcoming tree. Add a glass of wine and you're talking nirvana.

There's goes my ADHD brain again. I shake my head and focus, open the next folder that heads into the nineteen twenties and early thirties. Finally, Emma appears. There's a piece about her quilt being accepted into a Chattanooga art gallery, then one in Chicago. At the bottom of the pile I find an old press photo of Emma standing proudly—much like those men in the company brochure—next to an exquisite quilt. I say quilt but it's more like textile art, pieces of fabric making up a dreamy lake in the center surrounded by magnificent trees waving in a breeze. Tiny leaves float on the wind and those sparkles I witnessed this morning dot the lake's water. In the corner a woman gazes at the scene, her hair whipping around her face. I can't help feeling movement staring at this quilt, as if I'm there by the side of the lake, smelling the trees, feeling the breeze in my hair.

I close my eyes and suddenly I am there, standing in the exact same spot I stood in yesterday. There's no brown swath but no trees grow here either. I realize the loggers did choose this spot first, then cleared the land for the town. In fact, every-thing around me has been laid bare.

"It was to be a park for the children," the woman from the picture tells me, and there's a sadness in her voice.

I turn to spot the woman in the quilt but instead hear a knocking on the room's glass. I open my eyes and find my kind librarian opening the door.

"Are you okay?"

I shake off my vision, wish I could have had one more moment to see who was speaking, but I thank Camille and assure her I'm fine. She looks around and hesitates, then finally enters my room and closes the door behind her.

"I don't know if you know this but there's some history between this town and the Cove."

I want to laugh. "I've heard."

She doesn't sit down but rather leans in close. I gather she wants to impart some secretive information and retreat quickly.

"The part about it being a sanctuary of sorts is true. I lived there until I got this job and then I moved into town."

I'm not sure where she's going with this but she discreetly hands me a modern brochure, this one about women in abusive relationships and how to get help.

"I moved there because my husband is going to school at Rocky Mountain," I tell her.

She holds up her hands like a cop at a stop sign and backs up. "No need to explain."

I try to return the brochure, but she keeps retreating toward the door.

"Honestly, that's not why I'm there."

"Just FYI. The number's on the back." And then she's gone.

I slip the brochure into my backpack and do something completely against my ethics and morals, slipping Emma's photo in there as well. I can't believe I'm stealing from the library, but I assure myself I will return it once I scan it at home. No harm done, I tell myself. Besides, it's the photo used in the issue of *Life* magazine and the folder contains two copies of the magazine. But no matter how I spin my action, I can't believe

I'm doing such a thing. It's almost as if some power forced my hand when I had the chance.

The next folder I pull from the pile heads into the Great Depression with several articles critical of Emma's success. Lightning Bug leaders report Emma helping women from other places, neglecting Tennessee residents, and training them in jobs that should have belonged to locals. The writer of the opinion piece, a newspaper editor by the name of Wilton Delaney, demands that Harrington focus more on the immediate community.

"Mrs. Harrington has gained notoriety in august places such as New York and Chicago but she shares her success with every American town but her own," Delaney writes.

"We spoke with one of those women, a Mrs. Montclair, who hails from Indiana! This woman abandoned her husband and uprooted her children to live a life of luxury and debauchery by Mrs. Harrington's side in the now notorious 'Emma's Cove,' sharing her money with this unsavory woman that could be better spent on the poor citizens of our town. Or in her own town in Indiana."

Notorious? Unsavory? I flip through more articles and there's one of another cove woman returning home to her "grieving husband who was lost without the comfort of wife and children."

I'm starting to get the picture here. Emma found success as a single woman and wanted other women in similar situations or abusive relationships to learn how to be self-sustaining as well. And the good people of Lightning Bug weren't pleased.

Funny, how greed and jealousy can do that. I think back to Rosario, a friend who moved to New Orleans from Guatemala when her husband got work in the Louisiana offshore oil fields. To make ends meets, Rosario earned money cleaning houses in town. She was good at business and her cleaning service quickly expanded so she hired staff and made a good living. When her husband was laid off, he began beating her, stealing her money.

She had no legal recourse because of her immigrant status, but she tried living on her own. A competitive cleaning service owned by a prominent New Orleans man reported her and she ended up back in Guatemala.

"It's a man's world," Rosario told me the last time I saw her, when officials arrived at her apartment to take her to the airport.

I think of Rosario as I gaze at the last photo of Emma Harrington.

It's Emma's obit.

"Emma Harrington died Tuesday in her sleep at Emma's Cove. She was 101.

Harrington moved with her husband to the town of Everhart in 1912 when Clark-Everhart Timber hired men to work the land. Her husband moved on with the company but Harrington refused to join him, living in Everhart (now Emma's Cove) until her death.

She was a farmer, teacher and nurse but received notoriety as an artist, showcasing her work in galleries and art museums around the world.

Her most famous piece, 'Speak to the Trees,' hangs in the Hunter Museum of American Art in Chattanooga. The American Art Review called the piece, 'a breakthrough in the use of color in textile arts, a true masterpiece.'

Harrington offered a haven for female runaways and abused women, teaching them skills to become self-sufficient. She was accused of harboring undocumented workers and female criminals and of committing tax fraud, routinely investigated by the FBI and the IRS, but never found guilty. In 1937, she was arrested for the murder of several Lightning Bug residents but was never convicted due to lack of evidence.

Harrington spent the last years of her life as a hermit.

A private ceremony is scheduled for dawn Thursday in Emma's Cove. In lieu of flowers, contributions may be sent to the Emma's Cove Foundation."

FBI? No wonder Maribelle was so suspicious. But murder?

There are two books related to Emma's Cove, one written by a local historian and another on the region's timber industry. It's approaching noon so I grab the books and head to the check-out counter. I hand Camille the pile of information and ask to check out the two books. Camille's still affable but she doesn't meet my eyes and I want to refute her suspicions that I suffer spousal abuse but a line forms behind me. I grab my books and go.

It's a good walk to Doctor Mahoney's office but I'm loving the gorgeous weather now that the cold front has moved on leaving a sunny but brisk day in its wake. This time, however, my Dillard's jacket adequately warms. I snack on nuts while strolling through town, then head down a small road that turns rural. As I stroll down the gravel road, Craftsmen houses with small yards turn to farm houses, some with horses and cows and some with long stretches of fallow fields. I relish in the peace and quiet but when it continues for more than a mile I'm convinced I took a wrong turn, Finally, I spot a sign announcing Dr. Mary Mahoney, general practice. Not what I was expecting, thought Dr. Mahoney specialized in babies, but I walk up the long driveway anyway.

I wonder if Mad Maribelle has called Mahoney, relayed what happened the night before and if I'm still welcomed here. Considering Mahoney's a GP, I won't mind searching for a new gynecologist and am now convinced a trip to Cleveland is in order. Still, I had hoped for answers today so I'm wishing I at least get that ultrasound.

The waiting room has two women seated who both smile when I enter and the tables contain intelligent magazines lying about so I'm hopeful. When I state my name to the nurse, however, hope fades. She avoids my gaze and tells me she suspects they don't take my insurance.

"You said you did when I called yesterday."

I put my backpack on to the counter and start rummaging through my notes and library books. Finally, I locate my wallet and retrieve it but the brochure on abusive relationships falls out onto the counter. I pull the insurance card from my wallet, but when I look up the nurse has the brochure in her hands.

"Let's trade," I say, taking the brochure from her and handing over my card.

She's now looking at me with what I suspect is empathy. I want to explain why I have that brochure but she quickly says, "Let me check," and heads toward the back.

I sit down and make myself comfortable, enjoying *National Geographic's* latest exploration of light pollution and how modern civilizations live without darkness and rarely see the stars.

"I see the stars," I think, remembering the first night we spent on our houseboat and how vivid the night sky shined down upon us. I really do love my new home, despite its history.

After twenty minutes—and thankfully after I finish the fascinating article—my name is called and I follow the nurse into the back rooms. I'm weighed and measured, asked a million questions, then head into a room where the ultrasound machine sits in a corner. I'm wearing loose pants so there's no need for me to disrobe.

A woman with long black hair tied in a ponytail enters the room and greets me, introduces herself as the doctor and places a hand on my shoulder while she asks about the baby. She's engaging and owns kind eyes. Despite my worries about being dismissed, I'm feeling at ease. I lean back on the table and expose my belly while she tells me the usual—that the gel will be cold and it may tickle.

"But you know the routine," she adds.

This doctor actually read my chart.

I'm holding my breath as she moves the wand across my stomach looking for a heartbeat and images of the child I will bring into the world. My body tenses and my head aches from the lack of oxygen. Just before I start to see daytime stars, I feel the doctor pat my knee.

"Relax, Viola. Everything's going to be okay."

How different, I think, as I exhale and try to relieve the tightness in my chest.

And then, I hear it. Loud and clear. Thumping to all the world.

"There she is," Mahoney says, smiling broadly. "There's your baby."

I look up and see a beating heart on the monitor, with two small arms protruding. As Mahoney moves the wand, the head appears, everything looking healthy and where it needs to be. Another slide and the whole child materializes on the screen.

"That's one very healthy baby."

I can't help it, I start to cry. Like bawl. For the past three months, I pushed the fear aside, trying not to think of what may happen bringing another child into the world. I wasn't ignoring the child growing inside of me, but I didn't want to image the worst. Imagine what happened to Lillye.

I feel Mahoney's hand on my shoulder. "Cry all you want, sweetheart. It's tough having another after losing your first."

I nod, thankful I'm experiencing this with an empathetic doctor, and continue my cry fest while she measures the baby and records the information.

"Everything's great, the baby exactly where she needs to be."

"She?" I finally ask, getting my emotions under control.

"I can't tell, just use that gender since men used theirs all those years." She sends me a fun smile.

"But what about that?" the nurse asks, pointing to what looks like an appendage near the baby's thigh.

Doctor Mahoney studies the scene and her countenance changes. She examine the screen and frowns and my heart constricts.

"What?" I ask.

She shakes her head as if she's pondering something, then rolls her chair to the other side of my belly and begins the process again. I spot a healthy heartbeat and the outline of my child but it looks different, like a photograph that's been flipped.

Mahoney takes more measurements and these appear to be different if I'm not mistaken, then she does a full belly sweep and there's that photo illusion again. Mahoney sends the nurse a look and the nurse smiles.

"What?" I say, feeling like my heart's about to be ripped from my chest.

Mahoney takes off her gloves and smiles. "Ms. Valentine, do you have twins in your family?"

CHAPTER 6

After my kind doctor and nurse fill me up with diet recommendations, prenatal vitamins, and a lecture on taking care of myself, since my blood pressure was higher than normal, I'm released. My backpack now has a variety of brochures on bringing twins into the world, but I plan to visit the source. As I'm walking down that long driveway back to the road, thinking of the call to my mom, I find myself dialing another number.

My brother picks up on the first ring.

"Vi! Weird."

"That's a strange way to say hello."

"I was just thinking about you."

"That is weird. I was just thinking about you too. Hence the call."

"Funny."

One thing I love about my twin brother, Sebastian, he gets my sarcasm.

"Why were you thinking about me?" I ask.

There's a long pause and I sense something's wrong.

"Sebastian?"

He exhales. "I quit my job."

My first question is why quitting a plum job as an assistant chef at Commander's Palace in New Orleans makes him think of me, but instead I ask, "What happened?"

There's that pause again.

"Sebastian?"

Suddenly, he perks up. "Wanna meet me somewhere? We haven't spent time together in ages and I need to get out of this town."

I perk up too. Road trips do that for me. Especially ones with my crazy twin.

"Why don't you come here? We have a spare room." Then I think of Emma's gorgeous artwork I saw this morning. "Or better yet, let's meet in Chattanooga and then come to the Cove. There's an art museum I really want to visit."

"I haven't been there since Dad took us to Rock City when we were little."

I can't help but smile broadly at the memory. "That was so much fun. Remember the gnomes inside the mountain?"

We both start laughing. Hard. Rock City offers gorgeous trails, flowers, and a view of several states from on top of Lookout Mountain but there's a section where you go underground and view little gnomes and fairy villages. My parents and older sister Portia thought the scenes ridiculously corny— all three are highly intelligent and look down on simple amusements—but Sebastian and I adored them. We created a gnome village in our backyard when we returned home to New Orleans.

"So, Chattanooga?" I ask.

"I'm on my way."

"Seriously, you're coming up?"

I'm doubtful because Sebastian evacuated to Atlanta during Hurricane Katrina and found a new life working for celebrity chefs. He would always say he was coming to visit but rarely came home, flitting in and out of our lives as he worked exciting jobs around the country, ending up in Hawaii as a contestant on a reality show. When our absent father came home last fall, and our parents looked like they might reunite, Sebastian showed up, announcing his new gig at Commander's. I always had a feeling he longed for family, but not New Orleans.

"I'll pack now," he says. "I'll find a hotel and text you the information. You have time to pop over?"

"I always make time for a road trip." I think about how much I miss my twin, especially these past three years. "And you."

I try not to cry, because I've missed him like crazy. I look up at the lovely maples at the end of Mahoney's driveway and wipe my eyes.

"Vi, what's wrong?"

One thing about being twins, you always know what the other's thinking. In our case, we're not identical—obviously since we're boy and girl—and this special talent hasn't worked well in the past few years since we were both traveling in different directions. But right now, I'm feeling his pain and he's picking up my emotions.

I swallow hard and push the tears away. "I'm pregnant. With twins."

There's a loud yell on the other end and I move the phone away from my ear.

"Vi, that's awesome!"

It really is, and now that I'm relating news instead of worrying, a broad smile stretches across my face.

"They have their own placentas, so chances are I'm having a pair like you and me."

"God help us."

We laugh some more and talk about how Mom laid guilt trips on us.

"'Y'all were double the trouble,'" Sebastian mimics.

"'If I had a nickel for every time y'all cried at the same time,'" I add.

We laugh at the memory and I conveniently ignore the fact that I'm in for the same scenario.

"Does TB know?"

Crap. He's on his way to pick me up after I called and said all was fine, that I'd explain everything when he arrived.

"I need to go, Sebastian. He's coming to get me at the doctor's and I should have told him first."

"Maybe. I am your favorite twin."

As if on cue, TB turns into the driveway. "Gotta go. My ride's here."

"See you tomorrow," he says and hangs up.

"Wait, what?" But Sebastian is gone.

I climb into TB's pickup and he looks at me with wide eyes, no doubt holding his breath like I did in Mahoney's office. I can't help but release a giant smile. TB instantly pulls me into his arms. We sit like this for what seems like an eternity until another patient trying to leave Mahoney's politely honks. We pull apart and TB backs down the driveway, turning on to the road toward home while wiping his eyes with his sleeve.

"So, healthy?" he asks.

"Very."

He's smiling for all the world and it warms my heart that we're at least past this hurdle. What's down the road may be another story.

"There is something I need to tell you." That smile doesn't budge so I gather up the courage. "We're having twins."

His eyes grow to the size of citrus and he looks at me with astonishment.

"The road, TB. Keep your eyes on the road."

My sweet husband, who was ever so happy a moment ago, starts to hyperventilate.

"Pull over," I tell him, and he does. When the truck comes to a stop I force his head down. "Breathe!"

TB slowly pulls in air and exhales but there's tension throughout his body.

"It's going to be okay, sweetheart. My mom went through this and Sebastian and I are just fine."

He finally regains control and sits up. "It's you I'm worried about."

"Me?"

He pulls a hand through that thick blond hair. "There's added risks when you have twins, isn't there?"

I think there are added risks for me and the babies, but I don't want to add fuel to his fear. I can't help wondering if he's picking up on something divine. Descendants do that, sense danger ahead of it happening.

"I'll be fine. I'm healthy. My blood pressure's a bit high, but that's fine."

He looks at me with concern. "That's not fine."

Again, that sense he knows something. A chill runs through me.

"Are you cold?" he asks.

I give him a look, but when we start down the road again TB insists I wear his jacket and he pumps up the heat. Now, I'm hot, but I say nothing.

"You have to stop traveling," he says after a while.

"What? No way."

He's dead serious.

"I'm not giving up my traveling, TB. That's insane."

"It's dangerous, Vi. And what if things progress when you get closer to the birth?"

"I'll deal with that then, like July. Jeez, TB, you're over-reacting."

We're silent for a while and then I think of Sebastian.

"Speaking of traveling, I talked to Sebastian and we're

meeting in Chattanooga tomorrow. I'm going to try to convince him to come home with me, if that's okay with you."

"Of course, but why not just let him come here?"

We pull into our parking spot and home. I grab my backpack but before leaving the truck, turn and gaze at my worried husband.

"I'm taking the train, the one the tourists use between here and Chattanooga. I doubt it will be an issue."

I thought logic would finally filter through but he's gazing at me like I'm piloting the Space Shuttle. The skunk crawls over my grave, as my Aunt Mimi likes to say, and I shiver again.

"It's cold. Let's go inside and I'll show you my ultrasound pictures."

We do just that but that uneasy feeling stays with me through the night, even as I'm calling every family member to tell them the happy news.

THE NEXT MORNING, I wake and pack. Sebastian texted me in the night to relate that he'll be heading out of New Orleans at daybreak and should arrive in Chattanooga early afternoon. The tourist train leaves Lightning Bug at ten so I should get to Chattanooga about the same time since the train inches along the mountain passage and there's lunch service. It's expensive, more focused on tourists with money, but I've connected with the Tennessee tourism folks and they arranged a comp ticket for me since I'll write about the experience.

TB drops me off at the Lightning Bug train station, but he idles the truck and doesn't say a word.

"We're not back to you thinking I should stay home barefoot, are we?"

He finally looks at me, a shocked look on his face. "I'm not like that, Vi."

I give him a sweet kiss. "I know, sweetheart, but your worrying is worrying me."

"I want you to be safe."

"And why do you think that's not so?"

He shakes his head, does that hand in the hair thing. "I don't know. Something feels off."

I kiss him again, take his face in my hands. "I'll be fine. I'll be with Sebastian."

"Oh, that'll make all the difference."

Did my husband just offer sarcasm?

I decide to change the subject. "Do you have your revised English paper with you?"

He nods but he's not smiling. I kiss him again before he has time to doubt himself. "Your rewrite was awesome."

"Thanks to your help."

"And yours! It reads great to me so I'm sure you'll do fine."

The train does its smoke exhalation thing. Time to go. I exit the truck and pull my small travel bag from behind the seat. TB rushes around and takes it from me.

"Don't be silly, I'm not helpless." But I let him, all the way to the train entrance.

We kiss again, I assure him for the umpteenth time I'll be safe and eat my veggies, then I enter the historic train, climbing aboard the metal steps like those women in the old black-and-white films. I turn to do the nostalgic wave but TB's already headed back to the pickup.

There's two families with children in the first car I enter and there's lots of noise so I keep walking. The next car contains two elderly couples and a gaggle of middle-aged women wearing tiaras with what looks like wine bottles peeking out of their bags. Since I'm looking for peace and quiet I keep moving, thinking I'll circle back to the second car if what's in the last doesn't suit me. But it does. There's a lone man in the front row and a quiet couple not far behind. The back stretches open with nary a person. Perfect.

I choose the back row—the only thing behind me now is the caboose—and get comfortable. It's an authentic train from the 1940s and I choose a section with one of those four seaters where four people can face each other. I prop my legs on the unused seat across from me and pull out my laptop. I still have that story to write about Wisconsin and I'll be taking notes as we travel to Chattanooga.

The conductor, or a man dressed in an old conductor's uniform, gathers tickets from the passengers, then a young man looking fresh out of college arrives with a cart, offering coffee and pastries. Of course, I take both, but make my coffee decaffeinated with cream, still thrilled to find the morning sickness gone. The conductor comes on the intercom and announces our trip to Chattanooga, the stops we'll take, and what we'll experience along the way. I must say, I'm excited as heck.

We start out, slowly at first, making a fuss with the train horn as we travel through Lightning Bug. We'll be stopping at the neighboring town to pick up passengers and then we'll pick up speed, the conductor explains. The couple in front of me jumps up to tour the train and I gaze out the window, legs stretched out in front of me on the seats, and wave to the children on the street.

It's then a shadow crosses my lap and I realize someone has taken the seat across from me.

I look up to find Dwayne.

"Hey there, Vi."

I jump to a sitting position, the laptop falling to the floor.

"You should be careful with that. Those things are expensive."

I'm staring into those cold blue eyes beneath a camouflage hunter's cap, that scar Stinky gave him stretching from one eye down to his chin.

"What are you doing here?"

"I was going to ask you the same thing." He shifts in his seat, getting comfortable. I panic thinking he may be traveling to Chattanooga.

"Don't worry. I'm getting off at the next stop so I won't be here long."

I keep my eyes on the man but reach for my purse with my left hand. It's on the seat next to me but I can't seem to locate it.

"I wouldn't do that if I were you."

I pause in my actions. "Do what?"

"Grab your phone."

I swallow and move my hand back to my lap, but gaze over the rows of seats to see if that man's still in the front row.

"I'm not going to hurt you, Vi."

This makes me laugh. "Did you forget the knife you used on me in Natchez when you tried to slit my throat?"

"It didn't have to come to that, you know."

"Right, I just needed to steal a few souls from the ghosts I help to keep you immortal."

My voice has risen because I'm scared as hell. Dwayne looks around to make sure we're alone, then leans in close. I, in turn, lean back but there's nothing but seat behind me and a window to my right.

"I tried to help you, what did you expect me to do?"

I laugh again, but it comes out nervous. "Uh, not kill me?"

"You could have had everything. Seen your daughter. Be with your daughter."

That old pain returns full force. The one thing I desire more than life is seeing Lillye again. But at what cost?

I shake my head. "I'm not stealing souls for you."

He gives me a weird smile, one that chills me to the bone. "I think you will."

I slide my hand across the seat next to me but I still can't find my purse. I look over at the man in the front row and wonder if he'll hear my screams over the noise of the train.

"Vi." I look back at Dwayne, who's perfectly calm. "I need you to do something for me."

I huff. "Yeah, right."

"You owe me."

I'm starting to gather up nerve, although I have no idea where it's coming from. "I don't owe you squat."

He runs a hand across his scar. "You did this to me. And I'm not used to having my looks marred."

If I'm not mistaken, his confidence slipped a bit. And mine has lifted. A bit.

"Poor Dwayne. A cat messed up his pretty face."

He leans in closer and I can smell that heady aftershave he uses, the kind I once thought was intoxicating. Today, I feel like gagging and it's got nothing to do with my pregnancy.

"I need a soul to make this right. And you're going to give me one."

I wonder if he'll kill me if I say no but I shake my head anyway. I will never bow down to this man ever again.

"No way."

He smiles and leans back in his seat. "Thought you would say that."

"Then why are you here?"

"To convince you otherwise."

Now, I'm frightened down to my toes. He feels it, smiles knowingly.

"You're going to give me a soul or I'm going to make sure your daffy husband not only doesn't graduate from college, but has a nice tumble off a mountainside or an accident on the way to school."

"That'll never happen," I say with way more confidence than I feel. "He's a descendant. He'll know you're coming."

Dwayne cocks his head and grins. "He didn't know I was coming today, did he?"

I think back on how TB hesitated in the truck, but why didn't he follow through? Did he not sense Dwayne in the vicinity? I don't know how angel descendants work but I've seen TB's focus go elsewhere and then he disappears, only to return saying he saved a person from a car accident or something.

"He's an idiot and easily manipulated," Dwayne adds.

I want to dispute this fact and defend my husband but deep down I know Dwayne's right. TB isn't the brightest crayon in the box, even though he carries Archangel Michael's DNA from both parents. He loves unconditionally and is generous to a fault, but sometimes he can't manage toast.

"He's not much better than that stupid lumber jack FBI agent," Dwayne continues. "What's his name?"

"Clayton?"

Dwayne smiles as if he's enjoying this banter. "Clayton Ginsburg. Couldn't find me if he was sitting next to you right now."

"You're wrong. He's on your tail."

Dwayne's cockiness falters again and he turns solemn. "Get me a soul or dear dumb hubbie goes bye-bye."

I shake my head and lie. "I don't know of any ghosts."

Again, that creepy smile. "Find one."

"I can't just pull a ghost out of thin air."

"Oh Vi," he says, examining his fingernails. "You live in a town full of ghosts. Surely you know that."

I don't know jack crap about Emma's Cove but I would have seen ghosts had they been there. "You're wrong."

He stops picking his nail and looks at me with narrowed eyes. I used to be entranced by those deep blue orbs. Today, their gaze feels like ice water sliding down my back.

"You two. Such potential and yet so incredibly stupid. You haven't a clue what power you possess."

"I know I'm not going to be like you."

He leans in so close I can smell the mint he ate before.

"You're a medium and a witch, do you have any idea what you can do with that power? And I wanted to teach you, show you ways to hone your craft, develop your skills. You could have been awesome."

"I could have been a murderer, you mean?"

"The ghosts are already dead."

Dwayne's voice raises enough that the man in the front seat turns and looks. I want to shout out to get help but Dwayne immediately turns and apologizes to the man who smiles and continues reading his newspaper. When Dwayne looks back at me, the smile fades.

"Get me a soul, Vi," he says sternly. "Or the world has one less descendant."

And with those final words, Dwayne rises and leaves the car while the conductor announces our first stop.

I'm still shaking as I watch Dwayne through the window. He exits the train and heads toward the station and I watch his bright red flannel shirt and hunter's cap disappear among the hoard of people waiting to get on board. I sip my decaf coffee and try to relax—my heartbeat is pumping at an alarming rate—and feel much better when all those folks enter my train car and grab seats. So much for peace and quiet, but what I need now are crowds.

I take a deep breath and think about my next action. I need to call Clayton, but tell him what? He doesn't know about descendants. Do I tell TB what happened? He'll insist I never leave the house.

I'm confused as hell and not sure which action to take when I hear the ring tone of my phone belting out ELO's *Mister Blue Skies*. I locate my purse — it had fallen on the floor when I dropped my laptop — and pull out my ancient flip phone. I answer without looking at the source.

"Vi," my Aunt Mimi exclaims. "What's going on?"

I had phoned Mimi the night before to share the good news but she wasn't home. Thursdays are bingo nights in Branson and Mimi's their favorite bingo caller. I would love to gush out the exciting news about me giving birth to twins but a lump the size of Texas lodges in my throat.

"Vi, what's wrong?"

Like Sebastian, my witchy aunt senses everything.

It's difficult for me to talk but I manage to whisper, "Dwayne. He's back."

There's silence on the other end for a few moments, then a thousand questions. Mimi demands to know where and when I saw him, what he said, how confident he seemed, and how I reacted.

"I'm a mess," I say through tears that may soon develop into hiccups. "I don't know what to do."

"What do you have with you?"

I look around and spot my laptop, purse, and backpack, and relay that information.

"No, darling, what protection?"

I'm still in Lala Land so I'm about to tell her that TB and I didn't use protection, which is why I'm having twins.

"Did you mean like stones and herbs?"

I can almost feel her smiling. "Yes, darling."

I reach into the deep pocket of my purse and pull out a black stone polished and shiny. "Black tourmaline."

"Good, is that it?"

I pull out the remaining three. "Lapis, obsidian and angelite."

"Black tourmaline is tops in my book for protection, as well as obsidian, and I love lapis for a lot of reasons, but angelite isn't a protection stone, sweetheart. It's a good one for attracting the other world."

Might be time to rethink that one. The last thing I need right now are ghosts.

"I don't think stones are going to save me from him," I finally say.

"First of all, you need to work in threes and you have four stones there so when you get to Chattanooga, find a store that sells these things and buy an extra or two to get your numbers straight. Maybe a nice hematite necklace or a handful of crystal points for your pockets."

Anyone listening to this conversation would think we're nuts but I've seen her in action and trust her advice.

"And second, only you can save you from him." Mimi sighs. "We need to build your confidence."

"I can't possibly fight off this man."

"You can't if that's your attitude."

I love my aunt, I really do, and I believe with all my heart and soul she can commune with nature and work miracles. Teaching me these powers and either of us fighting off Dwayne? I don't think so.

"Maybe I need to give this up," I whisper. "Stop being a SCANC. Then he wouldn't have a reason to hound me."

She sighs again. "That's fear talking."

"Well, right now I'm scared shitless."

We talk logistics until one of the nursing home residents demands her attention; Aunt Mimi owns an assistant living facility. I can hear the resident in the background complaining about the toilet overflowing into the hallway.

"I have to go, sweetheart, but I'll call back as soon as I'm done. Make sure you're never alone."

"I'm going to see Sebastian in Chattanooga in about an hour and I'll call Clayton with updates. I'll figure something out."

"We'll figure something out," she says and we disconnect.

The more I think about it, the better giving up the ghost seems. It would solve a lot of my problems. Plus, I'm bringing two souls into the world. I have a family to worry about, not a few beings trapped on the earthly plane. Let some other SCANC solve their mysteries.

I pull out my laptop and try to write my story while the train chugs through industrial areas, but I can't focus. When we move past the towns and into the forested mountains, I stare out the window and enjoy the comfort of the trees, as if their branches are reaching out and enveloping me in a bear hug. My blood pressure drops and I remind myself I'm about to see my long-lost twin. But Dwayne's face, complete with hideous scar, keeps popping into my mind.

We finally arrive in Chattanooga but not at the famous historic station with the Chattanooga Choo Choo hotel. I'm a little disappointed but the train ride was exquisite, full of historic information relayed by the conductor and staff and a delicious lunch that I barely ate. I'm crushed that I didn't enjoy the ride more, vow to take the train again sans crazy relative of Lucifer.

Sebastian texts me that he's still at least an hour out so I text him back that I will find a taxi and head downtown. I text TB and Aunt Mimi the same thing, just in case. I still need to call Clayton but for the life of me can't think of what to say.

I arrive at the Hunter Museum of American Art and there are three buildings to choose from, an early twentieth century mansion with fancy Greek columns, a seventies structure, and a sleek modern building of steel and glass, all of which overlook the Tennessee River atop a dramatic bluff. It's all gorgeous and inviting and I long to absorb the museum's collections and exhibits, but I first ask about Emma Harrington's famous quilt and am directed to the second floor of the mansion. On one end of the room the windows overlook downtown Chattanooga and at the other end of the hall lies the river. In between, on a massive wall, hangs Emma's quilt.

It's enormous, filling the entire space with vibrant colors I could only imagine when I gazed at the black-and-white press photo the day before. In fact, it's so startlingly different, that I pull the photo out of my backpack to make sure.

Sure enough, I'm viewing *Speak to the Trees*, what Emma's obit called her most famous artwork. The lake's at the center of this masterpiece with old-growth trees surrounding the water, each one swaying in an invisible breeze. At the lower right-hand corner stands the woman, her hair skipping about her face, her eyes closed in deep reflection.

I read the art description:

Emma Harrington, 1898-1999

Speak to the Trees

Dyed fabric

Rich earthy tones make up Emma Harrington's most celebrated work, a scene she recreates from her long-time home of Emma's Cove, Tennessee. Named for the internationally famous artist, the hamlet located an hour outside of Chattanooga provided her constant inspiration. The artwork's fabric was dyed using elements from nature found in Emma's Cove, producing some colors modern artists have yet to replicate. This piece not only showcases the beauty of Harrington's work but her innovation with materials as well.

I walk backwards and sit on the bench in the middle of the room, letting the image sweep over me. The colors almost glow they're so vibrant and I wonder, no doubt like so many before me, how she produced such an art piece from nature.

And there's that woman, so peaceful, a resplendent look on her face. Was she one of the company's wives who arrived in the Cove in the beginning? Or was she one of Emma's many protégées, escaping an abusive past?

Once again, I feel sucked into the scene, as if the trees are beckoning me. I close my eyes and suddenly I'm at the water's edge, standing where the brown clearing exists today. No trees grow here. In fact, there's nothing but mud from the lake to the town. I turn and gaze up at the few buildings that make up Emma's Cove, namely the old empty buildings I found so intriguing and the one containing the library and post office. All appear new with bustling activity inside. The only thing missing in this scene is the diner, but I suspect it was built in the twenty-first century. And the motel and my houseboat, of course.

I shake my head. Where am I?

"It's nothing now," the woman in the quilt tells me. "But one day the trees will come back and the children will play here."

I turn and there she is, skirt hanging to her ankles, white lacy top, that long silky hair blowing around her face.

"Soon it will be lovely, the pride of southern Tennessee."

I have so many questions but the one that emerges first is, "Where am I?"

She smiles sweetly. "Why, Everhart, of course."

I own a head of wild curls so nothing's flitting around my face, but I feel the breeze just the same, hear trees whispering around me although I don't know why since the area has been logged.

"And you are?" I ask.

"Caroline." Again, that warm smile. "Caroline Montclair."

The name rings a bell but I'm not sure why.

A shadow falls across us both and Caroline's smile fades.

"They came here for me," she says softly. "They only wanted me."

"Who?"

"I didn't blame them for what happened, it was my choice to make. But Emma did. It was natural she would feel that way but she needs to let it go. Her anger keeps it there. We need to let the earth heal. Let the darkness fade away."

I have no idea what Caroline is imparting but when I try to inquire, the image fades away.

And the shadow remains.

My heart skips a beat and I open my eyes, expecting the worst. Instead, I find Sebastian looking down on me. I jump up and give my twin the biggest hug.

"What were you doing and why were you talking to yourself?"

I pull back and cringe. "Was it out loud?"

"A bit."

I loop my arm through his bent elbow. "Never mind. I'll explain all later. Wanna get some lunch or would you rather go through the art museum."

I almost laugh because there's two things my brother can't tolerate, art museums and plays. He's quite the literary man, enjoys novels and the food section in the Sunday New York Times, but he can't sit or stand still too long.

"What do you think?" he replies.

We turn to leave but I take one last look at Emma's quilt. I could swear the woman sends me a smile.

"Ask MB" is the last thing that skips through my mind.

CHAPTER 7

*I*t's a bit chilly at the outdoor café but I'm not missing out on Chattanooga's gorgeous view of the river and the late winter sun warming my face. My eyes are closed as I lean back and enjoy the moment, but those large red blobs beneath my eyelids have begun so I sit back up before I do permanent damage to my sight. I gaze at Sebastian through the sun spots that won't go away; he's shaking his head.

"Aunt Mimi says to commune more with nature, but I don't think I'm doing it right."

"I doubt there's a right and wrong way, Vi. But you might want to avoid looking straight into the sun."

Sebastian takes a long drink from his iced macchiato with almond milk and a hazelnut splash, topped with *hand*-whipped cream, mind you. His instructions for lunch nearly took twenty minutes. I want to enjoy being with my twin for the first time in years, laugh about his peculiar relationship with food, but the earlier incident hangs over my heart.

Sebastian studies me hard. "Vi, what's going on?"

The tears threaten and he takes my hand and suddenly the walls come down. I tell him everything, from turning into a

SCANC at the hands of Katrina to finding out TB is a descendant of angels. I mention Stinky showing up out of the blue and adopting me and the weird things that cat has done since. I relate my trip down the Natchez Trace and how I originally followed Dwayne with his promises to evolve my gift only to realize who he is and what he does to stay immortal. I end with our meeting on the train that morning.

"Oh, and according to Dwayne and Aunt Mimi, I'm a witch."

I say this with a smile because I'm still not sure I believe it. Aunt Mimi carries the family powers, ones her mother owned and shared at the old family homestead in Alabama. People came from miles around for divine advice from Grandma Willow. And my cousin, it turns out, who lives next to the old homestead, found powers of her own the last time I visited. I think to impart that news to Sebastian but I doubt he will believe that Tabitha reads energy only when she's wearing her Mardi Gras tiara.

I shake my head. "It's all crazy, isn't it?"

Amazingly enough, Sebastian doesn't smile back.

"You think I've lost it?"

Sebastian places his cup on the table, pauses as if collecting his thoughts. "Vi, we're twins."

Not what I was expecting. "Uh, I realize that, Sebastian."

"And did you not think that if you were a witch, that I might be too?"

I'm so stunned my jaw drops. "What?"

He looks around and leans in. "Why do you think I'm so successful in my career?" Then, with a shrug, adds, "At least some of the time."

It takes me a while for this to sink in. "Your magic is cooking?"

He grins slyly. "Well, I'd like to think my brain adds something to the equation, but yes."

I'm confused and when my brain doesn't work at top speed,

I add coffee. I call over the waitress and this time ask for a caffeinated cup.

"You shouldn't drink that," Sebastian warns.

"Okay," I tell the waitress. "Make it half decaf and half regular and bring lots of cream."

"What's with you and coffee?" Sebastian asks.

I point to his intricate glass of a thousand ingredients. He laughs. "Noted."

"Must be a witch thing."

We turn serious, both of us gazing at each other as if seeing our truths for the first time and wondering what to do next.

"I don't understand," I finally say. "You're an amazing cook. You went to school for it. What about that is magical?"

He leans his head one way and then the other and I can hear his neck cracking.

"When I'm creating and I'm allowed to let go and follow my bliss, magic happens. When I'm working a job, I'm using my brain and that's all there is."

"I still don't understand."

"It's a long story."

The waitress brings me my cup and I get comfortable. "Spill."

Sebastian explains how he could create dishes that were out of this world, mainly when he was in charge and allowed free rein. In school, things were different, everything precise and controlled.

"I made terrible grades the first year. Y'all thought I was doing an internship in Atlanta but I actually escaped there to stay with a friend, trying to figure out what to do since I flunked out of the Louisiana Culinary Academy."

"What?"

He shrugs. "Turned out to be a good thing. My friend introduced me to a culinary school that was more experimental. Still a lot of regulated classes, but I managed to pass. But that's why when I came back home I had those crappy jobs. I wasn't good at being a sous chef and the guys I worked with and for were assholes. Looking back, I can't blame them. I was bored and it showed in my work."

Now that I think about it, Sebastian never seemed happy in those restaurants. I used to think it was because they were entry-level jobs but now I realize he was creatively stifled.

"Katrina was a blessing for me," he continued. "When I evacuated to Atlanta, that same friend introduced me to chefs he was working with and they gave me freedom to create my own dishes. And that's when I blossomed."

I take his hand. "All this time I thought you were being a brat, basking in the limelight and forgetting you had a family."

"Well...." He smiles. "It was nice being the center of attention."

"And now?"

The smile fades. "I came home because I was lonely, missed y'all, but it was back to the same grind. Working at Commander's, what a dream job. Chefs would kill to have that opportunity."

"But not you."

He shakes his head. "Not me."

I know what it's like to be miserable in a job. I despised writing about school board meetings and murders, although in hindsight that cops beat gave me knowledge I now use in solving ghost stories.

I squeeze his hand. "No worries. Let the other chefs have that job. Your dream position is somewhere up ahead."

"Sounds like the opening of *The Twilight Zone*."

"If it has something to do with me, it likely is *The Twilight Zone*."

We decide to skip the hotel for the night and head back to Emma's Cove, mainly because TB and Clayton Ginsburg have called numerous times, no doubt because Aunt Mimi called them. We had hoped to walk around town and enjoy ourselves and pretend the real world doesn't exist for an hour or two but the cell phone constantly beeping was driving us nuts. We find a New Age shop where rocks and other spiritual products are sold and lo and behold they have a hematite necklace.

"Of course, they have one," Sebastian says, when I hold it up for his inspection. "Aunt Mimi sent it."

I want to laugh but there's a seriousness about his comment. I wonder if she's been giving him lessons in the Craft too, will pick his brain on the ride home.

I adore rocks, always have, could always feel their vibrations. The store hums with their magic and I'm as happy in this rock heaven as a possum eating a sweet tater. I think back on Mimi insisting on the power of three so I peruse the store to round out my collection.

"Looking for something in particular," the store owner asks.

"Protection?" I ask shyly.

She doesn't inquire further, leads me to a table containing the rainbow-esque labradorite, glassy obsidian, and other black stones such as onyx and the popular black tourmaline, plus a lovely collection of moonstones, one of my favorites.

She picks up a smoky white stone. "I use selenite for removing negative energy."

"Get that one," Sebastian calls out from behind the bookcase. "I don't want your bad juju in my car."

"Kyanite holds up against bullying," she explains, showing me a collection of the stones. "It lets you keep a clear head when you're being assaulted."

I hold a lovely piece of raw kyanite, its blues rich as the lake outside my window back in Emma's Cove. "This will be a nice change from all that black."

Sebastian peers from behind the bookcase. "Maybe you aren't a witch, after all, if you're only concerned with color."

I'm embarrassed that the shop owner heard that remark, but she doesn't change expression. Guess there are more like me than I realize, even if I'm a witch-in-training with color on the brain.

"I'll take these two and that hematite necklace," I tell her and she gathers up my purchases and heads to the register.

"Does a necklace count when you're doing the odd number thing?" I ask Sebastian.

"Not if you add some earrings," the lady behind the counter inserts with a grin, as she pushes a pair my way.

We leave the store loaded down with items. I have six stones in my purse for protection, I'm wearing a hematite necklace with matching earrings, and Sebastian nabs a Saint Michael candle, medal, and statue for his dashboard. He peels off the adhesive on the bottom of the archangel statue and attaches Michael above the radio. Michael now guards over us with a sword in one hand and his foot on the devil. I look at this mighty angel and it's hard to imagine my husband one of his heirs but then I witnessed TB saving my life from Dwayne's knife in a flood of intense white light. And there was the time he stopped a convenience store robbery with a tub of Blue Bell ice cream.

I laugh at the memory, relate to Sebastian what happened in Texas last fall. He shakes his head.

"Superman TB. Never saw that coming."

Before we head out, Sebastian smudges the car with burning sage and I place my stones in my palm for their cleansing as well. I always found "cleaning" stones silly, felt they came to me for a reason in all their natural beauty and I didn't need to erase the former owner's energy, if there was a former owner. But I bought a haunted photo once and became one with its story and Gorton followed me home, so keeping my aura clear of these spirits might be in order after all.

We head toward my new home and call everyone along the way. Clayton insists on me relating every detail and I oblige. He will be checking in with "his guys," which makes me wonder how I'm being watched by the Feds and if them hanging around will cause Maribelle more grief. Aunt Mimi demands an update and I explain the stones I purchased and she congratulates me on my choices, tells me to put my crystals out when I get home. When I talk to TB and explain how I met Dwayne on the train, I hear him gasping and wonder if he's hyperventilating again. I tell him to sit down and place his head between his knees and Sebastian looks at me and shakes his head. When I finish the call, he says, "Michael descendant, huh?"

"You'd be surprised." But deep down I'm still wondering why TB didn't know Dwayne was at the station.

We arrive at the houseboat as the sun's setting over the lake, casting rays of auburn, amber, and bronze. The night brings a deep chill so I'm thinking a fire in the Franklin stove might create a nice cozy atmosphere. Sebastian grabs his suitcase while I gather my backpack and as I'm throwing it over my shoulder I spot Maribelle through her kitchen window. If I'm not mistaken she's watching me. I think to wave but what good will it do? Even if she waves back, what will her feelings toward me be tomorrow; the woman's personality changes as fast as the weather.

Sebastian follows my line of sight but when he sees Maribelle at the window, pauses and stares.

"She's my neighbor, owns the motel."

He doesn't say a word, so I tug at his sleeve. "Come on, TB's got something hot on the stove." Sebastian groans so I swat his arm. "No complaining about what we feed you. Or you cook everything from here on out."

"I can do that."

I smile because that's exactly what I was hoping he'd say.

TB opens the door before our feet hit the deck. I know what's coming so I hand Sebastian my backpack and seconds later TB envelopes me in a massive hug.

"I'm fine," I mutter into his flannel shirt.

He pulls me back, examining me from head to toe.

"She's fine," Sebastian reiterates, "and she's well-armed with magical stones."

TB doesn't get my rock fascination but that's okay. If he mans the skies, I'll take the earthly plane and we should have most of life covered.

"It's cold," I tell my husband who's still giving me the once-over.

"Right." TB pulls back and opens the door wide. Stinky's waiting for me and if I'm not mistaken, he's checking me out too.

"This is home," I tell Sebastian. "And that's our cat, Stinky."

I show Sebastian my office, which doubles as a guest room, while Stinky follows behind, sniffing everything Sebastian lays on the floor. Without even looking his way, Sebastian leans down and scratches Stinky behind an ear. Stinky immediately starts purring and eventually rolls on his back so Sebastian will have access to his belly. I know where my cat will be sleeping tonight.

We settle in and grab a bowl of TB's jambalaya, forgo the small four-top we bought at a garage sale and sit cross-legged on the couch and accompanying chair, bowls in our laps. The Franklin stove hums away, producing a cozy warmth that makes me forget all about evil men on trains.

Sebastian breaks the silence. "We have to figure out what to do about Dwayne."

So much for me forgetting my troubles.

"That reminds me," I say, placing my bowl on the coffee table and rising. I head to the bedroom where I keep my precious stones and return with my bag of quartz crystals I've had for years.

"I'll be right back," I tell the men and head outside before either can object.

I place a crystal every few feet on the deck surrounding our houseboat, so that when I return to the front door I've created a rectangular circle—and yes, I know that's a contradiction. I chant the words Mimi taught me, asking the Goddess and Mother Earth to protect this home, what's inside this circle, these lives. I also repeat a few prayers I learned in Sunday School, asking God and the angels for the same.

As I say the final words, I spot him, Gorton watching from the woods, the trees closing in around him as if to protect my Wisconsin ghost. I want with all my heart and soul to head there and find out what he wants, who MB is, why that person matters. But it's cold, the woods are dark without the aid of a moon, and for all I know Dwayne waits for me there, hoping I'll transition Gorton and he can steal his soul.

Gorton and I gaze at each other for a few seconds, then I head back inside and resume my seat.

"Finished with your woo-woo?" Sebastian asks.

I say nothing, try to eat, but my appetite's long gone.

THE FOLLOWING morning I'm not feeling so hot, thinking that maybe coffee wasn't such a good idea the day before. TB and Sebastian had stayed up talking until the early morning hours but I hit the hay before midnight and now, since the men are still sleeping, the houseboat's nice and quiet. I decide it's time to finish that Wisconsin story so I reluctantly drink Maribelle's tea and feel much better after twenty minutes. I grab a blueberry muffin, enjoy it while I'm typing away, and shake out crumbs from the keyboard.

It reminds me of when I worked at home and Lillye would climb into my lap, food falling everywhere, her grimy hands all over the desk. But even with the mess, I used to love typing my stories with that little head of soft brown curls beneath my chin.

I miss her so much my heart literally aches and I have trouble breathing. I know this pain will never disappear but that shrink my mom insisted I see after Lillye died swore that time would make my grief bearable. And, it has. Sort of.

I think about the twins and wonder if Lillye approves. Having two babies feels like I'm betraying her, moving on, finding new children to love. Of course, that's ridiculous but what I would give for a sign from my firstborn, something to tell me it's going to be all right. But that's the big hope, isn't it? We all want to know that everything's going to be okay.

Wisconsin story finished, I pour myself another cup of tea—it's growing on me—and gaze out the window toward the woods. No Gorton. But a face suddenly appears and I shriek.

Maribelle holds up her hands, looking equally frightened. "It's just me."

I open the door and Stinky goes flying out, heading toward the woods.

"What do you want?"

I don't mean to sound snippy but Maribelle's been a roller coaster from day one.

She glances around the room. "Are you alone?"

"The men are sleeping."

"Can I come in?"

I nod toward the living room and she enters cautiously. I offer her some of her magical tea and she accepts so I head to the kitchen to pour a cup.

"I saw you putting crystals out last night," Maribelle offers, still gazing around my living room. I can't believe we've been here two months and this is the first time she's been inside.

I hand her the cup. "Like I said, I have a man stalking me so it's a protection thing."

She nods, glancing toward the back bedrooms where both doors are closed. She leans forward and whispers, "If you're worried about protection, you might want to place the stones inside your house."

I look around and wonder if I'm missing something.

"Has someone been here when we've been out?"

"What? Not that I've seen."

I exhale. I should have borrowed Sebastian's sage and smudged the house.

Maribelle takes my hand and I nearly drop my cup. "I'm talking about you being protected. Here." She nods towards the back bedroom. "From anything he's capable of."

I immediately think she knows of TB's divine lineage, but that's highly unlikely since I didn't know for most of our marriage. And if she did, she'd realize he's the best protection I have.

"I'm confused. What are we talking about?"

Maribelle pulls me over to the couch where we both sit down. "I know about the brochure. The nurse at Dr. Mahoney's told me about it."

"What brochure?" She gives me a look, so I think back to Thursday and my visit to the kind doctor. I shake my head. "What brochure?"

She leans in closer and whispers, "The one about calling for help, should you need it."

Again, I immediately think she knows about Dwayne but how could that be? But then, she smelled the Feds when Clayton arrived.

"How did you know?"

She takes my hand. "The bigger question is why didn't you tell me?"

I pull my hand away. Now, I'm the one being cautious and suspicious. "Tell you what?"

She nods toward our bedroom again.

"TB?" I ask.

"He seemed so sweet. I have to say I was totally thrown off by him."

My jaw drops open when the pieces finally fall into place. The brochure Camille gave me in the library. The nurse seeing it when I pulled the mess out of my backpack. The Cove being a haven for abused women.

"It's okay, you can talk about it with me," Maribelle says.

Just then Sebastian emerges from his bedroom, heading to the hall bath. He's busy yawning and scratching his mess of hair but stops abruptly when he spots Maribelle on the couch.

"Oh, hello."

Maribelle blushes at the sight of my half naked brother and Sebastian, in turn, grins seductively. There's chemistry happening here, can feel the air change like we've been invaded by a thousand lightning bugs.

"Sebastian, this is Maribelle Greene, our neighbor. She owns the motel." To Maribelle, I introduce Sebastian.

"Nice to meet you," she says.

Do I detect some nervousness? So unlike the tough businesswoman.

Sebastian's still smiling, holds up one hand. "If you'll excuse me," he says, and disappears into the hall bathroom.

I look back at Maribelle and she's smoothing down her thick gray hair that I've admired ever since arriving in Emma's Cove. It's completely gray, hangs short about her neck, which makes her look older than I suspect she is. If she colored her hair, I'd swear she was my age. But it's gorgeous and I hope she never does.

"I should go," she says, and I wonder if I'm right in sensing she's attracted to my brother and feeling self-conscious about her looks. She's dressed in jeans and an old flannel shirt, a wool vest on top that's worse for wear.

We both rise from the couch and I walk her to the door. This time, I take her hand.

"I'm not in an abusive relationship, Maribelle. TB is the sweetest man and would never harm anyone or anything. In fact, just the opposite."

She's not buying it, or at least still suspicious. "I'm here if you need me."

I have to laugh. "Since when?"

My last comment stings and she straightens her back. "We have reasons why we're this way."

I wonder how many women in Emma's Cove are victims of domestic abuse, think of how Maribelle lost her career because her obsessive husband wouldn't let go and died tragically. I think of Dwayne and how I jumped when Maribelle walked by my kitchen window.

"I understand."

"Maybe we can do breakfast sometime or talk about it?" she asks.

"Absolutely." Then a brilliant idea comes to mind. "Why don't you come over for dinner tonight. Sebastian's a chef and I'll get him to make something special."

Finally, a smile, accompanied by a soft glow on her cheeks. "That would be lovely."

"We can talk about that man I told you about. You should know the details, in case he shows up here." I swallow hard because the likelihood Dwayne might visit, despite Clayton's guys watching the house, are pretty damn good.

She nods, brushing a loose hair behind an ear. I really hope she doesn't go home and color it.

"I'll bring wine."

"And more of that tea?" I ask sheepishly.

We smile and for the first time I feel like we're friends.

I head back inside as Sebastian's entering the living room, pulling on a shirt. "Where did she go?"

I laugh because my twin's cheeks are blushing pink.

"Home. But she'll be back for dinner. And you're cooking."

As he buttons up his shirt and stares out our big picture window, I can almost see the wheels spinning inside Sebastian's head. "Is there trout in that lake?"

"Absolutely. And it's delicious."

"Meunière sauce. My special asparagus. Crab and corn bisque if I can find some fresh crabmeat in this wilderness. Bananas Foster for dessert."

"Okay, stop. I'm getting hungry."

Sebastian finally looks my way. "I'll do breakfast."

"Music to my ears."

After eggs Benedict, toast and Cajun hash browns cooked with red peppers, onions and Tony Chachere spice from home —my mom sent it along with Sebastian in addition to several other Louisiana food products—the three of us head into the tiny downtown of Emma's Cove. I show Sebastian the diner and mention its fantastic biscuits and gravy, the library and post office combination, and the lovely old buildings lying vacant. Sebastian pauses in front of the historic two-story building with its elegant cast iron metal façade, studying it carefully. As if on cue, we both peer into the front window and the inside appears as healthy as the exterior. The ground floor consists of a large room with fireplace in the center of one wall and a counter at the back. Shelves cover the opposite wall, many of which look to be in good shape. I'm thinking this was Emma Cove's general store.

I place a hand on his shoulder and lean in close, whisper in his ear, "Would make an awesome restaurant. Especially one without a set menu, where the chef would create masterpieces for his visitors."

A smile begins at the corners of Sebastian's lips and I detect he's thinking the same thing.

"Bet the second floor would make a nice living area too," I add.

"Would need some money and a lot of help."

I squeeze his shoulder. "I know a carpenter."

We look at the building next door but it's much smaller and in need of structural support, lacks the other's charm. One exterior brick wall slants slightly and there's a major hole in the second-floor roof.

"We tackle that one once we've made the big bucks," I say with a grin.

We walk down to the edge of the lake, stand on that brown patch of earth. We're all admiring the beauty of our cove, especially now that the rain has passed and the sun's warming us all. The men pull off their jackets and spread them on the ground, then sit down and let the sun warm their faces. I stand, watching the sun play tag with the lake waters, still thinking about that vision I had in Chattanooga.

"Aren't you going to join us?" TB pats the empty space next to him where his jacket lies.

I sit down, lean against my husband and try to forget about Dwayne, ghosts, and the dark history of this cove. The peacefulness of our new home warms me as much as the sun and I place a hand where two children are growing, thinking that it's time TB and I start a new life. Maybe it's also the perfect opportunity to stop chasing ghosts and demons, attempt to lead a normal existence. Once Dwayne is out of my life for good, we can become a real family, without the supernatural drama that's been plaguing us since Hurricane Katrina.

As soon as that thought flits through my mind and I smile thinking of the possibilities, I'm thrown back to a different time, sitting alone at the lake's edge and staring into the face of Caroline Montclair.

I sit up and gasp, feeling like I descended the peak of a roller coaster.

"Where am I?"

Caroline kneels in front of me, studying me as much as I'm studying her. She's not dressed in lace and a long skirt this time, but rugged pants and a man's shirt with a bandana tied around her head. I immediately think of Rosie the Riveter from the World War II posters.

"You're in Emma's Cove."

Around me the woods are still sparse but thicker than my earlier vision at the museum; trees have returned. And there's grass beneath my feet. But it's the green eyes of the woman before me that captures my attention.

"Are you in need?" she asks.

"Always," I say with a grin, but then regret my flippancy. "I mean, I'm pregnant."

I don't know why that blurts out of my mouth.

"The stones will help, but he's coming."

That roller coaster plunges again.

"Who?"

"He won't be alone. They always come in packs. They're afraid, you know?"

I sit up straighter. "Who?"

Caroline stares off toward the lake. "Such a gorgeous day. But the storms will return. Trust your instinct and rely on what's inside you. You're stronger than you'll ever imagine."

"Who?" I ask more intently.

Caroline sighs. "Men. They fear our power."

I suddenly want to defend the two at my side, wherever they are. "Not all men."

She nods and smiles. "No, not all men. And that's good to remember because they can help."

I lean in close, touch her arm and amazingly enough, it's flesh and bone. "What men are coming?"

She sighs. "Ask MB. She'll know how to help."

This MB mystery is getting the best of me.

"I keep hearing that but who is she?"

Caroline keeps staring off into the distance as she slowly dissolves into air. "Ask MB."

At this point, I'm frustrated as all get-out and even though I sense this vision fading, I yell out, "Who the hell is MB?"

I feel someone shaking my shoulder, hear TB call out my

name. I look over and find TB and Sebastian staring at me with concern.

"What the hell, Vi?" Sebastian asks. "Where did you go and who are you shouting at?"

"What just happened?" I ask them.

"You were screaming about someone named MB," TB says.

Sebastian straightens, looks over my shoulder and smiles. "Oh hi."

I turn and spot Maribelle not one hundred feet away with a basket filled with a teapot and cups and what looks like scones. Her hair's still gray but combed out smooth with the sides pinned up with cute little barrettes. She's changed into nice jeans and a mahogany peasant shirt. Despite her appearance and proximity to Sebastian, she's not smiling, only has eyes for me.

The knowledge hits me like a landslide.

Maribelle. As in Mari-Belle.

"Oh my God," I think to myself. "Maribelle's MB."

CHAPTER 8

I stand up quickly but the vision has slammed my energy and I nearly fall back to the ground. TB catches me as I'm sliding, holds my shoulders and gives me that once-over again. I want to explain that I'm good, that I'm channeling this woman who used to live here, but I'm so flabbergasted that I finally found MB.

Maribelle, on the other hand, rushes over to see if I'm okay.

"What's going on?" she asks.

There's so many questions but I'm afraid to blurt out that two non-humans are pushing me in her direction. I'm worried she will call me crazy and storm off yet again. Especially, since "MB" and Sebastian are sneaking gazes at each other. I haven't seen my brother smile this much in ages.

"I'm fine, just got up too fast."

She relaxes. "I brought tea."

What I really need is a stiff drink but I've a year at least between me and a bottle of bourbon.

"Why don't we head to a better place?" Sebastian suggests. "The ground here is pretty damp."

Maribelle's smile fades as she gazes at the brown patch where we rested. "Why on earth did you choose this place?"

"Pun intended?" I ask with a grin, but no one gets it.

I gaze at my brother who usually picks up my weird humor but he's frowning, pulling his jacket close over his chest.

"Yes, we definitely should move away from here," he says solemnly.

It's then I feel it. That darkness that surrounded me a couple of days ago when I walked down to the water's edge. Something angry and mean. TB senses it too, catch him looking around nervously, his body tense.

"What is it?" I ask him.

Maribelle's suspicions return. "What's the matter?"

TB attempts to shake it off but I know he's worried. "Let's go back to the houseboat."

"Yes, let's," Sebastian agrees.

We walk up the bank in silence and each step away from the lake's edge feels infinitesimally better. By the time we reach the back of the library and walk single file through the alley between the library and the diner, we're back to our old selves. At least, I am. As we emerge on to the street, we all sigh as if we've walked up a steep flight of stairs.

"Who owns those buildings?" Sebastian finally asks Maribelle.

She laughs. "I do."

"What?" we three ask in unison.

She slides the tea basket into the crook of her elbow, getting comfortable as she examines her property. "I thought one could be a lovely bed and breakfast and the other a shop for herbs and teas, maybe serve tea in the front."

I can definitely see that. "What happened?"

She shrugs but a sadness sweeps over her face. "Nothing. Everything. Lack of funds. Lack of time." Under her breath, she adds, "Touché."

Sebastian studies her intently and I would love to climb inside his brain right now. Finally, Maribelle lightens and moves the napkin from inside the basket, exposing several beautiful pastries. "Scones anyone?"

We're stuffed to the max after that big breakfast Sebastian made, but we all agree and walk back to the motel. The two motel buildings facing each other hug a pool and central patio with tables and umbrellas so we make ourselves comfortable there, choosing sunlit chairs and grabbing scones, still piping hot and smelling delicious. Maribelle pulls out cups and pours us some of her "magical blend." The way she explains the ingredients I know she's super proud of her creation.

"Grew every one of the herbs," she says, beaming.

"Where?" Sebastian asks, looking around.

Visitors access the motel off the main road and spot Maribelle's place via a large retro sign that reminds me of motels my parents took me to along the Mississippi Gulf Coast when I was a child. It's a short drive from the road to the two motel buildings Maribelle owns, one containing the office and Maribelle's apartment, the other closer to piney woods that stretch toward Lightning Bug for miles. The two buildings offer long lines of identical accommodations, and allow visitors to park directly in front of their rooms, again a throwback to the days when motels were popular. I'm suspecting only twenty rooms total as I gaze around and make a count.

The view's gorgeous from our patio oasis with motel rooms on either side and a lake view straight ahead with a dock stretching out into the water. Even now with winter still in full force, there's greenery around a cast iron set of patio furniture, a self-contained swing, and a pergola overhead with dormant vines clinging all over.

Maribelle touches some of the plants in a nearby planter as if she's caressing her child's hair. "Some are here, but I only bring them out when the weather's good this time of year. The rest are in my house right now."

"I'd love to see them," Sebastian says while sipping his tea. I notice a shy smile behind that cup. When I glance at Maribelle, she's blushing. Holy shit.

I turn away to give them privacy. "It's so pretty here," I mutter, looking around.

It's the second time I've been on this side of her motel; from my houseboat all I see is the backside of the building containing Maribelle's apartment and half of the accommodations. The first time I entered the full motel property was in January when we moved in and I brought her a basket of freshly made beignets. She merely thanked me for my kindness, took the basket, and shut the door. How lovely it would have been if Maribelle had befriended me then and we could have enjoyed tea out here on a regular basis, me getting to know her and this crazy town.

I get the feeling Maribelle's thinking about that day for she looks at me with what I suspect is regret. I'm right for she says, "Sorry about our first meeting."

I don't get a chance to reply for Sebastian pipes up. "What happened on the first meeting?"

I smile which puts Maribelle at ease. She takes a sip of her tea and gets comfortable. In fact, it's the first time I'm seen her this relaxed.

"I don't know what Vi told you but Emma's Cove has a history of being a sanctuary for women escaping one thing or another." She darts a stern look at TB and TB's eyebrows raise.

I reach over and take his hand. "Abuse, bad marriages or families, that sort of thing," I tell my husband.

"That's terrible," he says, and I hope Maribelle believes the sincerity of those words.

"The first woman to make her home here was Emma Harrington, an entrepreneur and an acclaimed artist."

"She did the quilt," Sebastian inserts.

I stop nibbling on my scone. "How'd you know that?"

He shrugs. "My sister's channeling a woman inside a quilt and you didn't think I'd look at the art description."

Maribelle looks at me with that now all too familiar discerning gaze, but Sebastian thankfully keeps the conversation going. "Go on," he says to Maribelle.

"Other women came and Emma took them in. They had a co-op going, making textiles and other items to sell. They enlarged Emma's cabin and built other buildings so it became a compound."

"They made a living doing this?" TB asks.

She nods. "They did very well. Raised chickens and sold the eggs, grew their own food, sold their artwork at Chattanooga markets. Emma became famous with her art. They all rode through the Depression without a blip in their income."

Sebastian helps himself to another cup of tea which makes Maribelle happy. She's practically lit up inside. "What happened?"

"Let me guess," I say, "people in Lightning Bug who did have a blip in their income weren't happy watching women living well."

Maribelle turns solemn. "That and one of the husbands showed up."

That dark feeling I felt at the brown patch returns, can almost feel it howling through the trees. At the same time, TB squeezes my hand and when I gaze over at my husband see him watching the tree tops. Then, within a heartbeat, it's gone.

"One of the women at Emma's compound left behind a prosperous family and the husband hired numerous people to track her down. Cost a small fortune. Finally, they found her here."

"And he wasn't happy," Sebastian adds.

Maribelle smiles grimly. "Not at all. He enlisted the aid of the Lightning Bug sheriff's department, riled up a bunch of the local men, and they came up to Emma's Cove ready to bring Caroline home, no matter what."

A lightning bolt jolts through me. "Wait, who?"

Maribelle doesn't get why I stopped the conversation. "What?"

"Caroline Montclair?"

Maribelle shifts in her seat and her eyes narrow. "Something else you read?"

It's an appropriate question but I gather she suspect there's more to me than I'm letting on. For not the first time I wonder if Maribelle suspects I have paranormal talents, especially after Sebastian's remark.

"I'll explain later," I say, because I don't want to get into the MB thing just yet.

Maribelle leans forward as if to impart some dark secret and we all do the same. The wind's kicking up again and the massive oak trees around us appear as if they're fighting it off. I wonder if we're in for another storm. I shiver and pull my jacket back on.

"The group of men carrying weapons and torches stormed up the mountain to Emma's compound and demanded Emma release Caroline," Maribelle starts. "Emma and the other women came outside and stood their ground, told the men to go home, but the men had been drinking and turned violent. One of them starting shooting out the windows."

"What happened then?" TB asks.

"The women grew frightened, naturally, and one of them was injured when a window shattered next to her. They moved inside and started discussing plans to either surrender or flee into the woods, even though Emma begged them not to, said they had to face their fears or they would be running for the rest of their lives."

"Or get killed," Sebastian says. "I suppose they didn't have phones to call the police?"

Maribelle nodded. "They did. And they called. But no one came."

"Did they run?" I ask, thinking of how proud Caroline appeared in that quilt.

"Caroline came out on to the porch, said she refused to give in to the men's demands and reiterated what Emma had said. She told the men she would rather die than return to her husband, who had beaten her on a regular basis, she told the men. Her husband called her names, said her dying was fine with him."

TB's eyes enlarge and turn moist at this story and I hope Maribelle finally realizes my husband's a puppy.

"Did they back off?" Sebastian asks.

"Her husband argued with some of the men who thought women shouldn't have to die, or be abused for that matter, but he grabbed their torches and set the house on fire. It went up fast and spread. Some of the other men joined in and the compound was done for."

I wonder if that was the end to Emma's haven but she lived to be one hundred and one on the Cove.

"Caroline?" I ask.

"The women came out of the house and tried to put out the fire, but the men grabbed them and held them back." Maribelle takes a sip of her tea and swallows hard. "Caroline never did. She never left her position on the porch, stared at those men as the fire burned around her."

At this point, TB's eyes are glistening. "How awful." I squeeze his hand.

"What happened to the men?" Sebastian asks.

"Some went home, disgusted by the whole affair, but most of them were drunk, oblivious to the fact that they killed a woman or just didn't care. It had been storming that week so they were full of mud and soot so they made their way down to the lake to clean off."

The wind's really picking up now and TB looks up at the treetops with concern.

"What is it?" I ask but he doesn't answer.

"There was one man who stayed on shore," Maribelle continues. "The rest of the men were in the water when another storm arrived. A lightning bolt hit the water and shocked them all."

"Wow," Sebastian says. "Killed them?"

Maribelle shakes her head. "No one knows. The man who survived told authorities that they were knocked unconscious, that he called to the women to help him get the men out of the water and no one did."

"Understandable, considering," Sebastian says.

Maribelle looks down into her cup. "From what I've heard in the Cove, the women did help but it was too late."

"And the surviving man said otherwise."

Maribelle leans back and the wind calms down. I feel the sun on my face, as if the trees took control and all is well. Weird.

"Lightning Bug residents came and gathered the bodies, told authorities the men were killed with witchcraft. Emma was arrested but never tried due to a lack of evidence and the fact that the rest of the women were telling authorities how Caroline was killed. And there was the burnt compound to prove it."

"And the men who left?"

"Those men disputed that the fire was started by Caroline's husband. One even said lightning caused the fire and that the women made the whole thing up."

"So, that was that?" TB asks incredulously.

"They dropped the case and that was that," Maribelle says. "And the people of Lightning Bug never trusted the women of Emma's Cove again."

"Even today?" Sebastian asks.

Maribelle sighs. "Even today."

I place my cup on the table. "But you forgot one thing. The women of Emma's Cove don't trust anyone."

Maribelle runs a hand through her hair, disrupting one of the barrettes. "True. But we have our reasons."

"Well, I hope you trust us," Sebastian says, showing a toothy grin.

Maribelle smiles back but I know the jury's out on that one. The comment also leaves behind a pregnant pause and Sebastian looks at me as if silently asking what he said wrong.

I wipe the crumbs off my lap and try to lighten the mood. "How about we tour those buildings you own on Main? I'd love to see what's inside."

Maribelle isn't expecting this. She gazes at me unsure of what to do next. "Oh, okay. If you want."

"I'd love it," Sebastian says.

I lean down and whisper in Maribelle's ear, "He needs his own restaurant and I think he should move here. You might get a tenant."

Sebastian gives me a "get real" look. "Emma's Cove? Me?"

I stand to prove that I'm serious about seeing the buildings. And when I gaze at my twin, I know he's just as curious.

"Okay," Maribelle says reluctantly. "I need to get the keys."

She gathers up the teapot. "Let me help," I say, picking up the cups.

Honestly, I really want to see inside her miniature apartment. I'm dying to check out all those plants growing in her window, to see if she's as magical with greenery as I suspect she is. Once we get inside and I spot the greenhouse within, my suspicions are confirmed.

"Oh, my goodness," I exclaim. "You must meet my Aunt Mimi. She's a wiz with plants as well."

For the second time that day Maribelle turns on her inner lightbulb. Out of the darkness that I'm used to, her light is almost blinding.

"Do you like plants too?" she asks. "I'm happy to share some."

I twist up my face. I know I'm a witch and all but I've been known to kill plastic. "Uh, not really."

The light fades. "Oh, okay. Just thought maybe I had found a plant buddy."

A thought emerges. "Maybe you can teach me."

And I can figure out why I've been called to you.

She smiles. "Absolutely."

Maribelle heads to the kitchen and unloads her basket items into the sink while I look around her tiny living room and pretend to admire her plants, none of which I recognize. I love plants, I really do, but I don't feel the connection like Aunt Mimi does. Trees I get, majestic beings who are on this planet to offer us shade, a cooling breeze in summer, and oxygen to live. But an African violet or a philodendron? Can't relate.

And it's also not the same as my connection with rocks. I don't feel vibrations from plants in the same way. Aunt Mimi insists I can learn but I'd rather play witch with my stones.

"Check out the herbs on the window sill," Maribelle calls from the kitchen. "I've got some unusual ones there."

I head to the bay window that overlooks the small office parking lot, a window big enough to greet the sun and allow plants to absorb sunlight until noon, Maribelle instructs me from the kitchen. I must say the smell is delicious and I would love to have some of that sweet aroma in my houseboat.

But then I get distracted by photos on the nearby desk. There's a photo of a woman with two kids with one of them looking like Maribelle as a teenager. What must be her parents have their hands on her shoulders, smiling, while an older boy on the side stands with his arms crossed about his chest, scowling.

"My rue is really taking off," Maribelle calls out from the kitchen.

"Awesome," I pipe back, leaning down to check out the

photos at the rear of the desk. There's another of people I don't recognize and a small one of a wedding couple with the man in uniform. I assume the latter is Maribelle's parents for they own the same facial attributes.

"I have lots of mint, too, if you just want something for iced tea," she continues.

"Okay," I say absentmindedly, reaching to the back to pull out a photo hidden by the others.

"And spearmint."

I pull the photo free and stand straight, move toward the light to better make out the image. There, staring back, is a wedding couple standing on a deck with commercial fishing boats in the background. Maribelle's dressed in a short lacy dress, pearls and high heels—so unlike her—and she's not smiling. Next to her is a ruddy bearded man in a suit.

It's Gorton.

"That was my husband," I hear her say behind me. "On our wedding day."

I swallow hard but I can't look at her. I don't know what to say. I need to find the right time to explain how I've been seeing her dead husband and how he insists I speak with her, but TB and Sebastian are waiting outside.

I place the photo back on the desk. "Lovely couple," I manage.

Maribelle grabs the keys, we join the men, and head back toward town but I'm stunned to say the least. I've had ghosts appear asking that I contact loved ones but never ones who have followed me around the country. And to have Caroline restate a request to speak with Maribelle has me befuddled.

We walk to the center of town and the worst-off building, which takes a good shove to get the front door open. The inside reveals a front room that's been gutted to the studs and cleaned, a hint of Pine Sol permeating the air. It's not as quaint as its neighbor, doesn't include the beautiful brick and wood as the other, but it's homey.

"It needs some structural work and the roof needs replacing but I've kept it in stable condition," Maribelle tells us. "I was hoping to make this the tea shop and I would live on the second floor. It's actually quite cozy up there with a fabulous view of the lake."

We head next door to the building I'm personally enamored with where the first floor has also been gutted and restored, just needs paint, Maribelle tells us.

"Except for the left wall, of course." She runs a hand over the rustic brick. "I left this exposed along with the wooden floors and beams."

I sneak a glimpse at Sebastian and he's checking out every inch of the place. I can see round tables throughout, with a couple of cozy two-tops by the fireplace, all covered in magenta tablecloths and candles.

"Where would the kitchen be?" I ask him.

"Kitchen?" Maribelle repeats.

Sebastian shrugs. "Vi thinks this would make a great restaurant."

The light comes on again and Maribelle smiles. "Follow me."

We head to the back and find a large room with massive sinks and a drain in the middle of the concrete floor. It, too, has been gutted but could easily be converted into a commercial kitchen.

"This was the commissary for the timber company," Maribelle explains. "They cooked and served the meals here. And there's an old mill in the woods behind this place so the company ground its own cornmeal and grits."

I adore freshly ground meal, makes the best bread, and the thought of stone-ground grits has me dreaming up a savory plate of shrimp and grits. I imagine Sebastian would love getting that mill back on line, but more importantly I would.

My brother's gazing around the kitchen with a smile, no doubt thinking where the appliances would go, and I'm about to burst. I know I'm ahead of myself, plus imagining my twin in tiny Emma's Cove after his experiences with famous chefs is hopeful at best. But I ask Maribelle anyway. "What's the second floor look like?"

We follow Maribelle upstairs through a back staircase off the kitchen and the second floor has been gutted too, although nothing more has been done. It's a blank slate except for the bathroom fixtures sticking out of the wall toward the back, connecting to the plumbing coming off the kitchen.

"I left this open, thinking whoever bought the building might want to live here and design it however they want." Maribelle again lovingly touches the exposed brick. "The bathroom must be back here because of the plumbing, but the rest is fair game."

We walk through the massive room, admiring the raw wooden floors, the tall ceilings graced with thick wooden beams and the oversized windows exposing a breathtaking view of the lake. The fireplace from the second floor has an opening here as well, and I imagine a cozy blaze on a cold winter night.

"Why didn't you want to live here?" Sebastian asks. "This view has to be better than the other."

She joins him at the window and from behind they look like the perfect couple contemplating their first home together. And yes, I'm way ahead of myself.

"I wanted to run the herb shop so it made more sense," she says. "And I thought about making this a bed and breakfast but I can't cook, so I figured I'd have to hire someone to run the kitchen or lease this out to someone who might want to use the ground floor and live on the second."

Like Sebastian.

As if he read my mind, Sebastian looks back at me and his eyes narrow. I can't help myself, send him a wide smile.

TB, on the other hand, isn't subtle. "You should open a restaurant here, Sebastian."

My husband's late to the table with that remark, to borrow a restaurant pun.

Sebastian laughs nervously, looking from us to Maribelle. "I just got here, y'all."

There's a bit of a blush on Maribelle's cheeks, but she adds a finishing comment. "I upgraded the plumbing."

TB starts talking carpentry to Maribelle and the two walk around the second floor examining her handiwork. Meanwhile, Sebastian sends me the evil eye.

I shrug. "Think of the quality time you could spend with your niece and nephew."

Maribelle turns around abruptly. "Twins?"

TB takes my hand and we smile for all the world and for the first time feel unconditional joy at our future. My mind starts to remind me that Dwayne is out there and the world is anything but safe but I brush the image away.

"Yes, twins. Doctor Mahoney thinks it's a boy and a girl."

Sebastian seems happy we're on to a new subject but after a few minutes of Maribelle's maternal questions and suggestions and the placing of hands on my belly, he's ready to move on.

"Where do the people of Emma's Cove live? Or are there people living here, besides you three."

"They live all over the mountain," Maribelle says. "Wanna see?"

Finally, I think, I'll get to find out where these people reside.

We climb into Sebastian's Toyota, Archangel Michael guarding us from his place on the dashboard. Sebastian insists Maribelle sit in the front passenger seat since she knows the way—at which time Sebastian sends us a hostile look daring us to comment—and we head west through town. As soon as we leave the lake's edge the road ascends and we're enveloped into woods, old-growth trees growing high, blocking out the sun with the lake peeking through the woods every few yards. I can easily see why women on the run loved this place, so isolated and yet peaceful and green.

As we drive through the Tennessee back roads, I spot a house or a trailer off the road, partially hidden behind the trees.

"The owner of the diner lives there," Maribelle says, when we pass a quaint little cottage nestled deep inside a stand of sugar maples.

She points out several other residents' houses, some hardly visible from the road, then the road ends in a cul de sac with a ranch-style house at the far end.

"After the men burned Emma's compound, she thought it best if the women of the town had their own places." Maribelle turns in her seat to make sure we're hearing her. "And over time she purchased plots of land for them where they built their own homes."

"Is that what the Emma's Cove Foundation is?"

Maribelle looks impressed. "Yes, exactly. It still exists."

"But who lives there?" TB asks, pointing to the house before us.

We look through the trees at the home that I assume is deserted, but there's a lovely garden plot in front, now dormant. If someone doesn't live here now, they did last year.

"That was Emma's house," Maribelle says softly, as if in reverence. "Now, it's a community center."

TB perks up. "Can we go see it?"

Maribelle gazes at the house in contemplation and I'm wondering if she still distrusts us. Finally, she digs the keys out of her purse and motions for Sebastian to drive. All the while I'm thinking, she has keys to this place? Was she leaving behind an abusive past, sugar-coating her story?

Sebastian pulls into the driveway and parks and we all head to the house. Now that we're closer, it's clear someone uses this place on a regular basis because the driveway has recent tire marks, there's fresh trash in the can on the side of the house, and a light shines on the inside.

"We have community meetings here," Maribelle explains. "We used to do town business at the library but this aggressive writer from a regional website kept showing up looking to solve the mystery of what happened years ago."

I hold up my hands. "Not all journalists are bad."

Maribelle huffs. "I wouldn't call that idiot a journalist."

She opens the door and indeed, the insides are well kept up and furnished. The wood paneling and mid-century light fixtures date the house but the walls contain peaceful landscape artwork and lake photographs and the wall colors are soft and inviting. We head through the front room, which has a circle of chairs.

"We do a lot of counseling in here, some of it by volunteers from a few Chattanooga organizations," Maribelle says. "Another reason why we moved from the library, because the library is part of the county system and Touché insisted that if we use a county building we had to have certified counselors present. We always did, but he found out about the one night it rained and the counselor couldn't drive over and we had an informal meeting anyway."

"Who's Touché?"

"I'll tell you later," I whisper to Sebastian.

In the back is a large kitchen and several bedrooms. In fact, the house stretches back way farther than anyone could imagine spotting it from the road.

"We house women, too," Maribelle says, giving us a stern look. "But please keep that to yourself. It's nothing illegal but we want to keep their whereabouts private. That's why the place looks deserted."

"Of course," TB says empathically.

"We don't have anyone staying here right now."

Sebastian gazes through the kitchen windows that are so dirty I'm not sure he can make out the backyard.

"What's back there?" he asks.

I follow his line of sight and there's an old cottage beneath a small grove of trees.

"That was the caretaker's cottage from the timber days," Maribelle explains. "It didn't burn with the rest of the buildings."

I love old buildings, adore the smell of the ancient fireplaces, the mature wood. "Can we see it?"

Maribelle shrugs and we walk across the yard that's filled with leaves and pine needles.

"We use it now for storage," she says, unlocking the small cottage's door.

It's so dark inside we're not sure what we're looking at and its dank darkness gives me the heebie jeebies. Maribelle flips on the light switch and suddenly it's a house, living area in front, tiny kitchen in back and a room off to the side.

"No indoor plumbing which is why we use it for storage," she begins while I start snooping around for that historical fix. So far, the place has been updated and neglected and it feels like an average old home. I'm disappointed, and the mildew smell reminds me of post-Katrina homes, when mold crawled up the walls like spiders. After viewing the kitchen filled with yard equipment, I'm ready to go.

And yet, something draws me to the back bedroom. I slip around the corner and peek inside, but the room appears empty. All except something resembling clothes stuffed in the corner.

"No one stays here?" I call out to Maribelle.

"Oh no," she answers. "We hardly use the place. And that bedroom has floor issues so be careful."

I walk into the bedroom, avoiding the soft spots in the linoleum. There appears to be a leak in the ceiling which might be the cause of the mildew smell. I think to convey that information to Maribelle so no further damage is caused, but that pile of clothes in the corner demands my attention. I inch closer and discover what looks like a shirt and a hat. As I finally stand above it, with the light of the window allowing it to come into focus, I gasp.

It's a red flannel shirt and a camouflage hunter's hat.

"TB," I call out.

My fright must have leaked through my voice for all three of them come running into the room, TB in front. He grabs my shoulders and turns me around, once more looking me over.

"I'm fine," I say, which of course is a grave lie. I point to the pile in the corner.

"What is it?" Sebastian says with a smile. "A roach? A mouse?"

TB senses something else and I can almost feel the hairs on his arms rise to attention. He looks at me and I nod.

"Dwayne's been here."

CHAPTER 9

Everything moves into hyper-speed. TB calls Clayton with one hand while holding me tight with the other. Sebastian plays detective, moving us out of the cottage and insisting we not touch anything or step on floor marks resembling shoe prints. Maribelle follows behind locking doors and moving us into the big house all the while asking, "Who's Dwayne?"

When we finally stop moving and breathe, plopping into the circle of chairs, Maribelle stands in its center, hands on hips. "What's going on?"

"He's on his way," TB tells me, flipping his cell phone closed. "Amazingly enough, he's in the area."

I nod, still trying to catch my breath. "Good."

"Who's on his way?" asks Maribelle.

"Are you sure those clothes were his?" Sebastian asks.

"Who's clothes?" Maribelle's getting pretty fed up.

"He wore them on the train."

"Who wore what?" She's shouting now so we all stop talking and look up.

"Maribelle, sit down," I say. "I'll explain everything."

But she doesn't want to sit down, starts pacing the floor, runs her hands through her hair pulling strands from the constraint of the barrettes. "I shouldn't have brought you here. The board's going to kill me."

"We won't tell anyone about this house," TB assures her.

She huffs. "And I should trust you?"

My husband looks like a puppy being scolded. "What did I do?"

Maribelle points at me. TB's still lost, looking from one of us to the other.

I stand. "We need to talk."

I take Maribelle's hand and lead her toward the kitchen, look over my shoulder and send TB a comforting smile. Once we hit the kitchen, I close the door behind me.

"He's not abusive," I say, not sure why I'm focusing on TB, but I need to build up to Dwayne and her fish stick husband haunting me. "You saw him in there. He's very protective."

Maribelle sighs and finally looks me straight in the eyes. "So was my husband."

I square my shoulders. "He's not the enemy. He's the reason I'm still alive."

Maribelle leans back against the sink and appears to be calming down, but she keeps repeating while shaking her head, "I shouldn't have brought you here."

"It's a blessing, really." I try to take her hand again but she pulls away. "There's a man stalking me and if he was here, we need to know. For everyone's sake. Including the women of this town."

That old mistrust that's her constant friend shines through the gaze she's sending me. It's now or never, I think.

"I'm a medium, Maribelle."

So far, so good. She's not called the authorities yet.

"There's a man who preys on people like me. If I solve the mystery of the people I'm seeing, the ghosts, they transition into this beautiful light. But, what this man wants is to steal the souls of those who are transitioning."

Her countenance doesn't change but she's not storming out either, so I continue.

"I'm a SCANC."

Her eyes narrow and she folds her arms across her chest. I forget the stupid acronym means something else.

"It's not what you think. SCANC stands for...."

"I know what it stands for."

"You do?"

She relaxes a bit. "When did this happen?"

I'm still not convinced she knows what I'm talking about. "Hurricane Katrina."

"Is this a water thing?"

I nod.

"Kinda weird that you would pick a houseboat on a lake to call home."

"That has occurred to me."

We stand for a while facing each other across the kitchen, letting all the revelations sink in. I'm stunned that she understands.

"So, this man...," she begins.

"His name is Dwayne Garrett."

"...is looking for you to steal the souls of people?"

It sounds so absurd I'm sure Maribelle doesn't believe me, but the look she's sending is not as distrustful as I would imagine. Again, I figure it's time to lay the cards on the table. If we had one.

"He's a descendant of...." I still can't bring myself to say it.

"Angels?"

I'm shocked because finding out TB's heritage stunned me to the core. I can't imagine anyone else knowing.

Even more shocking is Maribelle smiling.

"I'm a witch, Vi. Have been for a long time. I'm well-versed in the supernatural."

My mouth drops open. Not what I was expecting.

"But if this Dwayne is a descendant…," she begins.

"Of Lucifer."

Her eyebrows rise. "Holy shit."

"Yeah."

"And he's after you?"

"Long story."

I relate how I met Dwayne at the national SCANC convention in New Orleans last fall, how we ended up on a press trip together down the Natchez Trace and how, when I refused to help him in his nefarious deeds, he tried to kill me.

"TB saved me," I add, leaving out his angelic powers. "But Dwayne escaped police. And that's why the FBI came to my house the other day, because Dwayne's on the loose. I saw him yesterday on the train to Chattanooga."

"Hence the protection stones," Maribelle adds.

"Yes."

After a few moments of contemplation, I still can't fathom if Maribelle believes me or not, even if she is a witch.

"Do you believe me?"

She smiles but it's a half-hearted one. "Not totally sure. Give me time."

"Well, that's something we may not have." I touch her elbow. "There's something else."

She almost laughs. "More than devils, angels and SCANCS?"

I swallow. Hard. "I'm seeing your husband."

We're back to trust issues for she steps backwards, crosses her arms.

"I realized it this afternoon when I saw your wedding photo."

She shakes her head. "Now, you're pushing things."

"I saw him in Wisconsin, then again in the woods by my house. He's following me. He said his death was no accident." Maribelle moves to leave but I grab her shirt sleeve as she passes me. "He said to ask 'MB.'"

This stops her cold. I'm staring at her back, but I can tell she's relenting. Finally, after what seems like an eternity, she turns, her expression troubled.

"He's the only one who ever called me that."

Now, it's my turn to lean back on the sink. "Caroline Montclair said it too."

"Caroline's a ghost?"

I rub my eyes because saying all this out loud makes me skeptical.

"I'm channeling Caroline Montclair from Emma Harrington's quilt. Or maybe because I was at the brown spot in town. I don't know. But she keeps telling me to 'Ask MB.' And so does Gorton."

Maribelle shakes her head in frustration. "Who's Gorton?"

"Sorry, your husband looks like the man on the fish sticks box."

"His name is Jack Greene."

"Sorry."

Suddenly, I'm tired, weary of explaining this crazy trip I'm on, exhausted from the visions, and I have two people inside of me stealing my nutrition and energy.

"I met Gorton—I mean Jack—in Wisconsin and he told me a man was looking for me. I saw Dwayne the next day in the Atlanta airport. He and Caroline keep telling me to ask you."

"Ask me what?"

"I don't know." Now, it's my turn to sound agitated.

We hear commotion in the living room and an additional voice joining the others so we head back to the front of the house. Clayton has arrived, his large presence filling up the room, along with that delicious earthy smell. I turn to introduce

Clayton to Maribelle but pause when the two gaze at each other with disdain. If this was the Middle Ages, swords would have been drawn.

"Ginsburg," Maribelle says tersely.

"Greene."

"O-kay," I say. "Obviously, you two know each other."

Maribelle's back to being defensive, arms crossing her chest, eyes turning into little darts. I don't buy into the negative view of witches, know that the practice of Wicca concerns tapping into the divine through nature and not hags on brooms turning young virgins into newts. But right now, Maribelle's evil eye could kill. I wouldn't want to be on the receiving end.

"Why don't we all sit down," Clayton says, attempting a smile.

A long stream of expletives comes flying out of Maribelle in response to that suggestion.

"O-kay," I say again, touching her arm, which feels like steel. "I think sitting down, some coffee…." I look at Sebastian and TB who get the message and they both happily rise and head toward the kitchen. Wish I was heading there with them.

"I mean no harm here," Clayton says to Maribelle. "I'm here for Vi."

"Then why is it that I've heard you reopened my husband's case."

"Wait," I say, looking from one to the other. "What?"

Clayton's sighs. "Can we please sit down and discuss this?"

Maribelle looks out the front window. "Are your men out there ready to haul me off to jail again?"

"That wasn't us, Maribelle."

"Right." The sarcasm begins. "You weren't my enemy, just gave all kinds of evidence to the local police who read it wrong. And they hauled me off to jail."

I can tell Clayton's getting tired of the conversation. He

straightens, placing hands at his hips like a father finding his best tools left out in the rain.

"Sit down, Maribelle," he bellows in that daddy voice and after a few moments of resistance, Maribelle and I take a seat, Maribelle's arms remain crossed defensively across her chest and her gaze studies something in the distance.

Clayton joins us, those enormous legs stretched out in front. "First of all, we got a call from Touché."

Maribelle looks back and is about to retort, but Clayton holds out a hand. "We're not taking his complaints seriously. We know you're not practicing without a license."

More expletives from Maribelle. And I wonder, how does Clayton know this?

"But Vi said something about a ghost...." He looks at me, eyes narrowed.

"I told her who I was," I say.

"She mentioned that a man she's seeing in the woods near her house was wearing an earring in his right ear."

For the first time since spotting Clayton, Maribelle releases her arms. I'm not sure if she's surprised at the news of her husband's earring or that Clayton believes in ghosts and me seeing them.

"What about it?" she asks.

"Police found one matching that description on the dock and chalked it up to being a woman's. That, and what Vi said about him telling her it wasn't an accident made us think again about the case."

Maribelle leans forward, elbows on her knees. "I told you it wasn't an accident. The man was born on the water. He was half fish."

Clayton shakes his head. "That doesn't mean he couldn't have hit his head somehow, fell into the water."

"So hard it knocked his earring off?"

"Maybe."

She's not buying it. "Something happened, I just know it."

"Hell, he could have slipped."

"But there was no blood on the dock. There would have been if he had hit his head."

"It rained that night, Maribelle."

The two begin arguing while a buzzing starts at the base of my skull. I sense it sometimes when ghosts arrive but Gorton's nowhere to be seen. Some non-entity is here, something primal and unseen. The feeling's similar to that sensation I got at the brown patch of grass but on the polar opposite of the spectrum. This one feels positive. This one feels safe.

When Aunt Mimi instructed me in the ways of the Craft, she said to let go and let the universe and God show me the way. If messages come, let them out. So, I do.

"He didn't slip, he didn't hit his head," I say. "Someone killed him from behind."

Clayton and Maribelle stop their bantering and look my way just as Sebastian arrives with coffee and TB with five cups, all different shapes and decorations. One reads, "I survived Bourbon Street" and I want to laugh, but every person is staring at me, waiting for some explanation.

Finally, I shrug. "It just came to me."

Sebastian sends me a "Get real" look, Maribelle rubs her eyes in frustration, and TB asks if anyone wants sugar and faux cream.

"All I could find was the powdered stuff."

I send my husband an appreciative smile but Clayton's hard stare is like a laser burning a hole in my head. I know, too many similes. My journalism professor at LSU would have me hog-tied me for that. Wait, is that another one? Think that's a personification.

"Where did that come to you?" Clayton finally asks, bringing me back.

I shrug again because whatever floated into my dang ADHD

brain got sidetracked and is long gone. Wish Aunt Mimi was here. She offered me a crash course in Witchcraft on a road trip last fall, including a sexy moon ritual that got me pregnant, but what I really need is a doctorate program and Adderall.

Everyone's gazing at me for answers and I sink down in my chair. "Since when does the universe give you straight answers?" I plead.

Suddenly, two unmarked black cars pull into the driveway and everyone's attention turns to the front windows.

Clayton rises. "That'll be my associates." To the rest of us of he adds, "Don't move. We need to scour the place."

As Clayton heads out the door, I hear Maribelle mutter, "I should never have brought you here."

It takes hours to dust the place for fingerprints while members of the Emma Harrington Foundation Board insist the FBI not pass on information about the women staying here if their fingerprints match a missing person case. Clayton assures them he will use good judgment and extreme care but doesn't go so far as admitting complete concealment. The women know it and they send me angry gazes. I know they wish we had never arrived. Right now, I do too.

I lean against TB and put my head on his shoulder. I'm dead tired and really need a nap. "Any chance we can go back to New Orleans?"

He looks down at me. "Are you serious? I thought you loved it here."

I straighten, smooth down my shirt. "I do, but look at what's happened since we moved here. And now everyone hates us."

TB glances at the women arguing with the FBI, at Maribelle sitting in a corner with her head in her hands. "I don't think that's true."

At first, I'm sure TB's joking but when I study him harder I realize he's being his usual naïve self, gazing at life through an innocent's eyes. For the first time since meeting Dwayne and hearing his grim threats, I'm worried about my husband, scared he can't see danger coming no matter what DNA is running through his cells.

I think back on Natchez and how TB arrived in the nick of time to save me, instinctively knew where I was and that I was in danger. But does he sense that about himself? Will Dwayne sneak up on him and push him off a mountainside like he threatened on the train? Can a descendant do that to another? Or more specifically, does a Lucifer trump a Michael?

"I could go home and work until the baby comes," I offer, thinking that if I weren't around, TB would be safe.

He pulls back, eyes enlarged. "You'd leave me?"

I swallow hard. "I'm scared for you, sweetheart. Scared what Dwayne might do."

A big smile emerges that warms my heart. "He can't harm me."

"He's going to try."

TB feels it too, that doubt of confidence. After all, Dwayne walked on to a train right in the middle of the morning without anyone being the wiser. He's been living among us with the FBI in sight. And when I think of Natchez….

"He was arrested and thrown into jail, TB. And somehow he disappeared."

TB envelopes me into a tight hug, all the while insisting he's got the upper hand.

"The FBI has infiltrated the Cove," he says. "If Dwayne arrives and tries to hurt us, they would be here to nail him. And now we have Sebastian, an extra warrior in our corner."

"He's dangerous with a spatula," I add, sarcasm my old friend.

I look over at my brother who's trying to console Maribelle. I was so hopeful at the beginning of this lovely day, felt like a normal life was finally on the horizon. Sebastian would move here and build a restaurant that would turn the culinary world on its head. Maribelle would find love again and with our help renew her license to practice midwifery. TB would graduate with a library degree and head to graduate school, unless he wanted to test the working waters first. I'd continue my travel writing career while living on a houseboat raising twins.

And all those ghosts?

"I think I want out," I whisper.

"What?" TB asks.

"It would solve everything."

Clayton heads our way after his heated discussion with the women, looking like a hound dog left out in the rain.

"Again with the similes!"

TB and Clayton both look my way.

"What?" TB asks.

Did I say that out loud? What can I say, I'm exhausted. "I need a nap."

"I'll get you home soon," Clayton assures us. "In fact, we're about ready to wrap things up here."

"Great," TB answers and I can tell he's tired too.

"There wasn't much to go on," Clayton explains. "Lots of fingerprints but there are so many people coming and going through the main house. And practically nothing of real use in the back shed. Even the footprints were marred. All we have are a few fingerprints out back but again, so many people have used these houses."

"What about the clothes?" I ask.

Clayton sighs. "Tells us he was here. Might have his DNA. Nothing useful."

"Odd that Dwayne would leave them behind."

"I think he wanted us to find them."

I've been thinking the same thing. Dwayne would never be that sloppy. And he left clothes behind in Lithia Springs. Is this some message? Is he making sure we all know he's here, can't be found, and he'll create chaos if I don't give him what he wants?

"So, we know he came here but so does the FBI," TB says. "I don't get it."

Clayton glances at the angry women. Dwayne's playing with us, and right now he's winning. I could tell by the quiet, intense conversations Clayton shared with his agents all afternoon that Dwayne came and went under their watchful eyes, that he lived here among us and the sanctuary of women and no one was the wiser.

Suddenly, I'm so tired I'm not sure my legs will support the rest of me. Plus, I'm scared and want nothing more than to crawl inside the protection of my crystal circle and close my eyes to this madness.

"Can we go home now?" I ask.

Clayton ponders this and I'm thinking the answer is no, but he nods his head toward the yard and Clayton, TB and I leave the house, closing the front door behind us. Once we get there, I realize three of the Foundation women have gathered at one end of the driveway, huddled in a heated discussion. One of them looks my way and the hairs on my arms stand up. I pull my sweater close across my chest.

"There's something you should know," Clayton says softly. The women are too far away to hear us, but he pulls us close anyway. "It's about Maribelle."

I shiver and wonder if it's bad news coming or the fact that the sun's setting and a cold dampness has permeated the woods.

"When her husband's body was found, we searched the motel property, the neighboring woods, even your houseboat."

Oh no, I'm thinking, please don't say you found evidence in our home.

"We never found anything related to the murder weapon — if he was murdered."

That voice returns, reminding me that Jack Greene was definitely murdered. For a moment, I swear it's a woman speaking but I hear a small child whispering, "Listen Mommy." Shivers return in a rush when I think of my baby girl on the other side, wondering for the millionth time where she is.

And if she's reaching out to me.

"Are you cold?" TB asks.

I shake my head and pull my sweater tighter. I move my attention to Clayton. "Focus," the voice says again.

"No murder weapon," I reiterate.

Clayton leans in closer. "But we did find his blood in Maribelle's bathroom."

The voices rise from the group of women, one among them rather upset, but in my little circle I swear I hear my heart beating.

"They had a huge fight the night he died," Clayton continues. "Two people staying at the motel reported them yelling and Jack storming off toward the lake."

I shake my head because I don't want to believe it. I can't imagine Maribelle, an out-of-the-broom-closet witch who's supposed to believe in the sanctity of life, capable of murdering her husband. Not to mention that Jack keeps sending me back to her.

"She can't be implicated."

Clayton inhales and exhales. Loudly. Then, he straightens, looking like a Southern pine in the apex of summer and yes, I don't care if that's another simile!

"I don't want to think she did it, but I can't rule it out either. I'm telling you this because you seem to be friends with her now and I want you to be careful, regardless of whether you believe her or not. Just in case."

"Are there other suspects?" TB asks.

Clayton shakes his head. "And you have to ask yourself, who would want to kill Jack Greene? Who had a motive? He kept to himself, never talked much to anyone. His parents were gone and he didn't have a job. He might have been something to Maribelle but he was nothing to anyone else."

"As far as you know." I can't help myself, I've seen too many English detective series. On TV, it's almost always someone you don't expect.

Clayton sends me a paternal smile. "Most of the time, it's someone they know. Well."

Several FBI agents emerge carrying bags and Clayton moves off to talk to them.

"It can't be Maribelle, can it?" I ask TB. "Jack could have nicked himself shaving in her bathroom."

But Jack keeps sending me back to her.

"Ask MB!"

Ask her if she killed him?

"She does have a temper," TB mutters.

That last thought hangs in the air between us like a worm dangling on a fisherman's line. Similes! Argh.

ONCE CLAYTON ANNOUNCES we are free to go, TB, Sebastian, and I gladly head to the Toyota. Maribelle waves us on, hangs back with the Foundation group still engaged in a heated discussion. No one speaks until we're inside the houseboat and crash exhausted on the couch.

"Well, that was a weird day," Sebastian says.

My heart sinks because for the first time since Katrina blew through my hometown I was hopeful my twin and I might reconnect and have a future together. The idea of Sebastian opening a restaurant here, plus my twins and a new life with TB had given me confidence in my future, even one with Dwayne lurking in the shadows.

Especially with Dwayne lurking out there. The more family and friends I have around me, the better, I reason. As much as I spin a good tale about being brave and not willing to stay cloistered in my houseboat for safety, deep down I'm pretty damn frightened. In fact, I'm ready to give up travel writing for a while, find some freelance work that allows me to stay home until the babies arrive. And maybe then some.

I mentally create a list: contact local newspapers and see if they need contract editors or writers, start scouring online journalism boards for freelance work that can be done remotely. Maybe create a website and do public relations for a new Emma's Cove business.

I look at my twin, deep in thought. "I guess the crazy idea of turning that building into a restaurant is out of the question."

To my surprise, Sebastian laughs. "No way. I love a crazy town and this one's off the charts."

TB and I look up in surprise, which makes Sebastian laugh again.

"Seriously, who wants to start a business in some boring place?"

Now, that I think about it, Sebastian said his passion lay in creating something magical for special people. If working at the most celebrated restaurant in New Orleans couldn't satisfy him, then tiny Emma's Cove might do the trick.

"Besides," he continues, "these women could use something lovely in their lives. And tourists will bring in extra money."

"You've been talking to Maribelle," I say.

He blushes. My semi-famous chef of a twin blushes.

"I think it could work." He grins like a schoolboy. "Maybe my carpenter brother-in-law could help with the renovation. And my journalist sister could do some public relations."

"I've already got the website planned," I say, returning the stupid smile.

"Happy to help." TB extends a hand.

The men shake and I place my hand on top.

"It's not a done deal," Sebastian insists, our hands still

entwined. "I have to work things out with Maribelle, release some money I have tied up."

I think of the possibilities: motel occupancy will improve, residents will have a place to dine after hours since the diner closes after lunch, the town's tax base will improve. Maybe Maribelle can finally have her tea shop. And if I'm right about the chemistry between Sebastian and Maribelle, their lives may be changed forever.

"We could build a park for the children where that brown patch is."

I have no idea where that thought came from, but it slips from my lips without much thought.

"O-kay," Sebastian says, looking at me funny.

I shrug. "Just a thought."

"And maybe we can expand the library," TB says.

"Yes!" I exclaim. "Give my husband a job."

We're still holding hands, but now we're laughing, just like old times when we would hang together and watch Freaks and Geeks on TV after Lillye went to sleep. Hope renewed, life may turn normal after all.

Sebastian releases his hands and ours fall away. He turns his chin up toward the side of the house. "Speaking of...."

Maribelle's at the door peeking in and I wave. I stand and open the door, moving back so she can enter and join in the fun, but she hangs back.

"Sebastian's making dinner," I encourage her.

"Can we talk first?"

She crawfishes toward the boat railing, allowing me space to emerge outside. I give the boys a look and follow her on to the deck, closing the door behind me.

"I think I know why my husband and Caroline want me to talk to you."

That warm fuzzy feeling I was bathing in only minutes before quickly drains away. "Why?"

She leans on the deck's railing, the one I've been meaning to repaint on a warmer winter's day.

"I think they want me to instruct you in the ways of the Craft."

The frissons run from my toes to the tip of my head, what people in Cajun Country call the shivers or a weird sensation. I would say I'm surprised at the idea but the truth is, it came to me as well. Can't explain it, wasn't like a message from the heavens or anything, just a feeling that resonated deep in my soul.

Which means it's divinely sent, right? And I should jump at the chance. It could be God speaking, for all I know.

And yet….

I can't shake that happy feeling from moments before. I won't let it go. It's been three years since Katrina and I need something normal and wonderful in my life.

"Not a good idea?" Maribelle asks, examining my countenance.

I let out a huge sigh. "Actually, it is. But to tell you the truth, Maribelle, I'm thinking of giving up mediumship and all that woo-woo for a while."

This is not what she's expecting. I hadn't noticed it when she arrived, but I now get the feeling Maribelle was itching for the friendship along with her instruction, to have someone to talk woo-woo to.

"Can I ask why?"

I place a hand on my belly. "I need to think of these guys, to keep them safe. And if I'm not transitioning ghosts, I won't have to worry about Dwayne."

Not to mention I won't worry if you killed your husband or not, because I'd rather not know.

"But what I can teach you, it will keep you safe."

"Maybe." I'm not convinced.

Her eyes narrow when she smiles. "That's fear talking. And

that's exactly what I can offer. How to build your confidence, find your feminine power."

I think about how Dwayne nearly killed me, how he deceived us all while following me on the train, living among us. How could my feminine power save me from such a force? And how did Maribelle's feminine power save her from the FBI naming her the number one suspect in her husband's death and Dr. Touché stripping her of her license?

"I need to back away from this for a while," I tell her. "I need to let this go for now."

A silence falls between us and I hear frogs below our deck announcing more rain, their calls rhythmic, then out of sync, then together again. Finally, Maribelle lovingly touches my arm.

"He's out there, Vi. The dreams won't go away just because you want them to."

"How did you know about my…?"

"Fear is a monster, like a bulldozer rolling over everything in its path. You have to learn ways to combat it."

I think back on my reaction traveling back from Wisconsin, when the angel in uniform saved me from disintegrating on the terminal carpet. If you'd have asked me how I would have reacted to seeing Dwayne again, I never would have said peeing on myself and crying in the middle of the Atlanta airport. And now I have two lives to protect. Do I turn my back on the three souls closest to home?

"You need to learn how to work with the gifts you have," Maribelle says softly. "Maybe that's why Jack and Caroline sent you to me."

She's right about me facing my fears, know it deep into my soul. I close my eyes because that fleeting feeling of turning away from my gifts had felt so freeing, so peaceful.

On the other hand, maybe Maribelle can help me contact my precious angel. The thought takes hold of my heart and grips it like a fist. Yes, maybe the universe is finally allowing me contact with Lillye.

"Fine," I mutter, then open the door where the warmth of our wood stove and two male smiles greet us. I let Maribelle go in first, then turn to follow. Out of the corner of my eye, I spot movement in the woods.

It's Gorton.

CHAPTER 10

"Two macchiatos, a latte and a regular coffee with extra sugar," announces Brett Abernackie, handing out cups of Lightning Bug Latte's best. The high school intern turns to me with a scowl, placing the cup on my desk and backing away. "And one decaf."

I rise from the copy desk of the *Lightning Bug Chronicle* to remind him of my girth, a middle growing enormous and rock hard solid. I pat the bowling ball that's now my constant companion, hoping little feet start kicking so I resemble a victim from the Alien movies. Brett's heading into his senior year at Thomas Jefferson High School and an only child so my pregnancy freaks him out. He thinks I don't notice him walking aisles away to avoid passing me in the hall or that he's popped his head inside the lunchroom, caught me inside and done an immediate about-face. It might be because he touched my belly once and I let out a yelp, or that I swallowed a whole jar of olives, juice and all, gulping it down like a dog; I have weird cravings.

But today, the joke's on me. The belly kids refuse to move and I shudder recalling those horror films, ones Sebastian thought would be funny to show me now that I'm well into my third trimester. I've had nightmares ever since.

Not to mention the other dreams.

I push that thought aside, thanking Brett for the coffee to his retreating back and inviting him to my gender reveal that includes vivid copies of my ultrasounds. Carol Winn to my right starts laughing.

"I fear for the time he gets a girlfriend and she mentions tampons for the first time," Carol says.

"In all fairness," I reply. "I am the size of a small RV."

I've missed the newsroom, a sacred space considering the U.S. Constitution, but full of dark souls making fun of just about everything. It's how we cope after witnessing dead bodies, environmental disasters, and kids storming schools with guns. Even the food editor, usually so prim in her bright yellow suits, has her moments. Yesterday, we heard the long stream of expletives before we smelled the smoke emerging from the practice kitchen.

These people are my clan, my tribe, wordsmiths who know a little about a lot of things, and use sarcasm and humor as a shield. I once had a friend comment that my colleagues were badly dressed, uncouth frustrated novelists with weird senses of humor. Looking around the *Chronicle* newsroom, and excluding the food editor who's always well dressed, I see her point. Considering I'm clothed in what resembles a potato sack— maternity pants from the Target sales bin and a stretchable top I nabbed at Goodwill—my friend's probably right.

I'm grounded from travel writing because my blood pressure continues to hover threateningly above normal. The part-time, copy editing gig's enough to pay bills and allow me time to do travel puff pieces on the side, the kind I can develop through phone calls, keeping my hand in the game. But, I miss the road. And because TB's so freaked out about my health, he's anxious about me driving to someplace close like Gatlinburg or Atlanta for a weekend. I managed to convince him I'd be safe accompanying Maribelle to Chattanooga to purchase supplies for her herb shop and we leave this afternoon as soon as I finish my shift laying out the weekend features section.

"Page eight out the door," I tell Carol, sending the final page to the press.

As if Maribelle reads my mind, wherever she is, my phone lights up. "I have to go," I add, grabbing my purse.

"Have fun," Carol says without looking up. "And I love that new shirt."

Like I said, my tribe.

Suddenly, the pop culture editor prairie dogs above the cubicles, his eyes enlarged and his mouth hanging open.

"On my God, Michael Jackson's dead."

The newsroom turns into a mosh pit, news reporters asking questions and Carol scouring the Internet while Brett appears about to cry, and even though I long to know the details, I escape the chaos and head out; Maribelle's waiting for me downstairs. I waddle to her car and climb in, hear *Billy Jean* on the radio.

"Michael Jackson died."

"Yeah, I heard."

"Weird."

"Weird how?"

She shrugs and turns off the radio. "Who knows?"

That's Maribelle in a nutshell. For the past few months Maribelle has been teaching me lessons in the Craft and I, in turn, have been peering into her psyche, trying to establish how this plant witch operates. Whereas my brother seems to be making strides delving into her tough exterior, I'm still chipping away, like a child with a plastic knife trying to make a dent in a brick wall.

"You sleeping okay?"

And that's another thing, how does she know about the

dreams? I've never told her about Dwayne's nighttime invasions. Clayton insisted the horrid man left the area months ago and the dreams have lessened since the winter, but last night's was a doozy.

"What's the lesson for today?" I ask instead.

"Have you noticed anything different about Emma's Cove?"

"That's our lesson?"

Maribelle pauses checking both lanes and pulls out of the parking lot. "I don't know. Maybe I'm being paranoid."

I want to laugh because that's the town's MO for sure. Naturally, I can't blame them for being cautious considering what the women have been through, but most still don't talk to me, still angry over what happened at the Foundation house. Emma's Cove residents warmed up to Sebastian and TB as the temperatures rose in the spring, but their unfriendly behavior has returned of late.

"What I want to know is when does the interrogation stop? TB and I have lived here for months now and they still treat us as if we carry the plague. And Sebastian? He's renovating two derelict buildings and is about to open a restaurant that will bring money into the town, not to mention that you'll finally have your herb shop."

I'd say it took some convincing for Sebastian to remain in Emma's Cove—I spent a good week working on him while he argued against me, mostly to convince himself since the town's population hovers around fifty-six. But one night with Maribelle and he was sold. The two have been inseparable ever since, constantly working on opening "The Hearth," Sebastian's new restaurant in Maribelle's building with that ancient brick fireplace as its centerpiece. The objective, according to my brother, is for his restaurant to deliver signature dishes that change daily depending on local produce and fish from the lake, all served at candlelit tables.

"It'll be like the old days, like in the beginning of Emma's

Cove when people would travel by horse or stage and arrive tired and hungry," Sebastian told me. "The Hearth will be a place to find solace near a wood fire, enjoy a great meal with fresh ingredients."

Sebastian made friends with Mountains Spirits located near Lightning Bug and will carry its alcoholic products, along with fine wines from the Georgia mountains. Another friend from Alabama who's big on getting back to the basics in food production agreed to take over the mill, will be producing fresh-ground grits and corn meal. Sally will use the grits in the diner, Sebastian will serve both in the restaurant, and Maribelle will sell bags of the stuff in her tea shop next door, in addition to the tea collections she's amassing.

"Maribelle's Herbs" is on schedule to open the same time as Sebastian's restaurant with her apartment moved to the upstairs' space, although I've heard the two of them secretly discussing moving in together above the restaurant and turning the herb shop apartment into a home for TB, me and the kids. Sebastian and Maribelle are worried about our children's safety growing up on a houseboat but TB and I have that under control. We love our new home and have no desire to move anywhere.

"Paranoid how?" I ask Maribelle.

She shrugs. "Just a feeling. It seems like everyone's on edge."

Including you, I think. For the past couple of weeks Maribelle's been getting odd phone calls, ones she's not happy to receive. The first call came when I brought sandwiches to the restaurant and found her whispering angrily into her cell.

"I'm not selling," she argued to someone on the other end. "Threaten me all you like, it's not going to happen."

Of course, when I asked, she shrugged and changed the subject.

Another time, I spotted her pacing the patio area of the

motel, same tone, same whispered anger. This time I heard a lawyer mentioned.

"Does this have something to do with Clayton?" I bravely ask as we head toward the highway.

She straightens and it appears as if every muscle in Maribelle's body tightens. "What's that man got to do with anything?"

He's curious if you killed your husband. As am I.

I push that thought away, pray it's not true, that this plant witch passing on knowledge of love, communing with nature, and tapping into the feminine spirit didn't hit Jack Greene from behind while in her bathroom, then haul his limp body to the lake to die by drowning. Because no matter what happened to Jack Greene, twin to the Gorton's fish sticks mascot, he perished in the water, which is why he's visible to me.

I've thought about this scenario so many times I'm convinced it doesn't make sense. First, a blow to the back of the head produces a ton of blood, more than the FBI discovered in her bathroom. I realize Maribelle could have cleaned up the mess, but then she'd have to drag a full-grown man's body through the motel parking lot and down the dock and what trail would that have left?

She could have had an accomplice, but who would that have been? Clayton said no one wanted Jack Greene dead, nor did they miss him after his death, so who else had a motive besides Maribelle? Maybe Jack was just in the wrong place at the wrong time, but that's unlikely in most murders. As Clayton said, it's usually someone they know. Someone close to them.

"Where's your family?" I ask Maribelle.

"My family?" She looks surprised I would bring up the topic.

"You know, mother, father, sister, brother."

She says nothing, stares toward the back of the pickup in front of us, one loaded down with fishing tackle and coolers.

"You've met my parents and my twin brother," I say, hoping

this might open a door. "My crazy sister Portia will be here next month. They're what you call family."

She swallows—hard—and sends me a weird look, akin to grief but laced with fear as well. "My parents are deceased."

"I'm so sorry, Maribelle. How?"

I was right about Maribelle being close to my age. She's only thirty-two, looking older because of her gray hair. I'd add grumpy attitude but that's impolite and she's been much happier since Sebastian rolled into town. Right now, the subject's putting years on her face.

She attempts a smile but it's feeble. "Are you hungry?"

"Of course, I'm hungry," I say, watching the fishing pole in front of me bounce up and down and I suddenly long for a plate of fried catfish. "I'm always hungry."

"I was thinking about Public House in Chattanooga…."

"I'm not going anywhere with you."

We pause at a traffic light so Maribelle turns my way with surprise. I wait a beat, then look back, giving her ample time for suspense.

I cross my arms. "We have been having these 'lessons' for months now and, although I appreciate everything you're teaching me, I know absolutely nothing about you."

"Since when is that so important?"

"I'm Southern and down here we value friendship and family. If you can't open up a tiny bit, then why should I trust you?"

"You don't trust me?"

"Give me one reason why I should?"

"I'm dating your brother."

I shake my head. "Exactly why I need to know more about you."

We hit the open highway and Maribelle sighs. "I'll never understand the need for people to know a person's private history."

"How else will we Southerners know to bake you a cake on your birthday, anniversary, or other important event?" And yes, I realize my curiosity goes way beyond that.

Now, it's Maribelle's turn to shake her head. "I hate cake."

I laugh. "Of course, you do."

We ride in silence for several minutes and I'm about to give up learning anything about the woman, but finally, after we reach the countryside and the cityscape turns to farms, Maribelle speaks.

"My parents lived on a large piece of property in Maine, right on the water. They died after I got married."

"What happened?"

More silence, but this time, shivers run up my arms.

"They killed themselves. Together."

I turn in my seat. "What?"

She cringes. "The maid came over to clean the house one day and found them in the basement with a generator running, died from carbon monoxide poisoning."

"Wow, Maribelle, how horrible. Did you see that coming?"

For the second time since I've known Maribelle her face transforms into intense pain and grief. She turns away and looks out the driver's side window, but not before I spot tears in her eyes.

"I don't like talking about it, Vi."

I reach over and touch her shoulder, give it a nice squeeze. "But you need to talk about these things, *mon amie*. You shouldn't keep something this traumatic bottled up inside."

As soon as those words emerge, I think what a hypocrite I am. I crawled into a snail shell when Lillye died, refused to face my grief, receive help, even talk about it. Finally, my family convinced me to visit a grief counselor, which helped a great deal, but I'm a slow work in progress. I still expect Lillye to come running down the hall, still reach my hand out expecting to pat a soft head of curls. Sometimes a pain so intense falls on to my heart that I sob uncontrollably. So, I get it.

"I'm here if you need me."

Maribelle smiles grimly and wipes her eyes. She doesn't say more and I don't press. Finally, she pulls out a sheet of paper from her purse and asks my opinion about the list's items. We discuss the décor of the herb shop, what items need to be purchased today, and if I have time to scour antique stores for furniture ideas. I answer and offer my two cents but all I can think about is a couple so despondent that they took their lives, huddled together in a dark basement in Maine.

And just what made them do it?

We enjoy lunch with me almost licking the plate clean— twins really demand sustenance—and we're off hunting shop items. Maribelle starts in a furniture story filled with cutesy doo-dads and country apparel. I'm surprised at her choice but what do I know about selling herbs.

"If this is your style, Cracker Barrel carries a lot of similar items," I say.

Maribelle sighs. "It's not my style but I think an herb shop in south-central Tennessee should probably feel more country and less witch."

"And those in the know will buy theirs under the counter? Or maybe you can have a secret drive-through window in the back."

She looks at me with a frown.

"Selling herbs doesn't scream witch. I doubt the town's people will arrive with torches and rakes."

"Remember our cove's history?"

"This is 2009," I tell her picking up an oversized tea cup with a giant rabbit in glasses. It brings a smile.

"I guess you're right," Maribelle says. "I should be myself."

I spot a corner filled with rustic furniture and items suited for a cabin. "How about something veering more towards woods, loons, and a lake?"

Maribelle picks up a miniature canoe sitting on the coffee table. It's being used to hold remotes which distracts from its rustic appeal.

"Call me crazy but this would be a great centerpiece," Maribelle says. "I could fill it with tea."

I try to imagine her bare space mirroring the trees and lake surrounding the town, smell the herbs and maybe some tree scents as well. "Works for me."

Maribelle grazes the items, checking tags to find those made in the U.S.; she refuses to buy anything made in China in honor of those crafty American women who founded the town. A friend of a friend swore this store sold items made by Tennesseans, which is why we're here.

While Maribelle examines a side table crafted from maple, I check for the nearest bathroom.

"Okay, kiddos, which one of you is playing with mommy's bladder?" I mumble as I head toward the back of the store, my children in front of me by a foot.

The store offers different decors every few feet. Whereas the front of the store showcases a country style, followed by the rustic cabin items, now I'm passing a beach display, then a collection of retro furniture. Just before I hit the bathroom, I spot the deer head on the wall surrounded by camouflage jackets and hats and several flannel shirts hanging on a makeshift wardrobe.

I stop dead at the sight in the middle of the display. It's a flannel shirt folded neatly on top of khaki pants, topped with a camouflage hat. At the base of the chair on which this collection lies is an angel statue. Only the head is missing.

I can almost feel my blood pressure rising as my heart rate accelerates and my breathing becomes erratic. I place a hand over my heart as if that might stop the panic rising in my chest, but of course it does nothing. The world begins to spin and I start gasping, afraid if I don't pull oxygen into my lungs I will faint for sure.

"Ma'am," I hear a voice say behind me. "Are you all right?"

Suddenly Maribelle's at my side grabbing my elbow and muttering something. I'm too busy focusing on the image in front of me, the exact set of clothes Dwayne wore on the train and were left at the Foundation house. As I gasp for air, all I can do is point. Maribelle turns briefly and looks at the pile Dwayne left me again, then grabs both my elbows and leads me into a nearby chair.

"Should I call 911?" the voice asks her.

"I've got this," she answers, forcing me to lean back in the chair, placing a hand on my chest and whispering calming messages into my ear. "Breathe," she says softly. "In and out. In and out."

It takes me a while but I feel the tightness in my chest ease and my heart rate slow down. The voice returns—it's a man named John Peterson; it's on his nametag—and he brings me a glass of water, which I down like a desert rat.

"What happened?" he asks, but Maribelle doesn't take her eyes off me, bless her heart.

"She just had a scare," she says.

"But she's pregnant."

She finally turns to the nice man. "It's okay, small panic attack. It happens."

John absorbs this explanation but he's gazing at me with alarm, no doubt worrying I'll go into labor. Finally, when I've regained a normal breath, I smile up at the nice man and say, "I'm fine now, thank you."

I'm not, of course. Dwayne's back in the area and somehow knew I would be coming here today. And he left me a message.

I look back at the small angel statue lying there cockeyed, its head missing. I pull out my cell and call TB but it goes to voice mail.

"I'm sure he's fine," Maribelle says.

The tightness returns and I kick myself for being so complacent. Time passed with no sign of the man and our thoughts turned to baby-proofing the houseboat, renovating Maribelle's buildings for Sebastian's new endeavor, enjoying my part-time job back in a newsroom. We were all so blessedly happy.

"Stupid, stupid," I say to myself.

Maribelle finds a chair and pulls it up beside me. "Don't do that. We had no way of knowing."

I shake my head and groan. Loudly. "What did we think? That Dwayne would just waltz away and leave us alone?"

Maribelle looks at the pile of clothes and the horrible disfigured statue. "How did he know we would be here?" She rubs her forehead as if the movement might bring about the answer. "Who knew we were going to be here today?"

"Sebastian," I mutter, no harm there. "TB, but he definitely wouldn't tell anyone. You know how protective he is."

Maribelle stands up suddenly. "The bank."

"What?"

"I was at the bank this morning, before I picked you up. I took out a loan for the herb shop and the lender and I were going over the itemized budget. I might have mentioned that I was coming here. In fact, the lender recommended the place."

I don't know if it's the aftershock of my panic attack or me putting two and two together, but the thought of Lightning Bug's citizens learning of Emma Harrington's wealth and holding it against her runs through my mind. History repeating itself?

But it's a different world, isn't it? Bank lenders don't share proprietary information.

"Like I said before, it's two thousand and nine."

"What honey?" Maribelle asks.

Her reply is just what I need to jolt me from my funk. "Did you say honey? A Yankee turning Southern. What's next? Y'all?"

"Never." She's still not smiling—neither am I for that matter—but the shock of finding this altar to evil is dissipating.

Maribelle holds out her hand. I take it and struggle to stand, what with my enormous belly. The man returns and hands us both business cards with something written on one side.

"Anything in the store, twenty percent off," he says.

I smile warmly at the gesture and am about to politely decline but Maribelle beats me to it, accepting the business cards.

"Thank you, that would be lovely. We're opening an herb store near Lightning Bug and we could use every penny."

The man brightens. "Have you seen the displays in the front of the store? We have some adorable tea cozies."

"Actually, you have a gorgeous handmade table made of maple that I have my eye on. And as soon as I get my friend to the ladies room, I'd love to speak with you about it."

"Yes, of course," John agrees.

We head toward the bathroom but as we pass the corner display, Maribelle checks to see if anyone's looking, then knocks over Dwayne's pile with her foot, offering a few choice expletives in the process.

When we return, Maribelle selects the table, miniature canoe, and a lamp with three trees sculpted from metal and John heads off to ring up the sale, minus twenty percent. I'm sprawled out on an oversized arm chair, cell phone gripped tightly in my hand.

"Feeling better?" Maribelle asks.

"I'd feel better if TB would call me back, tell me he's safe."

Maribelle studies me with an expression I've come to know well. She scrunches up her mouth and her eyes narrow, like an artist studying an image to paint.

She gets in my face. "Stand up."

"What?"

Before she can respond, she grabs both elbows and has me on my feet.

"Pretend I'm attacking you."

I back up, feel the arm chair at the back of my knees. "What's going on?"

"First of all, you did the right thing. You backed up. The best way to fight evil is to avoid it to begin with."

Now that she's out of my face, I move forward and relax. "My mom used to say the best way to face a dark alley is to not go down it to begin with."

"Smart mom. But if danger approaches you and puts you in harm's way, you have to fight. Show me what you would do."

I swipe my hands in front of me in a gesture that says fight with this bowling ball?

"Come on, Vi. Pretend I'm attaching you. What would you do?"

I sigh. "Oh, I get it. This is another one of your lessons."

I start to sit down, but Maribelle stops me, her tone more urgent. "What would you do?"

I ball my hands into fists and pump them in front of me like an old-fashioned boxer, one arm extended farther than the other, one foot in front of the other.

"Good," she says. "Feel how balanced you are?"

"I feel like a fool," I tell her, but the old boxer stance gives me confidence. Yes, I do feel balanced. Bring it on.

Maribelle picks up a handmade purse for sale. "Imagine this purse is your fear." She hangs it over one arm, which throws me off-kilter and I stumble.

"What'd you do that for?"

"To show you how fear changes everything."

"That's not fair," I say, pulling the purse off my arm and trying to regain my balance. "You threw me off."

"Exactly. That's what fear does. It throws you off center."

Maribelle picks up a little bird house and hangs it off my other arm, which, of course, forces me to lean in that direction. I lose my footing and almost fall into a display of jewelry.

"Understand it yet?" she asks.

I pull the bird house off and place it back on the shelf. "Yes, Obie Wan."

"Yoda, if you please."

John hands Maribelle her packages and orders an employee to put the table in Maribelle's trunks. Once we enter the car and John waves us on, she turns to me.

"Lesson number one: The best way to avoid evil is to avoid it."

"Huh?"

"You know what I mean, like your mom said. Lesson number two is to find your center and remain balanced."

"Fine, can we go home now?"

We head out, driving straight home with me calling TB every five minutes.

"He's not answering." I chew my thumbnail and chew down too hard, breaking the skin.

"Remember what we learned about fear?"

"You can't possibly compare meeting evil head-on with worrying about my husband."

Maribelle thinks about this. "You're right. I guess I'd feel the same way if it was Sebastian."

It warms me inside to think my brother and Maribelle have found happiness, but I keep thinking of Dwayne's words on the train, about how TB might drive off a mountain one day. That old friend fear creeps up my spine and squeezes my chest and it's all I can think about.

"Call Clayton."

I can tell from Maribelle's tone that she isn't happy about bringing her nemesis back to Emma's Cove but it is the right course to take.

"The best answer to worry is to do something constructive."

I flip open the phone and Clayton answers on the first ring.

"Vi, what's wrong?"

I explain what we found at the Chattanooga store, including the disfigured angel statue and the bank lender. I end with mentioning TB's not answering his phone.

"He could be in class, studying," Clayton says, his tone like a father's calming down a nervous child. "But I'll make some calls to the school to check."

"I'd appreciate that."

"Meanwhile, we'll call this store, find out who's been in today and see if they have security cameras."

"Appreciate that as well."

There's a long pause and I hear Clayton sigh. "Regardless, Vi, we need to meet. Can we get together in the morning?"

"Yeah, sure. But you said regardless. Is there's something else going on?"

Another pregnant pause, and yes, I'm probably using that phrase because of my condition.

"Is Maribelle with you?"

"Yes."

"Then it needs to wait until the morning."

A shiver runs down my back all the way to my toes. "Some reason why?"

"I'll explain more in the morning."

We exchange goodbyes and I hang up, call TB one more time, then a couple of his college friends, but no one has seen him since he left campus two hours earlier.

"He said he was heading home to study," his math study partner says.

"He could be at Sebastian's," Maribelle adds. "If they're busy doing carpentry work, they won't hear their phones."

Maybe I'm overreacting, I think, trying to steady my anxiety as we drive homeward. Finally, we pull up to the motel and my neighboring houseboat but TB's pickup truck is absent from the driveway. For that matter, so is Sebastian's Toyota. Maribelle and I stare at the empty spaces and I swear she's thinking the same thing.

"Something's wrong, I can feel it," she whispers.

Suddenly, my cell rings, startling us both. I flip it open immediately.

"Sebastian," I say.

And then my whole world comes crashing down.

CHAPTER 11

I run down the hospital hall like a lopsided penguin but I can't get to TB fast enough. I enter his room to find Sebastian off to the side, arms wrapped around his middle, while a doctor and nurse huddle over TB's bed.

"He's my husband," I exclaim as I squeeze in between and reach his side, my fearful voice scaring me as much as everyone else in the room.

I have no idea what to expect. Sebastian had told me that TB's truck hit a bad patch of road a couple of miles outside Emma's Cove and tumbled down a ravine. The impact totaled the truck but TB never lost consciousness, was clear-headed enough to call Sebastian who immediately dialed 911, then me.

"It can't be that bad," Sebastian told me on the phone as Maribelle and I rushed into Lightning Bug. "He called me first, expecting me to drive over and get him. But I called an ambulance anyway."

TB lights up when he sees my face, but my blood pressure soars when I see his. There's a large bandage around his head and both eyes remind me of the makeup LSU frat boys wear on game days, a dark shade of purple.

164

"Hey Babe," he says, trying to smile but the cut on his lip makes him grimace.

I take his hand and examine him like a mother, checking arms, chest, peering under the blanket.

"He suffered a head wound," the doctor says, "but otherwise he's fine."

"Air bag saved me," TB mutters.

"That's where he got the black eyes. We think he hit his head on the truck window when it flipped over."

That panic friend returns. "Flipped over?"

"It was long ride down," TB says with a slur and I realized my husband's drunk with drugs.

"We'll keep him overnight for observation for the concussion but otherwise he's a very lucky man."

Lucky? In the last few years we've lost a daughter, our house and city to an overgrown hurricane, and now we have a lunatic on our heels threatening to kill us. My breathing intensifies and I feel the nurse to my right gently pushing me into a chair that she's pulled up next to the bed. I'm starting to see stars again but I hear Sebastian on my other side telling me to relax, all is well.

"But it's not well," I manage through my ragged breathing. "It's never going to be well."

"Is she okay?" the nurse says over my head.

I feel Sebastian squeeze my shoulder and the two begin a conversation but it all blends into the haze.

"Vi," a voice whispers.

I look over and TB's trying to rise on his elbows, studying me intently. "What's wrong? I'm worried about you."

I let out the breath I'm holding and laugh, think back on the years since TB and I met at LSU, how I chalked up our relationship only to sex, our marriage because of Lillye. Right now, witnessing the care in his eyes, his unconditional support and love, I can't imagine a moment without this sweet person in my life.

I lean my head onto the bed, feel his chest beneath the blankets, and start to cry. TB's hand strokes my hair.

"It's okay, Vi. I'm fine."

But it's not okay. I did this. I failed to take Dwayne seriously, thought he was gone for good, and now the son of Lucifer's playing his cards.

I lay there forever, comforted by the rhythm of TB's chest, his hand petting my hair, the soft voices above me discussing TB's care. I wonder where Maribelle wandered off to, what caused TB's truck to roll off the road. I think back to our lesson in the Chattanooga shop. Find my balance. Don't let fear push me off center. Right now, with my breathing still labored, I can't imagine pushing fear aside and facing Dwayne. All I can think about is packing up the houseboat and getting the hell out of town, giving up the ghost forever.

When TB's hand goes still, I realize my husband's drugs are doing their job. I look up to find him fast asleep.

Sebastian tugs at my sleeve. "Let's go get a coffee."

I shake my head, not wanting to leave TB's side.

"He's out for at least a few hours. Nurse said so."

I stand up but I'm not leaving. I might resemble the Karate Kid before he learned to stand on that pole like a bird in flight but I'm determined to face whatever or whomever tries to hurt my family.

"I'm not leaving him alone," I tell Sebastian.

My brother nods toward the hallway where Clayton's enormous outline fills the threshold. He's standing with his back to us, hands firmly planted on his hips. Over his shoulder, I spot Maribelle's face, angry and frustrated, as the two engage in a heated, although quiet discussion.

"What's going on?"

Sebastian sighs and looks at his feet. "I don't know. Maribelle won't tell me. But Clayton assured me he or another agent would be here until we got back from the cafeteria."

We head out, careful to step around the two gazing at each other like foaming mouth pit bulls. When we hit the cafeteria, we both exhale.

"What the hell?"

"Something Clayton found out about Maribelle, something to do with Maine. She's royally pissed."

That old fear returns, causing a rush of shivers through me.

"She didn't kill her husband," Sebastian insists emphatically, as if he reads my mind.

I think back on that old Shakespeare saying—our mom's one of the world's foremost Shakespeare scholars so these things are branded into our brains. When I would argue something of dubious worth that I knew was wrong, my mom would quote from *Hamlet*, "The lady doth protest too much, methinks."

"Has your love of Maribelle clouded your thinking?" I ask softly.

He huffs and shakes his head, turns toward the coffee carafes.

"I care for her, too, Sebastian, but maybe we're not thinking clearly here."

Sebastian pours himself a coffee while I choose a decaf loaded down with milk. A painful silence falls and he's avoiding my eyes, silently angry, but I can't help wondering if he's thinking the same thing. We pick a table away from the crowds, mainly two nurses huddled over sandwiches while badmouthing a boss, and a doctor chatting on a cell. Neither of us says a word until finally Sebastian breaks the silence.

"She's under a lot of stress right now."

"About Jack?"

Sebastian shakes his head, plays with the salt and pepper shakers on the table that, I realize, are bright orange and sport the University of Tennessee logos with the word "Volunteers" blazoned across.

"There's a group of investors wanting to buy the property

next to the motel," Sebastian tells me. "They want to turn it into a resort, the kind with zip lines, spas and motor boats. Mare is freaking out about it."

Mare?

"She took out a loan for the herb shop and the renovations of the buildings so she doesn't have the money to hire a lawyer and fight this."

I lean forward. "Fight what? It's her land."

Sebastian finally looks up and meets my gaze. "These men are ruthless, Vi. And the thing with Jack? If Clayton finds evidence they think links her to his death, and they arrest her again, it could unravel everything." He turns the pepper around and around. "And I mean everything."

I could argue that *Mare* might be guilty and worthy of arrest, could inquire if Sebastian's money is tied to hers and therefore subject to his unraveling. But I'm of like mind, don't want to think worst of my friend and neighbor. Even if that gnawing suspicion sits in my belly, punching me in the gut.

Or maybe that's a tiny foot. I shift in my seat trying to get comfortable now that the twins are up and moving.

"You okay?" Sebastian asks.

"August can't get here fast enough. I think there's a hand inside my rib cage playing with my liver."

"Your liver isn't inside your rib cage."

"Uh, it kinda is."

"Whatever.'

I take his hands and push those god-awful orange shakers aside. What the hell are "Volunteers" anyway? I've always wondered. And just what does a Volunteer mascot do? Come on to the football field and sign up for something?

"Vi."

Sebastian brings back my wandering brain. How did he not become as ADHD addled as I am?

"I have to do something tomorrow, Sebastian. Once we get

TB home and settled, do you think you could watch him while I go to work?"

"I thought you were off on Wednesdays."

"I am but there's something I need to do, something important."

Sebastian shrugs. "Sure."

"I made a protection circle around the houseboat and so far, I think it's worked well. Aunt Mimi taught me so I'm confident it's done right."

Sebastian squeezes my hands. "There's no wrong or right way, Vi. You need to believe in yourself and your abilities."

Tears rush up so fast they choke me. "Like keeping TB safe?"

"You didn't cause this."

"Didn't I?"

I remove my hands from his, turn away, and take a large gulp of coffee but it doesn't relieve the lump in my throat. I hear Sebastian call my name but the world turns blurry. Finally, I feel a finger at my chin and Sebastian turns my gaze back to his, wiping the tears that have fallen on my cheeks.

"This wasn't an accident, Vi. Someone messed with TB's truck and he never saw it coming. There was nothing anyone could do to stop him from rolling down that ravine."

"But Dwayne said he would harm him, Sebastian. He warned me."

"There's more to this than Dwayne."

"What do you mean?"

"We're being attacked on all sides, Vi. Can't you feel it? Dwayne's at the center of it all but he's only part of the problem. Something's brewing and it's only going to get worse."

"Like what?"

Sebastian shakes his head looking down at what's left of his coffee. "I don't know, Vi. Maybe Dwayne's talking to the developers, maybe he's stirring up trouble in town."

I think back on the bank lender who may have told Dwayne where we would be today.

"Wouldn't Clayton know if Dwayne was around, if he was influencing people?"

Sebastian's eyes turn dark. "If he's looking in the right place. He seems dead set on putting Maribelle in jail."

History repeating itself? I wonder, thinking of those angry men jealous of the Cove's success, storming Emma's homestead and killing Caroline. What evidence does Clayton have? And will it unravel us all, as Sebastian predicts?

"Thanks for the inspiring talk," I whisper.

Sebastian attempts a smile but fails. "We have to be vigilant and we have to be fearless."

I think back on Maribelle's lesson, given an opportune time after witnessing Dwayne's little altar at the rear of the store. I rub the back of my neck wondering about the coincidences when my twin makes a comment that sends shivers through me, no doubt my twins feeling every one.

"There are no coincidences, Vi."

I believe that, I truly do, but what if Dwayne isn't involved and Maribelle planted the altar and harmed TB to distract the FBI and the men trying to purchase her land? Dwayne would be the perfect diversion from a murder investigation, allowing Maribelle to remain free to fight off the resort and finish her herb shop.

But if that's the case, a murderer is shagging my twin brother.

We finish our coffee and return to TB's room where an agent is standing watch at the door. I look for Clayton but Agent Sheridan—it's on his lanyard—informs us the boss has retired for the evening and will visit again tomorrow. I spend the night in TB's room while Sebastian leaves to check on Maribelle and our houseboat.

"Be careful," I practically yell as he leaves the room.

There's a pull-out sofa by the window so I make myself comfortable, which is a relative term. Nothing is comfy these days due to the enormous belly protruding from my middle, but I make the best of it.

TB wakes at the crack of dawn, complaining that his head might split open, but still all smiles. The man amazes me. The nurse gives him a thorough going-over and more drugs—this time the pill form—and we're released, required to exit the hospital by wheelchair. Where I would balk at being wheeled to my car like an invalid, TB enjoys the ride, waving to the little kids in the waiting room like a float rider at Mardi Gras. Everyone laughs but me, the worries of the world still firmly planted on my shoulders.

Plus, I have to visit the bathroom for the tenth time this morning.

Sebastian's waiting for us at the exit and we pile into his Toyota, Michael gazing down from the dash toward his heir in the passenger seat, his angelic foot still firmly planted on the dragon, sword held high in his outstretched hand.

"I'm sorry about the truck," TB tells me as I lock his seatbelt into place.

"What? Who cares about the truck?"

For the first time this morning, his smile fades. "I do. That was my first truck, saved for years and bought it when I graduated high school."

I gaze into his French chocolate eyes and wonder if he realizes what happened here.

"You could have died, sweetheart. The truck doesn't matter."

There are times in winter when the sun shines brightly on your face and it warms your soul, but then a cloud passes over and chills invade. That's how I feel looking at my husband who's now realizing he lost control of his beloved truck. My angelic husband who routinely sees trouble coming and works to save those in its path.

I place my check close to his and whisper, "It's okay, my love. We'll figure it out."

We drive back to Emma's Cove in silence, TB's cheerful attitude long gone. Sebastian notices and glances at me through the rearview mirror. I shrug from the back seat but I know what TB's thinking, that somehow he missed the danger, like when he had failed to sense Dwayne at the train station. He's failing to conquer the dragon.

We pull up to the houseboat and get settled inside after a careful search of the place, Sebastian insisting we wait in the car until he determines the coast is clear. It is, my protection circle working—that or Dwayne isn't chancing visiting our home. Once inside, we settle TB on the couch with a soft pillow while Sebastian cooks up breakfast. Stinky immediately jumps into TB's lap, smelling him up, checking him out. My psychic cat turns to me as if I have the answers.

"Not yet," I say. "But I'm working on it."

"Working on what?" TB asks.

I smile. "Nothing."

There it is again, that haunted look. I sit next to TB on the couch and do my mommy thing again, check him out all over.

"I didn't see it coming," he whispers to me as I'm examining his arms for bruises.

I sigh, try to diffuse the topic. "I know, sweetheart. You were probably worried about your upcoming math test."

He shakes his head. "My brain is muddled, Vi. It's been that way for a while."

I pull the couch blanket over his lap, even though it's warm outside, and Stinky immediately starts kneading the material, purring like an engine.

"College will do that to you," I say, trying to keep the subject in one direction.

The smile's not returning, so unlike my happy-go-lucky man. "You don't understand, Vi. I can't feel anything."

I look him over with alarm. Did the doctor miss something?

He leans forward and runs a hand through his thick blond hair. "No, not like that. I can't feel danger coming." He looks at me to make sure I understand. "It's like there's a fog inside my brain."

I'm seriously worried but I don't want it leaking out into my countenance.

"You've been working really hard at school. The whole reason we moved here was for you to do an accelerated program so you could graduate in nine months. That's hard for anyone and you especially, since you were out of college for all those years we had…."

I look away, wonder for the ten millionth time when speaking her name won't cause me such pain. TB leans forward, wrapping an arm around my shoulders.

"That's just it, Vi. I'm worried sick about you, the babies. What if…?"

I shake my head. "Don't go there."

"I can't help it. I'm telling you this fog, this worry has taken over. I can't sleep at night, I can't concentrate."

"It's natural, sweetheart. We lost a child. How do we stop worrying about the health of our kids? Don't you think I'm feeling the same? But the ultrasounds have been normal and the two of them are kicking the hell out of my insides."

I send him a warm smile and he absorbs it. Sort of. I still see the confusion brewing behind his eyes.

And I can't stop recalling what Maribelle said the day before, that a sense of paranoia has taking over the people of Emma's Cove.

We enjoy Sebastian's breakfast spread that includes farm eggs from a neighbor, homemade biscuits, and strawberry jam Maribelle created the summer before. I'm constantly amazed at how Sebastian produces meals from the freshest ingredients found locally and "Mare's" genius with plants.

TB turns sleepy, lies down on the couch and falls into a deep slumber while watching This Old House on PBS. I look at Sebastian who nods toward the door. Without another word, I slip away, take his Toyota into town to the newsroom of the *Lightning Bug Chronicle*.

It's heading toward ten a.m. so the morning budget meeting's in progress. The section editors, a few reporters, and the managing editor pile into a tight meeting room and discuss what's brewing in the news and where these stories might be placed in print. They'll do it again at three, when stories are more developed, and that's when the front page gets finalized.

I wait outside until I hear chairs being pushed aside. Finally, the door opens and Olivia Bradley emerges, her arms full of newspapers and the initial story budget.

"Hey Vi," the managing editor tells me as she sizes up my large belly. "You must be due any day now."

"I wish. Another month."

"You're kidding," my skinny boss exclaims, which makes me cringe.

"Yeah." I place a hand at my lower back which is killing me today. "Can't arrive fast enough."

"Don't push it. You'll have twins to take care of. That can't be much fun."

Funny how when you're pregnant people say the most encouraging things.

"Pick out names yet?"

"Not yet." TB and I have been going round and round trying to whittle down the field.

"Olivia's a great name." Then my editor bursts into laughter.

I smile and slip behind her and into the meeting room, quickly close the door. The other editors pause in their socializing and look my way.

"I need all y'all's help."

Carol looks past me to the closed door. "Why the secret?"

"It's a favor and it's not *Chronicle* business, although it could be a very big story if we discover something."

I'm waiting for someone to object, some conscientious person to remind the group they don't work for me, they answer to Olivia, but the mention of a big story ignites the room. I seize the moment and explain Jack's unsolved murder, the strange deaths of Maribelle's parents, and a group of investors looking to place a modern resort at the edge of Emma's Cove. I also mention Sebastian and Maribelle's new businesses, so everyone knows I have a personal part to play.

"And my husband's truck went off the road yesterday," I add, trying to keep the catch from my throat. "I don't think it was an accident."

"Why would you say that?" Carol asks.

I shake my head because I have no evidence to prove foul play but I offer a few theories. I don't mention Dwayne's name but I do explain how a man tried to kill me in Natchez and has been on the run ever since, threatened my family earlier this year.

"The FBI's looking into that but I'd like to know what's going on in town, what happened to Jack, who these developers are and what, if any, this has to do with me and my brother's new business."

"What do you need?" Carol asks.

The room becomes a symphony of suggestions. Nellie Ridley, who covers the cops beat, will call Maribelle's hometown and see if she can obtain police reports. She will do the same locally about Jack's murder and TB's accident from the night before. The business editor, a stout balding man in his fifties named Morgan Culotta, will dig into the group looking to develop Emma's Cove, do a title search on Maribelle's properties.

"I'll use the newspaper archives to see what I can find on Maribelle's parents," I add.

"Those are at the library," Carol tells me. "Talk to Camille Smith over there. She can help you."

I smile gratefully at my tribe, feeling like the day TB and I were rescued from our roof after Hurricane Katrina. The National Guard pulled us into a helicopter and then landed on the nearby elevated interstate where we were immediately surrounded by first responders, each one offering water, food, medical attention.

"Thank you," I tell my friends. "Thank you from the bottom of my heart. Or belly as it were."

The business editor laughs. "Thank you. This might be a great story."

The door opens and Olivia sticks her head in. "Everything okay?"

"Fine," Carol says with a big smile. "We're planning the Fourth of July potluck."

Olivia brightens. She might be a hard-nose editor but she adores free food in the newsroom. "Ooh, do bring your deviled eggs."

"You bet," Carol says, and it's all we can do not to laugh.

I waddle through Lightning Bug's streets towards the library but I have another person to contact. My sister Portia answers on the second ring.

"Is the baby coming?"

"Four more weeks."

"Oh darn. I was hoping to get a vacation."

"You can still do that. In fact, I wish you would."

I'm trying to be funny in a serious way, but what emerges sound nervous and scared. Portia doesn't miss a thing.

"Why? What's the matter?"

I explain the accident but insist TB's fine, resting at home with Sebastian.

"Where are you?"

"In town. That's why I'm calling. I need your help."

Portia and I have never been close, have butted heads our entire lives, but we've reached a truce since taking a long road trip through Texas last fall. In fact, things have improved so much we actually call each other now and catch up. She still doesn't know the extent of my ghostly and witchy talents, nor that TB's a descendant. Or that Dwayne tried to kill me in Natchez and is at it again.

Maybe we still aren't that close. But, that's all about to change now.

"Portia, there's something I need to tell you," I begin, pausing in front of the library. "I can do it now or in person. I think being here and sitting down might be preferable."

There's a heavy pause on the other end.

"It's a long story and Sebastian's involved," I add. "And we need a good lawyer."

Finally, I hear her exhale. "I'm on the next plane, but at least give me some information."

I take a deep breath and begin. "There's a man I met on a previous press trip who's dangerous. He attempted to kill me then and may want to try again. The FBI's involved but it's possible he could have been the reason TB had the accident. Our neighbor, who Sebastian is in love with, is a suspect in the murder of her husband last year, and we're not sure she's innocent but we hope she is. But if she goes down, Sebastian may lose the restaurant. There's also a weird history in Emma's Cove and a group of developers may be conspiring to run Maribelle off her land."

Another pregnant pause, and yes, I'm using that metaphor again.

"Is that enough?" I ask. "We can get into details when…."

Finally, she laughs. "Is that it? Sheesh, Vi, why don't you call when you have a serious problem?"

Did my stalwart sister, nicknamed Jackie McCoy by her

colleagues in a nod toward Law and Order, just offer sarcasm? I'm so shocked I have nothing to say.

"I'll make flight arrangements now."

Family. So crazy, so infuriating. And yet, so reliable when you need them the most.

"Thank you, Portia. I know it sounds insane."

"If you're involved, it's always insane."

True dat. "Sorry."

"Just stay safe."

"Will do."

"Keep the FBI close."

"Yes ma'am."

"And don't tell Mom."

And with those final words, my sister hangs up.

I enter the public library and ask for Camille, find my helpful friend alone in the genealogy room restocking books.

"More research?" she asks with a smile.

"Actually, I need to check old newspaper articles."

"You know where those are located. Help yourself."

"From Maine."

Camille stops mid-reach, looks around the room, then discreetly closes the door. "What's the big deal about Maine?"

"What do you mean?"

"There were three men in here this week doing the same research."

It's hot in this stuffy back room but I shiver. "What men?"

Camille shrugs. "Guys in suits."

"Did they give their names?"

Camille thinks for a moment. "Not to me, but to use the library resources without a local library card they would have had to sign in at the reference desk." She gives me a wary gaze. "What's going on?"

I look around the stacks, even though I'm sure we're alone, then pull Camille toward the back of the room.

"Some people are trying to get Maribelle Greene's land, the property next to her hotel. They want to build some fancy resort there."

Camille crosses her arms about her chest. "Those gorgeous old-growth woods?"

I nod.

"But what's that got to do with Maine?"

A family walks by the room, the kids talking animatedly about the story time they enjoyed. I wait for their voices to die away.

"Maribelle's parents lived in Maine. They were found dead and ruled a suicide."

Camille utters a sentence in Spanish and performs the sign of the cross.

"I'm wondering if these men are looking for ways to tie Maribelle to the crime, compromise her finances fighting the charges and snatch that land."

"Or find a way that proves she doesn't own it to begin with."

I step back in surprise. "What?"

"You didn't find that in the folders I gave you on Emma's Cove? That once Emma Harrington became successful, the timber company tried to lay claim to the land?"

I think back on that newspaper article about litigation. "I did, but there was nothing else about it so I figured it was thrown out of court."

Camille smiles sadly. "Nothing rich corporations do gets thrown out of court that easily. They sue and hope you won't have the money to fight them and give up. But they underestimated Emma. She had support from her own rich friends in New York City. They took on her case and won."

Good for you, Emma.

"You think that's what these developers might do to Maribelle?"

The light that routinely shines in Camille's eyes fades. "I

think that when powerful men want something, they will do anything they can to get it."

We've never discussed Camille's background, where she came from, why she moved to Emma's Cove and then Lightning Bug and changed her name. I've always assumed there was a violent husband or boyfriend in her past, possibly someone who took her to court or vice versa. But she doesn't have to explain for me to feel the pain emanating from those eyes. I touch her arm and she acknowledges me with gratitude.

"You access the newspaper database through our computers," Camille explains. "I can show you how to do that on your own computer at home, but discretion is called for."

"That would be awesome."

"Don't tell anyone," she states firmly. "Library rules say everyone must do this in-house and I could get in big trouble."

I slide a hand across my lips pantomiming a zipper.

We head toward the reference desk and I wait on the other side while she writes me instructions. She passes me the information, then holds up a finger. While I slip the paper into my purse, Camille examines the sign-in sheet from the past week.

"Here it is," she says, then straightens as if a lightning bolt cascaded down her back.

"What is it?"

She leans across the desk, silently checking for anyone within earshot.

"Those three men," she whispers. "They were from Clark-Everhart."

"The timber company?"

She nods her head. "They're a major corporation now and have several divisions. One is a hotel chain."

I lean back, absorbing this news. "Any names?"

She glances back at the sheet and frowns. "Three. One is Dr. Patrick Touché."

"Shit." The word emerges before I have time to check myself.

"Sorry. But he's the man who stripped Maribelle of her midwifery license."

She shakes her head at the other names. "Gunnar Bronagh."

"What a weird name." Reminds me of a Masterpiece Theatre mystery series. "But it doesn't ring a bell."

Camille tilts her head and her eyes narrow. "I don't know this one, although it sounds familiar."

"Who is it?"

"Robert Johnson."

CHAPTER 12

can't flee the library fast enough with this information, calling Clayton on the ride home. He doesn't pick up so I leave a detailed message.

"Robert Johnson?" Sebastian asks when I enter the houseboat out of breath and relate all that occurred this afternoon. "Why does name that sound familiar?"

"Mississippi blues singer," TB mumbles from the couch.

His lip's still bruised on one side, making him lopsided like a hound dog. I'm surprised my husband knows who Robert Johnson is considering his seventies infatuation. He shrugs as if he's reading my mind.

"I visited Greenwood, Mississippi, with the high school football team. Seen his grave. The man has three, you know?"

"What?" Sebastian asks.

TB leans on an elbow and I notice the color blooming in his cheeks. The black eyes still break my heart but my husband's slowly improving. I wish I was sitting on the couch so I could cover those cheeks with grateful kisses.

"Robert Johnson died mysteriously outside Greenwood," TB tells us. "Some say by a jealous husband of a woman he was flirting with, maybe poisoned. Others think syphilis. No one knows for sure where he's buried and there are three gravestones in cemeteries in the Mississippi Delta that insist it's the place. I'm going with the one I visited."

Sebastian shakes his head trying to make sense of it. "Fascinating."

TB perks up. "It was. People visit his grave all the time, leave weird things like harmonicas and bourbon."

Sebastian turns to me. "Why would you think someone with a blues singer's name and three graves is Dwayne?"

I cringe remembering meeting Dwayne in the middle of the Natchez Trace, and what I had contemplated at the time.

"Because Robert Johnson was such an amazing musician people claimed he sold his soul to the devil at the Mississippi crossroads," I explain. "And I nearly did the same thing."

"What?" The color drains from TB's face. He never knew how close I came to giving in to Dwayne's insistence that he could help me contact Lillye.

"I didn't know what he wanted in return," I tell him, finding my voice taking on a desperate tone.

I nearly lost TB on that trip down the Natchez Trace, so desperate I was to reach my sweet girl, and now my husband's staring at me like I'm a lost cause. And maybe I am. Because I'd still offer my life for one more moment with my precious baby.

TB swallows. Hard. "Vi...," he begins.

I rise from my seat. More like slowly slide out of my chair, belly first, arm on the back for support. "Anyone want something to drink?"

No one answers as I head toward the kitchen and I swear I can feel TB's gaze boring into my back. Once inside the kitchen, the men begin to talk quietly and I let out the breath I've been holding. My heart's beating hard again so I set the kettle on the stove and pull out another Maribelle concoction, this one she swore would help with my high blood pressure. What would really help bring my heartbeat down, I'm thinking as a rush of anger creeps up my neck, is for someone to tell me how to contact my child!

TB's whispering to Sebastian and I grind my teeth. I'm suffering day and night carrying two of his children, losing sleep and having to pee constantly, not to mention the horrific heartburn I suffer after every meal and my back about to break in two. Here he is, sitting in the other room discussing me to my twin, no doubt expressing my insane determination to see Lillye. And what mother wouldn't move heaven and earth to see her child? God knows what Sebastian's telling him back, probably all kinds of nonsense from my youth.

I'm furious by the time I head to the living room with my tea, my heartbeat so intense I can feel it pulsating in my ears. But instead of discovering a conspiracy, I find the men debating whether Les Miles should coach another season of LSU football.

Sebastian looks up. "That better not be coffee, Miss Addicted to Caffeine."

TB adds a sweet smile. "Maybe next year we can take the kids to a game in Death Valley."

"Uh, a few years," Sebastian inserts. "Next year the twins will be one."

"Oh yeah," my husband retorts with a goofy smile.

"But we can go," Sebastian adds and the two of them laugh.

My heart plummets to my toes. Where did that paranoia come from?

The wind whips up from the lake and the woods to the left of our houseboat dance in response. It's so sudden, we all glance out the window, watching the tree tops sway frantically. Stinky jumps off the couch and scratches at the back door, letting out a plaintive howl.

"Clayton," TB says.

"How do you know?"

I see no one, still watching the trees rock back and forth as if they're waving at me.

TB rises from the couch and heads to the bedroom. "I can smell him."

Sure enough, our favorite FBI agent appears outside our door, waves at me through the glass. I welcome him in and while Stinky makes love to his ankles Sebastian merely shakes Clayton's hand and excuses himself, says he has important work to finish.

"Of course," Clayton says. "I'm sure Viola will relate anything we discuss here."

Sebastian heads to his room and closes the door and I glance down the hall to see that the main bedroom door is closed as well. I turn back to Clayton with a smile but I'm sure he catches both my shock at their rudeness and my embarrassment.

"No worries. I get it."

I don't. "Can I get you something to drink?"

He shakes his head and politely declines, walks through the living room clearly uncomfortable, glancing around as if he's looking for something. Stinky follows, rubbing his back against Clayton's legs, acting as if he can't get enough of the man. That delicious manly scent Clayton carries with him permeates the room but it doesn't alleviate the darkness following in his path.

"You have something to tell me. And it's not good."

Finally, Clayton turns his enormous brown eyes toward me, rubbing his forehead and grimacing. "No, I'm afraid it's not."

I motion for us to sit and Clayton chooses the sofa, his giant form encompassing most of the cushions, his knees sticking out at ninety-degree angles, bumping up against the coffee table. Would hate to sit next to this man on a plane. Stinky immediately jumps into his lap and makes himself comfortable while Clayton performs a massage on his head. I can hear the purring from my chair opposite the two lovers.

"Clark-Everhart's hotel division, called Tennessee's Best

Hotels, wants to purchase the woods next to Maribelle's motel," he begins. "She owns the property and has no intention of selling."

I gathered this much but I say nothing, let Clayton explain all in due time.

"Touché, whom you know, is helping them. He knows the area, knows the Cove, knows Maribelle's history."

"Right." Again, this is information I fed him in my long message after I left the library.

"The man called Robert Johnson…."

"Is Dwayne Garrett."

Clayton shakes his head, looking as lost as I feel right now when it comes to my nemesis.

"I don't understand it, Vi. No matter what we do, we can't catch the man."

I lean forward, as much as I can with a beach ball for a stomach, and touch one knee so Clayton looks me in the eye.

"There's something I have to tell you." I swallow hard, wondering how this news will go down. "Dwayne's not of this world."

Surprisingly, Clayton's countenance remains solid.

"He's a descendant," Clayton whispers. He nods toward the back bedroom. "Like your husband."

I'm so shocked I'm not sure how to respond.

"Well, not like your husband," Clayton adds.

I fall back into my chair and realize that not only does Clayton know about descendants who walk this earth, but so does the FBI. But, Clayton surprises me again, dropping his shoulders and offering a sad smile.

"I'm not of this world either, Vi. I'm surprised you haven't figured that out."

If I had time to think about it, I'd come up with some banal response, some repudiation. Instead, I blurt out what I've been thinking all along.

"I had a feeling, although I have no idea what it is."

Clayton smiles for the first time. "I figured."

"Think it was that earthy smell."

"Think your husband knows too."

What?

"Why would TB know?"

Clayton extends one arm across the back of the couch and pats the fabric. "I'll explain another time. Right now, we have bigger things to worry about."

I nod although I'm bursting with curiosity, especially wondering how my husband knew and why he appears to dislike the man. Instead, I relate what I found in the library.

"Touché we know," Clayton begins, pulling out a miniature notebook from his inner coat pocket. "From what we've uncovered, he owns a substantial amount in Clark-Everett's hotel division."

"Was that always the case? Do you think his insistence that Maribelle killed Jack was because he wants her land?"

"I'm not sure the idea of the resort goes back that far; we're looking into it. But Dwayne is now involved and likely helping them with the development. We can't comprehend what his role is in all this."

I'm racking my brain trying to see a connection. Dwayne wants me to solve a mystery and transition a soul to enable his immortality, so why would he be involved in a real estate transaction that pushes Maribelle off her land? Unless this results in the town's "unraveling," as Sebastian predicted, putting pressure on me.

"Is Dwayne trying to destroy my brother's business to get to me?"

Clayton rises, pushing Stinky off his lap, much to my cat's chagrin, and begins pacing the living room, filling up the space with his enormous body and causing me anxiety.

"You're scaring me."

He stops moving, hand through his thick brown hair, and apologizes. And yet, he still doesn't move, Stinky gazing up at him as if pleading for Clayton to return to the couch and his massage.

"Is this about Gunnar Bronagh?" I ask, probably destroying the pronunciation of his name.

Clayton silently looks down on me, hands on his hips, and I suspect he's wondering how much to divulge.

"Tell me."

He lets out a breath and returns to the couch, Stinky once again making himself at home in his lap.

"How much do you know about Maribelle?" Clayton says softly, looking off toward Sebastian's closed door.

I don't like the way this conversation's heading but I report what I know.

"She's from New England. Her parents killed themselves in a basement in Maine. She moved here to get away from a loveless marriage and purchased the motel next door to start over."

"And half the town."

I tilt my head. "Sorry?"

"She bought up half the town. The motel, the two historic buildings and the fifty acres of woods to the right of her business."

This takes me back. "Fifty acres?"

"All in all, worth about two million dollars."

"Where on earth did she get that much money?"

Clayton smiles grimly. "Where indeed? Kinda hard to believe she earned it working as a nurse."

I shake my head. "I don't understand. She bought it before her husband died so you can't think she killed him for money. Besides, he didn't have any."

Clayton leans forward, careful not to interrupt Stinky, and whispers, "She inherited it from her parents."

A chill settles over the room and I shudder.

"You have to ask yourself, Vi, why would two people who seemed happy to their neighbors and friends go into a dank basement and kill themselves by carbon monoxide poisoning? Together?"

I shake my head because I don't want to imagine Maribelle doing such a thing. Maribelle grows plants, welcomes the dawn, gives thanks to the compass points each morning. And she cried relating what happened to her parents.

"She couldn't have done it."

Clayton sighs. "One thing I've discovered in this job, Vi, is that everyone's capable of doing horrible things. It's not something I hoped to learn being in the FBI, wanted to believe that human beings were basically good. But as they say, just because you don't believe something is true, or hope it's not, doesn't make it not true."

I'm still not convinced. "But why kill her husband?"

"They weren't divorced yet."

"And?"

"If and when they divorced, he was entitled to some of her money. Like you said, the man owned nothing, worked for a fishing company, a job he lost when he moved down here trying to get his wife back. He rented an apartment back in Rhode Island so he truly owned nothing."

"So, Maribelle had a motive, kill her husband so he wouldn't be entitled to some of her inheritance? She must have known Jack would get some of her cash after their divorce when she bought the property. If that was such an issue, why didn't she divorce him first?"

"Maybe she didn't expect him to find her. Her property isn't in her name, it's in a corporation she created."

This doesn't sound good.

"I don't know, Vi, but killing him gets him out of the way, regardless."

Neither one of us says a word and I hear a pair of cardinals calling out to one another from the deck where TB planted three bird feeders. Suddenly, I remember something.

"So, who is Gunnar Bronagh?"

Clayton's cell phone rings and he rises, answers the call and begins speaking deferentially to a man's voice that sounds like a boss. He looks at me as if to indicate the conversation is important, then grabs his notebook and heads for the door, talking all the way. He pauses at the threshold, still in conversation, but leans down and kisses the top of my head. Placing a hand over the cell, he whispers, "Stay vigilant and know that agents are watching the house."

"I will."

"And stay away from Maribelle."

With those final words, Clayton exits the houseboat and I watch his long stride fill eat up the side of my houseboat. While I'm gazing at his retreating form, something to my right catches my eye. It's Jack Greene, standing in my neighboring woods, looking forlorn. He's been remiss all these months, thought maybe my friendly ghost had become satisfied that I'd befriended his wife, that he settled into an in-between land or moved on. I should have known better than to assume a soul stuck on this plane would disappear that easily. Or that Jack Greene would find peace with his death still unsolved.

The wind's blowing hard now, a thunderstorm rolling in. Where before temperatures reached into the high eighties and humidity pasted clothes to my skin, the oncoming storm's bringing a chill to the area. I button the top of my blouse and check the horizon, then head toward the woods. But not before calling Stinky for company.

My cat and I stride off the deck and into the grove of maples and oaks, enjoying the cool breeze coming off the water. I love my new home. In New Orleans this time of year, breezes are hard to come by unless a hurricane's brewing in the Gulf. Louisiana in July means stagnant air, high temperatures, and steam rising from the sidewalks. Even before Katrina came barreling through my hometown and taking what was left of my life, I wanted to move north, someplace with four seasons and summers that didn't steal your essence.

I look down at my cat who appears to be relishing in our new home as well.

"If only we felt safe here, huh Stinky?"

He looks up and winks.

When I reach the woods where I spotted Jack, my fish stick man's there, although the energy he's consuming to stay visible is taking its toll. I know I have minutes, if not seconds, before I lose him.

"I need to know," I begin. "What happened to you? How does this involve Maribelle?"

He stares at me with those pleading eyes, still unable to communicate well. But he pulls on the fish earring hanging from one lobe.

"What is it? What can you tell me?"

He points to Maribelle's hotel.

"Maribelle killed you?" I ask, which makes him stomp his feet in frustration. "Maribelle had something to do with it?"

He's truly agitated now because I'm missing something important. He pulls the earring again, frowning.

"What?" I ask, equally frustrated.

Jack fades, his face distorted in a mix of anger and disappointment. Stinky sniffs the spot where the ghost had appeared and begins kneading the area like he does after using his litter box.

"Vi!" I turn to find Agent Sheridan coming up the path. "You shouldn't be out here alone."

He's right, of course, and I'm not going to explain why I'm here so I nod and make my way down the path toward home, Stinky following behind.

"Don't you worry about that cat running off?"

I look back at Stinky who gives Agent Sheridan a get real stare.

"He's fine, kinda follows me like a dog."

Sheridan studies Stinky, watches us both as we make our way on to the deck. "That cat's not right," he mutters and then heads towards his car.

I open the door and let Stinky inside, but I've got other questions to ponder. I call out to the agent and explain where I'm heading, ignoring Clayton's last request. He follows me to Maribelle's door but I make sure he's out of sight before I knock. Maribelle opens before my knuckles hit wood.

"What's the matter?"

I'd normally laugh at her keen intuition but today there's too much doubt plaguing my brain.

"We need to talk."

Her eyes narrow in suspicion but she opens the door wider and lets me in.

"Tea?"

Only if it doesn't contain poison, I can't help thinking. "That would be lovely," I say instead.

I'm standing in her tiny living room, thinking how nice it will be for her to share that spacious second-story apartment with Sebastian, the one being renovated above the restaurant. But even though it's tight in Maribelle's motel suite, the numerous plants and homey furnishings make a visitor feel comfortable and welcomed.

"Have a seat," Maribelle calls out from the kitchen.

I realize I've been pacing the floor of her living area, wiping my damp palms against my mommy jeans with the giant waistband that's currently stretched to the max. I choose an oversized arm chair by the window—try not to break springs when I plop down —and her vast collection of herbs. She joins me and places two cups and a tea pot on the table next to me, sits on the ottoman.

"Tea will be ready in a minute."

I take a deep breath, which of course immediately conveys how nervous I am. I decide to come clean.

"Clayton came to see me."

Maribelle twists one side of her mouth into a grimace, causing a dimple to emerge on the opposite cheek. "And what did our FBI agent reveal this time?"

"Actually, it had to do with something I uncovered this morning."

I explain how I visited the library, leaving out the part about wanting to research her family. I relate how Camille and I discovered the three men who had been there before, looking into Maribelle's past.

"I called Clayton and he confirmed that Tennessee's Best Hotels plans to develop your woods at Emma's Cove. Plus, here's the bad news. Dr. Touché owns part of the company and Dwayne's involved."

Surprisingly, Maribelle doesn't react.

"You know about this?"

Maribelle stares off through the picture window toward the woods of mention. The trees grow so dense there so that lake breeze only stirs the top branches.

"The Clark-Everhart Timber Company started logging next to what is now the library," Maribelle begins. "They cut down all the old-growth trees and built the two buildings we're renovating. They built the employee cabins farther down the road because they thought the higher elevation would keep them from flooding."

The tea kettle whistles so she rises and heads to the kitchen, returns and pours the hot water into the tea pot between us. The sweet aroma of orange and spice emerges.

"Thankfully, the woods over there," Maribelle says with a nod, "were saved from the ax. Emma's Cove was too far from the railroad and getting timber to market was too expensive so they abandoned the place."

She pauses, tea kettle stilled in her hand. "Those woods are the reason I came here. There's something magical about this place, Vi, something healing. I think Emma Harrington felt it too. In addition to my motel and the future herb shop, I was hoping to offer nature retreats here, especially for women needing rejuvenation."

I think about the article I read recently concerning forest bathing, the Japanese practice of immersing yourself within forests and nature in an effort to restore balance and health.

"Trees carry powerful healing properties," I say.

Maribelle lights up, knowing I get it. "Yes, they do. Which is why I have to protect those woods."

I lean forward and take her free hand. "But you realize that there are powerful people behind the development. And Dwayne might be involved in a way to get at me."

Maribelle never falters, appears as confident as the moment I knocked on her door. "I'm not afraid of them, Vi. I refuse to live my life in fear. It only makes me stronger and more determined."

"But, how will you fight them?"

She heads to the kitchen, still wearing that smile, asking if I want lemon scones she baked this morning. Of course, I do, I tell her, but I'm worried for my friend. A major corporation with a legal department can attack with unlimited resources.

"Lesson number one?" she asks from the kitchen.

"You can't avoid these people, Maribelle. They are already coming down your dark alley."

I hear plates being moved from a cabinet. "Lesson number two?"

I sigh and do her bidding. "Center yourself and achieve balance before you face your enemy."

"Good!" She turns the corner, two plates of goodness in her hands.

"And three?"

"There was a three?"

She hands me the plate with a still-warm scone. I can't wait to slip that soft lemony pastry into my mouth.

"Fight them from a place of love."

I can't imagine facing Dwayne with love in my heart but I kinda get where she's coming from. Military generals might disagree but I think Martin Luther King, Jr. found the right answer, moving social mountains without ever pointing a finger of hatred toward his enemies. And he had plenty.

While I enjoy the most delicious scone I've ever tasted and Maribelle pours us both more tea, I glance at the desk full of photos and notice the smiling older couple, the man in uniform and the woman dressed in a tea-length dress carrying a bouquet of flowers. I lean closer to get a better look.

"My parents," Maribelle says, returning to her ottoman. "On their wedding day."

"They look so happy."

"They were."

The comment's stated so assuredly I can't help wondering about their strange deaths, what made them so unhappy.

"What happened to them?" I ask in a whisper.

Maribelle appears in a trance gazing at the photo and I doubt she will discuss the horrific event, not to mention her involvement. But, then she begins to speak.

"The maid came over in the morning as she always did, expecting to find my parents drinking coffee at the breakfast table, reading the newspaper. She called out their names as she entered the house. When she had no response, she started searching."

"How horrible."

"Police found the furnace exhaust pipe wasn't attached and

had been spewing carbon monoxide into the basement. That's what caused their deaths."

Maribelle pauses in her telling and neither of us says a word. I listen to the wind moaning through the trees and around the building, hear rain falling outside in large noisy drops. I wait for an appropriate amount of time, then decide to spill the beans. I feel horrible initiating this accusatory conversation but I must know.

"Clayton said you inherited their estate," I say softly. "He suspects you might have killed them for the money."

Maribelle turns her eyes to me, tears pooling. "I know. I didn't."

"I know you dislike him, but you must admit, the money gives you reason to kill Jack."

Maribelle smiles grimly, looking down at the cup in her lap. "Not to mention my parents."

Despite my doubts, I reach over and take my friend's hand. She squeezes back and the tears cascade down her cheeks.

"I'm not a fan of Clayton, as you know," she tells me, wiping the moisture away. "He's not the FBI's sharpest cowboy on the ranch. But I do understand why he thinks the way he does."

"You don't think your parents committed suicide?"

Her eyes enlarge and she shakes her head. "Absolutely not."

The wind howls again and I shiver. "Who would want to kill your parents?"

For the first time, I sense fear in Maribelle, as if an evil presence has entered the room, threatening to absorb us both. The fear in her eyes sends goosebumps up my back, that ole skunk running over my grave.

She looks past me to the desk full of photos, to the one I spotted that day in February, the first time I entered Maribelle's apartment. It's a photo of Maribelle's mother standing next to two children. One of them resembles Maribelle as a scrawny teenager, looking at her feet awkwardly, arms crossed against her chest. An older boy stands more confidently on the side showing a full set of teeth in a creepy scowl, reminding me of Jack Nicolson's character in *The Shining* when he pushes his face through a door and says, "Here's Johnny."

I shiver again. "Who's that?" I ask, pointing to the man.

Maribelle's countenance doesn't change. If anything, it turns darker. I don't know how I put the pieces together or if there's someone on the other side forcing the words from my lips.

"Gunner Bronagh?" I ask.

We lock gazes and the fear I sense emanating from Maribelle seeps into my soul.

"Yes," she whispers. "He's my brother."

CHAPTER 13

The rain's slowed down so I slip back inside my houseboat, wave to Agent Sheridan as I pass by. TB's waiting at the door, looking as frazzled as I feel.

"Where have you been?" he yells.

Now it's his turn to inspect me up and down.

"I'm fine. I was just talking to Maribelle."

Sebastian rushes in from the kitchen. "She's back?"

"Sheesh, guys, I just went next door."

The minute the words come out of my mouth I regret them. I should have told them where I was going. Of course, they have reason to be worried.

"I'm sorry, should have left you a note. But the FBI's right outside."

TB looks at Sebastian, his frantic worried expression never faltering. "We should get Sheridan."

"Or call Clayton back."

I shake my head. "Just because I went next door?"

Sebastian walks closer and holds out his hand. Inside his palm lies a brick with a string tied around the middle. There's a note attached.

"Someone threw this onto the deck."

I reach for the note but fear stills my hand.

"Sheridan would have seen anyone coming this close. He saw me walking in the woods."

"You were the woods?" both men yell at me at the same time.

"I took Stinky with me."

I didn't think Sebastian could appear more agitated and TB begins pacing the floor.

"I'm sorry, but Jack appeared and I really needed to speak to him."

They're still looking at me as if I've lost my mind, Sebastian holding the brick in front of him as if it's about to detonate. My back's killing me so I plop into the chair.

"If you hadn't been so rude and listened to what Clayton told me, you'd have understood why I needed to speak to Jack. But the two of you had to crawfish into your rooms...."

TB pauses, hands on his hips, gazing at me with eyes the size of saucers. "Are you kidding me? You could have been killed."

Sebastian sits on the couch, still holding the vandalizing instrument. "Vi, you need to read this."

I take a deep breath and let it out slowly. I lean forward as best I can and turn over the note. It reads, "We had a deal. Transition Jack Greene."

I jump back in my seat as if the note burned my hands.

"Bastard."

Now, TB's raccoon eyes are in my face. "Never leave this place without us."

I think back on Maribelle's "lessons" and understand how bad people win when good people let fear rule their thinking. But then, I failed the first lesson, not staying out of the path of evil to begin with.

"We can't give up our lives," I tell them both. "They're trying to intimidate us."

"And it's working," Sebastian says.

TB begins pacing again. "You're getting on the first bus out of here heading to New Orleans. I already called your mom and she's making up the guest bedroom."

I stand up so fast I surprise myself, considering my girth. "No way."

"You can't be here," Sebastian adds.

"I'm not leaving." I glance from one to the other. "No way."

TB grabs my shoulders. "Vi, he wants you. Dwayne's not going to stop until he gets what he wants. The best thing to do is put you someplace safe."

"New Orleans?"

"If that's what it takes."

I take my husband's hands and place them on top of my belly. "Sweetheart, I'm not leaving you."

TB's shoulders drop. "I'm coming with you."

"What?"

"I can finish at LSU."

My mouth hangs open and I look at Sebastian for support but he appears defeated as well. "You too?"

"It's better this way," Sebastian says.

"And Maribelle?"

Sebastian avoids my eyes. "You heard what Clayton said. She's not who we think she is."

So, Sebastian listened at the door, heard Clayton's theory of why Maribelle killed her parents, then Jack.

"Innocent until proven, Sebastian."

"Just until this blows over," TB inserts.

"And leave her here to fight off the allegations alone, to deal with a major corporation breathing down her neck with Dwayne and her crazy brother adding to the mix?"

Sebastian leans forward. "Brother?"

"Yeah, there's more to this story and maybe if y'all hadn't hidden inside your caves when Clayton was here or listened to

Maribelle's side of the story, you wouldn't be advocating running home with our tails between our legs."

Sebastian studies the lint on his jeans, no doubt wondering if he was quick to judge.

"I thought you loved her," I ask him.

He leans back on the couch and looks out over the water, the surface so still now that the storm has passed. "I do, but we hardly know each other. A brother?"

I fall back into the chair, this time without thinking and the force makes a plumping noise that startles us all. "Maribelle wants to talk to us. She said to meet her at the restaurant at seven and bring food."

No one says a word.

"I'd cook but I'd rather you would," I tell Sebastian.

He nods. "I'll heat up the leftover pasta."

Just the thought of that creamy pesto-infused fettuccini with heirloom petite peas from the farmer's market makes my heart swell. Why can't I stop dreaming of food?

I now have Sebastian on my side. I look up at my husband who's still shaking his head.

"I'm not losing my family," he says with a catch in his throat. "Not again, Vi. We're going home."

Don't make me stand up again, I think, gazing at my pain-stricken husband. But I so need to hold him close right now. I reach for his hand but he moves away, still shaking his head.

"Nothing you say or do is going to change my mind."

Just then, a startling knock comes at the door, making us all jump.

"What the hell?" Sebastian says.

Before I have time to turn my enormous middle around, a voice comes through loud and clear.

"Open up, you idiots."

Sebastian sends me a furrowed look. "Who told Portia?"

I attempt to rise but TB beats me to the door, opening to my sister standing there with three—yes three—oversized pieces of luggage. The designer kind, of course. She's dressed in jeans, a striped pullover and a Tommy Hilfiger jacket, looking like she's about to set sail on a yacht in the Hampton's.

Portia looks from one of us to the other. "You're going to make me stand out here all night?"

We all bolt into action, TB grabbing her suitcases, Sebastian rising and giving her a hug. I'm last to address my stalwart sister, mainly because it takes me forever to rise from my seat.

"Sheesh, you're huge," Portia tells me when it's my turn to hug. "You're as big as a barn."

For years, her comments unnerved me so much I would spend days chewing on the insults, wishing I had countered with some snappy comeback. Nowadays, I laugh them off.

"I'd say the same for you but that would be rude."

Sebastian laughs but Portia sends me the evil eye. She's always struggled with her weight.

"You know I'm kidding." I pull her farther inside the living room. "I'm so glad to see you. I need you on my side right now against these two."

Her evil glance turns to the men. "What did you two do now?" We all stand staring at each other, no one speaking, until Portia huffs. "Well, someone speak up."

"We're going home," TB says firmly.

My husband's usually so easy-going that he doesn't stand for much. If we head to dinner, he's up for any meal. "Whatever you want," is his typical refrain. When asked about a weekend getaway. "You're the travel writer, you pick the place." But right now, he's not wavering.

But then, my sister's no match for anyone. An hour in a courtroom and the opposition runs home crying.

"No one's going anywhere," she bellows. "The lawyer's here to save the day."

Sebastian remains skeptical, rubbing the back of his neck

nervously, and TB's not saying a word but Portia and I begin discussing dinner and for now, we're headed to the restaurant for seven.

By the time we leave, however, that old paranoia returns as Sebastian, TB and Portia begin discussing me. I'm in the bathroom for the ten thousandth time today and I can hear them tattling about how I waltzed off into the woods, visited Maribelle—a suspected killer (did Sebastian say that?)—and that I'm not taking the dangers of Dwayne seriously. Then TB mentions Lillye and my inability to let her go and a flush burns up my neck and my head starts to pound. How dare them?

When we gather the food together and head toward the restaurant, I realize I've been feeling this way a lot lately. One minute I'm waking up happy about the world and the next I'm ready to take someone's head off. Is it my blood pressure wreaking havoc with my emotions? Possibly. The pregnancy and those temperamental hormones raging through my body? Most likely.

And yet....

I follow my husband and siblings inside and note the progress made since my last visit. The brick walls now sparkle, the wooden floors have been restored but await a final coating, and light fixtures installed. TB's expert carpentry skills transformed a rough space into something magical. Even the back wall's elegant bar with its subdued lighting and intricate bookshelves for the alcohol inventory looks like something out of *Food & Wine* magazine.

"It's gorgeous," I say, reaching up to right one of the chandeliers hanging haphazardly above a table.

"Be careful," Sebastian calls out, moving me away as I return to earth from my toes.

I feel TB's hand at my elbow. "Watch out for the loose nails on the floor. We haven't finished installing the walls and the nails are everywhere."

I pull free of their grip. "Y'all stop manhandling me."

"I'm not manhandling you." TB appears hurt. "I'm worried about your safety."

"You mean you want me to go home, quit working, and be a good little mother."

Where on earth did that come from?

"I'm sorry," I begin but the apology fades when the anger returns, "but you men…."

"What do you mean, you men?" Sebastian asks, clearly unhappy with me.

"Always telling us what to do. Always grabbing us like we're a piece of meat you want to manipulate."

Sebastian appears as if he's been stung. He shakes his head and heads toward the back while TB stares at me with those sorrowful black eyes.

"Geez Viola," Portia says.

"What did I do?"

But I know what I did. Sebastian's not the enemy. TB either. And yet, there's this anger filling up my soul that I can't release. I know I should apologize again but the emotion's there, simmering, and my head's about to blow apart. And I can't shake TB's last words in the houseboat.

"Why should I let my precious angel go?" I tell my husband. "She's my daughter and it's perfectly normal that I would want to see her. Especially since that bitch of a storm made me see all these other dead people."

Now, I'm shouting. And it's scaring me. My body's vibrating with the rush of adrenaline but I can't seem to come down from this.

TB reaches for my arm. "I know sweetheart, we're just worried."

"I'm sorry," I say again, but it comes out hollow and insincere. "I really don't know what's wrong with me."

"I do," comes a voice from behind.

We all turn to find Maribelle entering the building, two bottles of wine and several glasses in her arms. She reaches my side, gazes into my eyes, and studies me.

"Not you, too," I say. "I guess you're also suggesting I head to New Orleans and spend the rest of my life in a closet."

"Maybe a broom closet."

Maribelle offers a warm smile and I feel the blood drain from my face. As the anger subsides, Maribelle calls out to TB and the two of them lead me to a chair, each one holding an elbow. I'm starting to see birds tweeting around my head but the world becomes clearer once I sit down. TB examines me again like a mom and Maribelle's checking my pulse.

"We need to get you back to Dr. Mahoney," she says. "Your pulse is racing."

Portia, on the other hand, is more concerned with my attitude.

"What the hell, Vi. Where did all that animosity come from?"

While everyone's huddled over me—except Sebastian, who from the sound of things is futzing in the kitchen—two women appear at the front door, knocking loudly and startling us all. It's Patrice from the diner and that unfriendly librarian.

Maribelle heads to the front and lets them in, but they're as pissed off as I was moments before. They march in, holding up a piece of paper as if it's the devil himself.

"Seriously, Maribelle?" Patrice asks. "First, you let these Louisiana people bring the FBI to town and now you've got Lightning Bug on our ass."

"What are you talking about?" Maribelle asks, and I'm surprised at how calm she is because Patrice is practically in her face.

The librarian extends an outstretched arm with the offensive paper in her hand, close enough to Maribelle's face that she likely can read it.

"The city says you're breaking all kinds of rules building this restaurant and your precious herb shop, and now they want to inspect the diner and library, claiming we're at fault too."

"That's ridiculous." Maribelle takes the paper and begins reading it, but not before Portia reaches her side.

"Did you get all the necessary permits?" my sister asks.

Maribelle doesn't look up, still reading. "Of course."

Portia looks from Patrice to the librarian. "And y'all?"

"I always get an A from the health department," Patrice says staunchly as if the question is an abomination.

The librarian's eyes turn to slits. "I'm a library branch connecting to the whole county."

Portia takes the paper. "Then what do y'all have to worry about?"

"Who's this?" the librarian asks Maribelle, and not in a nice way.

"Another *Louisiana* person," I mutter from my chair.

Portia and Maribelle instinctively know who the other is but they haven't been introduced. I struggle to rise and TB's immediately at my elbow, helping. I think to pull away again but now that the anger's retreating, realize how crazy I've been. I thank my husband, then waddle over to the group.

"Portia, this is Maribelle, the owner of the hotel across the street and the soon-to-be owner of the 'precious herb shop' next door, not to mention Sebastian's landlord."

Patrice huffs and Rude Librarian crosses her arms across her chest.

"Maribelle, this is my sister and one of the finest lawyers in Louisiana."

"Excuse me," my sister says. "Finest in the *country*. I'm well versed in both Napoleonic and common law."

For some reason, the librarian's starting to look human. "Napoleonic is the type of law they use in Louisiana," she tells Patrice.

I can't stand it anymore. "What is your name?"

Rude Librarian's demeanor changes drastically. "Kerry Hancock." She surprises me even further when she begins proudly relating family history. "My grandmother was one of the founding members of Emma's Cove. She knew Emma Harrington."

Growing up here might explain her unfriendliness.

"Nice to formally meet you, Kerry."

She smiles and I'm nearly thrown backward at the sight. And even though Portia's been reading through the document since the introduction to Maribelle, she doesn't miss a beat.

"Are y'all suffering from the same weird paranoia as my sister here?"

Maribelle's head juts up and the two make a knowing eye contact.

"Wow," I'm thinking. Who knew my witchy future sister-in-law—if Sebastian doesn't screw it up—and my sister with the rod of steel for a spine would instantly be a match? Maybe Portia, who insists she doesn't own magical powers like other members of the family, is holding out on me.

"They have no case," Portia tells us all, handing the paper back to Kelly. "This looks like the developers wanting Maribelle's land are putting pressure on members of the city council and they're trying to intimidate you."

"But they say we're in violation," Patrice insists. "And Touché is working with them."

"They say you may be in violation," Portia says. "Who's Touché?"

"A prominent doctor in town who bankrolls a lot of the council members," Patrice explains. "He practically runs Lightning Bug. He alone could shut us down."

"Not if you have all the proper permits and paperwork and you passed health inspections." Portia looks at Kelly. "And crap, you're part of the county-wide library system. You can't let fear rule your logic. They have no case."

Kelly shakes her head. "The library's been threatening to close our branch for years, supported by the city council. They say we don't have the numbers to justify the branch but our numbers are pretty strong. They chalk it up to budget cuts."

"I've always said we should privatize the library," Patrice says. "Screw them."

"We can't afford it."

"We can do anything. We always have."

The two begin arguing and Maribelle holds up her hands for silence like a kindergarten teacher.

"This is exactly what he wants us to do. How he wants us to react."

Everyone stops talking and I catch my breath wondering what Maribelle will reveal. With all eyes on my motel witch, Maribelle drops her shoulders and offers a sad smile. "I should have brought more wine glasses."

We make our way to the center of the building, TB pulling out chairs and placing them in a semicircle around the fireplace. Portia finds some extra glasses at the bar and Maribelle opens the wine.

"I'm on duty in an hour," Kelly says, turning down a glass.

Maribelle places a glass in her hands. "You're going to need this."

"No one comes in the library, anyway," Patrice says with a smug grin.

Finally, Sebastian appears, carrying a platter of steaming goodness and several plates and forks. Everyone oohs and aahs but I notice that he fails to acknowledge Maribelle, doesn't offer his usual kisses and affectionate name calling. Since their lovey dovey stuff drives me to puke, I relish the break, but something's not right here. When he sits as far from Maribelle as he can, I'm worried.

I choose the seat next to him and whisper in his ear. "What's the matter with you?"

"Me? You're the one who went off the deep end."

"I'm sorry. Truly. But why are you acting this way?"

"Ask her."

Sebastian's last words are uttered loudly enough for Maribelle to hear. Everyone stops talking and helping themselves to pasta and glances over. For the first time since she arrived, Maribelle's countenance falters.

"Why don't we start from the beginning?" I say, hoping we can clear the air and find a way to move forward together.

Everyone settles into their chairs with plates in their laps and glasses of wine at their feet. Maribelle and Sebastian send emotional glances at each other and TB takes my hand.

"You okay?" my husband asks.

I nod and try to appear normal. My anger has dissipated—thank goodness—but I don't feel well, my head still splitting and my stomach roiling. I think Maribelle's right about seeing my doctor again. Twins can pose a real threat to a mother and Doctor Mahoney insisted I take it easy, get off my feet, and avoid stress of any kind. Like that's going to happen in my life.

I place the plate of food on the floor near my glass of water. "Why don't I start?"

I explain how I came to know Dwayne, how he almost killed me in Natchez and how, even though he escaped from police after TB saved me, thought he was gone from my life for good.

"He's a terrible man," TB adds. "And he's dead bent on getting back at Vi and me."

Sebastian nods toward TB. "We think he caused TB's accident yesterday."

Patrice and Kelly look from me to Sebastian to TB.

"I don't understand," Patrice says. "Why does he want to hurt y'all? With the FBI sitting out front, you'd think he would be anywhere but here."

I exhale a long breath, lean my head back, and close my eyes. The thought of Dwayne watching our home, thinking of ways to harm my family frightens me to the core. Maybe TB's right, I should give up this crazy life and seek refuge in my parents' house in New Orleans. Then I wouldn't be sitting here explaining the insanity surrounding my life to a group of panic-filled women.

"The thing is," I finally begin, "I'm a SCANC. It means…."

"You see specific apparitions due to a trauma you've experienced," Kelly inserts. "Among other things."

I never stop being surprised at how many people know who we are.

Kelly shrugs. "I'm a librarian descended from a group of unique women."

"Living among witches," Maribelle adds with a smile.

Another thing I fail to get used to, women admitting to being witches.

"Anyway, I see ghosts who have died by water because of Hurricane Katrina," I continue. "But Dwayne was interested in me because…."

I glance at TB but he's shaking his head slightly so no one catches on. It's one thing to see ghosts, quite another for people to learn that angel descendants are walking the earth. My own husband didn't tell me who he was and the way he's looking at me now, I know he prefers it to remain secret.

"Dwayne taps into the spirits of ghosts as they are transitioning," I explain instead. "He uses it somehow."

I leave out my belief that Dwayne's stealing souls for his own immortality.

"Weird," Patrice says.

"He wants me to transition someone." Now, I look at Maribelle who immediately sits up straight in her chair. "I don't think he'll go away until I do that for him."

"No," she states firmly.

This gets Portia's attention. "What?"

"Yeah, what?" asks Kelly.

Maribelle leans forward, elbows on her knees. "Vi has seen the ghost of my husband in the woods next to her houseboat."

"Your husband's dead?" Portia asks, looking from Maribelle to Sebastian, but my brother is too busy staring into the bottom of a wine glass.

"The FBI thinks he was murdered," I tell her. "They suspect Maribelle."

All eyes turn to the town witch.

"And they have lots of reasons why," she answers with a grim smile.

Maribelle explains the suspicious death of her parents, how they changed their will before perishing in that horrid basement resulting in her inheriting several million dollars.

"The rest you know," she continues. "I moved here, bought this property and the motel and woods and started practicing midwifery on the side. Jack followed me here to convince me to stay married to him."

She glances at Kelly. "I wasn't here, what, a few months before he showed up."

Kelly nods. "Four months maybe?"

"And nothing I could do would make him leave. He was a good man, but so possessive. When he lost his job, I let him have a back motel room and he helped with yard work and renovations." The memory takes hold and she turns silent.

"What happened after that?" Portia says, bringing her back.

Now it's Maribelle's turn to gaze into her empty glass of wine. "He disappeared. We had terrible argument. I thought he had gone into town to drown his sorrows or...."

"Or?" Portia asks.

She looks up, smiling grimly. "I was hoping he had left and gone back to Rhode Island."

"They found him in the lake," Patrice says. "Wound on the head."

It begins to rain again, a soft patter on the trees outside. In the distance, faint thunder rolls. We all shift in our seats.

"Clayton found a tiny bit of his blood in my bathroom," Maribelle begins again. "I have no idea where that came from, he hardly ever visited my apartment but he did use it from time to time. They found blood on the back dock too, but no murder weapon. Everyone assumed at the time that I killed my husband to get rid of him, but the truth is, he was my best friend." Tears pool up in Maribelle's eyes. "He saved me once. Why would I kill him?"

Portia states what any legal or law enforcement personnel would think. "The money."

Maribelle wipes her eyes with the back of her sleeve. "My parents left me with a fortune. I used a good bit of it to purchase the Cove properties and renovate the motel. The plan was to get each property online while working in nursing until they all were renovated and open."

"But Jack would have wanted a piece of that," Sebastian says.

The light in her eyes dims and her face turns hard. "I had several hundred thousand in the bank. Anyone can check that. I saved it just for Jack, told him to take the money and buy the fishing boat he always wanted." She leans forward, looking straight at my brother. "I always—always—planned to give him part of the money."

"Why didn't he take it?" Kelly asks.

Maribelle closes her eyes and grimaces. "Because he wouldn't let me go."

She rises from her chair so fast the chair falls over backward, then heads to the enormous fireplace and leans against the mantle. I feel the tension shift and know that soon one of the women, if not Sebastian, will try to comfort her, which isn't what Maribelle needs right now. I know this woman, she'll want to remain strong throughout her story or the pain will unravel her for sure.

"Tell them why he wouldn't let you go."

All eyes turn to me, questioning, then Maribelle slowly turns, her shoulders dropping and her gaze vacant and dark.

"I married Jack to get out of an abusive relationship."

Finally, my twin straightens in his chair. "Who?"

She shakes her head sadly. "My brother."

TB still holds my hand and I feel it tighten.

Maribelle finally looks up, that tough exterior slipping as she recalls her past horrors.

"He was a monster. Used to terrorize me, both emotionally and physically."

"Where were your parents?" TB asks.

"They didn't believe me. Said I was being dramatic. When he sexually assaulted me, he threatened to kill my cat if I told them and when I did, I found my beloved pet in pieces in the back yard."

"Jesus," Sebastian whispers.

"I married Jack to get away from him. Jack and I had been friends throughout high school, where Gunner bullied him unmercifully. We eloped and Jack got a job on a boat in Rhode Island, far away from my family, and I went to nursing school. But, y'all know me, I'm an independent soul and I was never meant to be a fisherman's wife. Not to mention Jack fell in love with me and I didn't feel the same."

"That's when you moved here?" Portia asks.

"First, my parents came to see me. Apologized, admitted that I was right, that Gunner was ill." She picks up her glass and refills it with wine, drinks half the glass in one gulp. "We still don't know why he's the way he is. My parents were the finest of people."

"Except for the fact that they ignored a monster in their midst," Sebastian says with emotion.

Maribelle sends him a grateful smile, no doubt happy he's now convinced she's not the killer. "Except for that."

"What happened after that?" TB asks.

The rest of her wine disappears as she gulps the remaining half.

"They changed their will, told me I was to inherit everything. They tried to get Gunner into a hospital—they never explained what had happened that changed their minds—and that Gunner had left and they had no idea where he was. They begged me to come home, to leave Jack and go to college, which was my dream before things turned ugly at home. I told them I would but the next month they both were dead."

Maribelle recounts how the maid arrived one morning and found the couple dead on the basement steps. The police called it suicide but the case remains open due to some suspicious elements, one of which was the basement lock. Police suspected someone trapped them in the basement by locking them in, then changed out the lock to eliminate evidence."

Maribelle pauses while we imagine the worst, her parents likely clawing at the door, begging to be released.

"They suspected me, of course, because my parents had recently changed the will and here they were dead," Maribelle continues. "It's the main reason I came here. I needed to escape those memories."

TB releases my hand and rises, rights Maribelle's chair, then leads her gently into her seat. They silently acknowledge each other and I know whatever doubts Maribelle had about my husband, they are long gone.

"Where is Gunner now?" Portia asks.

I beat Maribelle to the punch. "In Lightning Bug."

Now, it's Sebastian's turn to rise, tipping over his chair. "What?"

"Maribelle's brother, Touché and Dwayne appear to be behind the hotel development."

"Holy moly," Patrice says, although she doesn't use the word moly.

"Touché?" Portia asks. "The doctor who runs the town?"

"Yes," I say.

"And the paranoia," Maribelle adds quietly.

Sebastian sits back down and we all lean in.

"I noticed it a few weeks ago," Maribelle explains. "Everyone on edge, acting suspicious. First, the farmer's market cancelled my monthly vendor permit, said they had too many stalls and I was one of the last to sign up so I had to be one of the first to go. The next time I went to the market, it was half full.

"Next, two of my best buyers cancelled herb orders. When I asked one why, she claimed someone was at the door and hung up. Finally, I cornered the other one in the grocery store and she turned ugly, said I was like all the other women in Emma's Cove, only looking after myself and not thinking of the bigger community."

"What does that mean?" Kelly asks.

"Not letting progress in. This woman thinks the development will bring jobs and tourism dollars."

"She's right," I add.

"No one's touching my woods," Maribelle states emphatically.

"So, these guys are stirring up fear in the town," Portia says.

"It's more than that." Patrice rubs her palms on the knees of her jeans. "People here have been acting strange. And I've been quick to anger lately."

"And judge." Sebastian offers Maribelle an apologetic smile and she, in turn, sends a grateful one back.

"Issues like these will do it to people," Portia says. "I've seen it time and again."

Kelly shakes her head. "It's more than that. There's a stagnant evil in Emma's Cove."

"Yes." Maribelle leans forward. "I think it emanates from that patch of ground where nothing grows."

The wind picks up and the rain intensifies, as if Mother

Nature's listening and she's letting us know we're on the right path.

"Wait," Portia says, offering that skeptical grimace I've seen since my youth every time I tried to tell her I saw the undead. "You're saying people are paranoid because of a piece of dirt?"

All my life I stood alone against people like my sister. Today, she's surrounded and I feel empowered knowing I'm among my own kind.

"What I think, Portia," Maribelle says softly, "is that Dwayne and my brother are tapping into something left over in this town from a horrific event that happened years ago and they are using it to get what they want. Which, in my case, is my land."

"In my case," I add, "it's Jack's soul or my life."

A stifling silence descends for what seems like minutes until Sebastian rises and stares off toward the kitchen.

"What is it?" Maribelle asks.

He says nothing, which unnerves us more.

"Are you just being paranoid now, brother?" Portia asks.

But then, we all smell it. Something's burning.

We bolt into action and head toward the back of the building. When Sebastian opens the door to the kitchen, a blast of hot air nearly knocks off our feet. The kitchen roars, engulfed in flames.

CHAPTER 14

TB slides two hands around my waist and firmly pulls me backwards into the main room.

"Get outside," he yells, then releases me and heads toward the kitchen.

I'm not about to let my friends and family fight this alone, especially since there's a handy paint tarp by the fireplace. Just as I'm about to grab the fabric, another hand grabs my elbow and pulls me back. This person, however, drags me to the door.

"Get outside," Agent Sheridan says.

"But...," I object, pointing to the tarp.

"I got it."

The next minute I'm standing in the building's parking lot.

I hear the sirens approaching, see members of the community running over with blankets. An unmarked car comes screeching into the lot, gravel flying everywhere. Clayton emerges and, once he makes sure I'm not harmed, rushes into the burning building.

I feel helpless, standing there watching everyone struggle to get the blaze under control. It's still raining, so that gives me hope, but I spot flames reaching through the back roof so I know the kitchen's a goner. When the fire trucks arrive, I'm pushed away from the scene, even have a fireman insist I go home and stop being a spectator.

"My family's in there," I tell him.

But as more and more people arrive and the parking lot fills up, sirens spin like a strobe light against the low-hanging clouds making the scene resemble a disco club, I retreat farther away. I find myself in the woods next to the buildings, watching the action like a movie. I strain my neck hoping to spot my husband, siblings, my favorite witch, but people are running every which way, disappearing into the building, running out the other side, a giant blur.

"Amazing what happens when you don't live up to a bargain."

My heart rises in my chest and lodges somewhere around my throat. I'm afraid to turn around, afraid to look Dwayne in the eyes.

"Poor Vi, your life is disappearing around you."

I scan the chaotic scene before me hoping to spot Clayton or Sheridan, but there's no one in the parking lot now. Everyone's inside fighting the fire. Dwayne inches closer and I can feel his breath on the back of my neck.

"All this goes away if you give me Jack."

I close my eyes, trying to find that balance Maribelle insisted would give me strength, but my words come out hollow and scared. "I'm not giving you a thing."

"Fine." Clayton emerges through the building's front door and I feel Dwayne move backward. "Then your family's next. And maybe Gunner would like a turn with your cat?"

It feels like an eternity before Clayton looks my way. I stand there numb, scared to call out, afraid Dwayne will stab me in the back. Finally, Clayton spots me, notices my panic, rushes over.

"What is it?"

I turn for the first time but Dwayne's long gone.

"He was right here!"

Clayton pulls out his gun and rushes into the woods, motions with his hand for me to head toward the building so I do. When I reach the front door and the safety of the firemen, I look back. Clayton's disappeared and the woods suddenly appear agitated, as if the storm's returning.

I remember Dwayne's last words and even though I shouldn't be doing this, head toward the houseboat. I feel more confident once I'm inside my crystal circle of protection, but my heart's beating rapidly as I try to remember if Stinky remained inside or out when we left for the restaurant. I open the door and call his name but receive silence in return. I waddle into every room, check under the bed, look through closets—even open and inspect the kitchen cabinets where he likes to hide when the weather turns hot. Nothing. As an afterthought, I grab a knife. I return to the deck and call his name. A distant roll of thunder answers but no orange-and-white cat.

"Stinky!" I call out frantically.

I hear steps running up the deck and turn, brandishing the knife in front of me. Clayton holds a hand up, his other gripping a gun.

"What the hell are you doing here, Vi?"

The tears follow the panic. "I can't find Stinky."

Clayton approaches the scene like cops in TV series, checking around corners, pistol to the ready. When he finds the area safe, he places his gun back in the hip holster.

"Your cat can fend for himself," he tells me, checking me out as well. "You, on the other hand."

"Am helpless."

Now, I'm really crying because I can't do anything. I can't help my family and friends save their business, can't protect my precious pet or home, can't face the person who is wreaking havoc on my beloved community. I can't even solve Jack's mystery so he can transition. I'm totally useless.

Clayton pulls me into his chest and I let loose into hiccupping sobs, my hands gripping his shirt to steady myself. I'm heaving so hard my bones ache.

"I've got you," he whispers into my hair, patiently waiting for my jag to subside.

I'm so thankful for this rock-solid man, grateful to lean on someone in my pain, but the truth is Clayton hasn't been there for me. Dwayne has repeatedly come and gone in Emma's Cove without the FBI's knowledge, even standing within sight of the restaurant blaze. If Dwayne can reach me in a firestorm of firemen and FBI agents, what chance do I have in battling this man?

I pull away, averting my gaze. Am I being paranoid or is Clayton working with the other side?

"I'm fine now, thanks." I start to crawfish back to the front door. "I think I'll go in and rest for a while."

And pack my bags.

Clayton senses something's amiss and reaches for me, but I retreat farther, try to find the doorknob without turning around.

"Vi, we should talk."

I attempt a reassuring smile but Clayton's not buying it. He takes a step forward and I grab the doorknob behind me, open the door.

"Another time," I say quickly, cross the threshold and close the door with a bang. I lock both the knob and the deadbolt, lean my pounding head on the doorframe, and wait for the giant shadow to leave. After a few seconds, the shadow moves and I hear his footsteps head down the deck. It's only then that I exhale a long breath.

I look around at my sweet little houseboat and begin crying again. I hate leaving my precious oasis but I brought tragedy to this cove and I need to take it away. I head to the bedroom and pull suitcases from under the bed. I begin emptying my closet, throwing my clothes in without much thought, adding toiletries and my prenatal vitamins. Once everything's finalized, and I zip up my laptop and notebooks into another bag, I grab my phone to call for an Uber. I'll catch the first bus out of here, drawing away Dwayne and his evil.

But where am I supposed to go? Home to my parents, where I might put them in danger? If Dwayne follows me there, how will I protect the lives within me?

I fall into the living room's easy chair still clutching the suitcase and the laptop bag, tears dripping down my cheek, creating polka dots on my maternity shirt. I'm screwed if I stay and dangerously on my own if I leave. There's no way out of this mess and no one to save me.

The footsteps return but this time there's more than one. A knock sounds on the door and I spot two shadows on the other side. I wipe the tears from my face and look around for the knife, find it resting on the coffee table before me. I grab the instrument of protection and stare at the door, but I refuse to move, even when the knocking becomes insistent.

"Vi?" Carol asks from the other side.

I drop everything and head for the door, pull it open and find my tribe.

"Why are you here?" Carol asks me. "There's a four-alarm fire across the street."

Nothing like journalist friends smelling a hot story—pun intended—to knock me out of my pity fest. I can't help but laugh. Carol notices the tears lingering on my cheeks, however, so her smile fades as she comes inside, followed by Morgan.

"What's going on?" she asks.

While I relock the door, I explain how family members, TB and three women in the community and I were having a private conversation at the restaurant when we smelled something burning and discovered the kitchen ablaze.

"The fire chief said the kitchen's a mess but the rain helped them get it under control fairly quickly," Morgan says. "Nellie's on the scene."

Carol's worried about me, pacing the living room, studying my packed bags and the knife on the coffee table.

"What's going on, Vi?"

I swallow the lump the tears left behind. "I'm leaving."

"What? Why?"

The tears threaten again and it's hard to talk. I shake my head instead.

Carol takes my hand and leads me back to my chair, sitting opposite me on the couch. "Tell us what's going on."

I explain how everyone pushed me out the door and that's when Dwayne found me, threatening me and my family.

"And my cat," I whisper when the lump reemerges. "I can't find my cat."

Carol shivers and sends Morgan a knowing look. "Like the Greenes' cat in Maine."

My adrenaline shoots high. "What?"

Carol exhales and her shoulders drop a good inch. "We found out quite a bit about Maribelle Greene, her husband Jack, and some lunatic she had as a brother. Apparently, he did some horrible things to their cat."

"And the neighbors," Morgan inserts. "There's a warrant out for him from the Portland Police for breaking and entering and animal cruelty."

Now I rise and begin pacing. I'll die if anything's happened to Stinky.

"It gets worse," Carol says.

I turn and laugh nervously. "How?" Although, I dang well know how.

"Nellie got your husband's accident report from last night,"

Morgan tells me. "It looks like someone tampered with his brakes."

My old resolve to leave this place resurfaces. "I have to get out of here. Dwayne Garrett is after my family. He started the fire."

"The guy you told us about?" Carol asks. "The one who tried to kill you in Mississippi?"

I nod. "He's here in Emma's Cove, sneaking around under the FBI radar although God knows how, unless...."

I hate to throw suspicion on Clayton and his men in case I'm wrong.

"Unless what?" Carol asks.

What the hell? I trust my friends to dig into things in an honest, balanced way.

"They're either the most incapable FBI agents ever or they're working for Tennessee's Best Hotels trying to nab Maribelle's property next to her hotel."

I leave out the paranoia sweeping the town, and the other supernatural information. Journalists deal in facts and logic so it's best not to include ghosts, demons and bad juju in brown patches.

"I got the scoop on Tennessee's Best," Morgan adds, pulling out his reporter's notebook. "They've been donating vast amounts of money to city council members' reelection campaigns. Word on the street is that Touché's spreading bad information about Maribelle, trying to get the community to pressure her to sell."

"The lunatic brother is working with them," I add.

"Damn." Carol leans back on the sofa.

"It gets worse," I tell them. "We think her brother may have killed her parents."

Either that or Maribelle's the best liar in Tennessee and we've all been sucked in.

"This is a great story." Morgan looks pleased, and if I wasn't a journalist who might have reacted the same way in the same situation, I would stab him with that knife.

Copy Desk Carol, on the other hand, who didn't go into journalism to discover the next Watergate, sends him a reprimanding look.

New footsteps sound on the deck so I grab the knife and face the door, feet splayed.

"Okay, you're scaring me," Carol says.

I think to mention the crystal protection circle that's kept Dwayne away but I doubt she'd understand. And I'm not sure it's working, considering Dwayne has bypassed the FBI, my vigilant feline, and my husband who can sense danger within a one-hundred-mile radius.

Someone's fiddling with the doorknob and all three of us hold our breath until the door flings open and TB steps inside. He only has eyes for me.

"Vi, where the hell have you been?" He grabs me in a tight embrace, ignoring the knife in my hands, which I immediately let fall to the floor.

"I'm okay," I mutter into the crook of his shoulder.

But I'm not, still determined to leave this place. And that thought makes the tears fall again.

"I'm Carol from the newspaper," I hear Carol say behind TB. "And this is our business editor Morgan."

TB pulls back and acknowledges my colleagues politely, although he never lets me go, holds me tight with one arm around my shoulders. I can't stop the pain breaking through, thankfully not sobbing like when Clayton visited but the tears keep falling in an endless stream I can't control.

Bless her heart, Carol comes to the rescue, hands me a tissue while she explains to TB what information they found on Maribelle and her brother, the developers trying to infiltrate Emma's Cove, and how the police report suspects someone tampered with his pickup truck.

"Your wife thinks this Dwayne fellow caused the fire," Morgan adds.

TB releases me enough to gaze into my eyes. I think I finally have the waterworks under control so I tell him the bad news.

"I saw him in the woods next to the restaurant."

I feel the muscles in TB's body tense. "When?"

"During the fire. He said he wouldn't stop until I gave him Jack."

"Gave him Jack?" Morgan asks.

"It's a long story," I tell him.

Not what you want to say to a journalist. Both Carol and Morgan cross their arms and wait for me to spill the beans.

"You really don't want to know," TB tells them.

"Oh, yes they do," I answer.

More footsteps and Nellie appears in the door.

"Hey Vi, got a laptop I can use? The night desk is waiting for the story. I have one in the car but it's way on the other side of the action and the parking lot's jammed with cop cars."

"Yeah, no problem."

I slip out of TB's embrace and grab the bag that's been left on the living room floor, pull my laptop out and hand it to Nellie who thanks me and immediately gets to work. TB notices the suitcase lying by the chair and sends me a questioning look.

"We're leaving," I tell him and he nods.

"Oh no, you're not." Now, it's Portia's turn to come waltzing through the door, leaving a long line of dirt and ashes in her wake. "The son-of-a-bitch responsible for burning my brother's restaurant is going down."

Sebastian's right behind, but he had the forethought to shake the mess off his shoes before entering.

"Kitchen's gone but we hadn't installed the new appliances yet, thank goodness," Sebastian tells us. "Good thing we have insurance."

Suddenly, the living room's Grand Central Station. TB starts asking our guests for drink orders. Nellie grabs his sleeve and nabs a few quotes from him as a witness, then requests a Diet Coke. Portia calls her law firm and begins a long conversation with someone about arson cases. Sebastian introduces himself to Carol and Morgan and they fill him in on what they found. The noise resembles my family dinners at holidays, events that would send my friends and old boyfriends running screaming from my home. Today, the cacophony comforts my bruised heart.

I feel a nudge at my elbow. TB's nodding toward the bedroom. If I was in the right frame of mind, I'd make a sly joke but today my thoughts run more toward slipping under those sheets and wishing the world away. I follow him to the back of the houseboat, TB closing the door to shut out the noise from the living room and conceal our conversation.

"What happened?"

I plop down on the bed, grateful to be off my feet.

"I kept getting pushed out of the way and the next thing I knew I was in the woods by the restaurant. I didn't see Dwayne, was too afraid to turn around, but it was him. He said if I didn't give him Jack he would come after my family and Gunner would have a turn at…."

The tears fall again. "TB, have you seen Stinky?"

He sits next to me on the bed, shaking his head. "I let him out before we headed to the restaurant, figured we'd be home before dark."

I deflate like a balloon, lean forward and pull my hair through my hands not caring that I'll resemble the Wicked Witch of the West afterwards. I'm so incredibly tired, so heartbroken I imagine myself melting into a puddle at my feet. And yes, I know, too many metaphors.

"We need to leave," TB whispers.

"I know."

"We'll head to my parents' house in Florida."

Now, I really want to cry. It's the best idea considering both parents contain Michael DNA, so three angel descendants against a Lucifer progeny makes perfect sense. It's just that Angela and Richard Boudreaux lack creativity and color, literally live in a house that's completely white inside and out. And I mean everything. They can discuss the day's weather for an hour—God helps us if a hurricane's coming,—and read nothing but non-fiction and ancient history texts, then corner you to relate every chapter ad nauseam. The TV's always on, news channels analyzing one story for an entire afternoon. And then there's the grandchildren. I'll endure several scrapbooks filled with photos and examples of their accomplishments, which are many. Descendants, as you may guess, are overachievers.

Only occasionally will they ask others what they're doing and usually make some excuse as to why they can't stay and listen. And because TB didn't inherit the gray matter his brothers and sister received, there are always remarks about TB's shortcomings. They're still insistent my husband made a crazy mistake coming here to study library science when he could be raking in money working for his uncle or "getting a real degree in something important."

They're really wonderful people but after twenty minutes I want to stick a fork in my eye.

"We have to find Stinky first," I tell him. "I'm not leaving without my cat."

The noise level in the living room rises a notch, someone new has arrived.

"Why do you distrust Clayton?" I ask TB.

TB doesn't answer right away and I'm pretty sure it's Maribelle's voice I'm hearing so I exhale the breath I've been holding.

"It's not that I don't trust him," TB begins. "He smells strange."

I lean forward and tilt my head so I can get a good look at the man sitting next to me on the bed. "Seriously?"

"You don't understand, Vi. It means he's a supe, but he's one I can't figure out and that unnerves me."

I shake my head trying to make sense of it. "A supe?"

He winces. "Crap, I shouldn't have said that."

"Shouldn't have said what?"

He won't look at me. "I'm not supposed to talk about it."

Turning my enormous body sideways to view my husband better gives me a crick in my neck. It's times like these when I cannot for the life of me remember being thin.

"Thibault Jeremy Boudreaux," I say using my mommy voice, "if you are holding back information from me, like you did with your angelic powers, I will curse you the rest of your days."

He hangs his head. "I'm surprised you didn't sense it too."

"Supe? As in supernatural?" Clayton did mention being someone "not of this world."

TB still won't meet my gaze, looking at the floor like a dog caught peeing on the rug. "Forget I said anything."

"What is he?" I ask. "And why can't you talk about it?"

He sighs and stares off toward the bathroom. "It's one thing being a SCANC, Vi. Everyone knows about ghosts and a good many people believe in them. The world won't react too kindly if they knew there are supernatural people walking around. And descendants would rather not let the government, especially the military, know what kind of powers we possess."

He finally turns my way, which gives my neck a break. "Descendants don't talk about any of this, not even to their spouses."

"Yeah, I got that. Took another descendant to spill the beans on you."

He shrugs. "It's for the best."

I laugh. "I'm about to possibly birth one. I think I should know."

He considers this and I realize my husband's probably regurgitating instructions from his angelic family.

"For the record, as for Clayton," he says, "I can't figure him out, just know he's one of them. Something earthy and primal, I suspect. But you can't mention that to anyone."

My neck's about to break so I stand and stretch my back. "But do you trust him?"

He goes quiet again, thinking it through, and I hear Portia relaying some information in the other room.

"I don't know. Right now, I don't trust anyone."

What a world we live in, I ponder. Greed threatening to infiltrate this town, jealousy keeping people from living their dream, fear running rampant, and a man so determined to live forever he will destroy anyone in his path.

"Tomorrow, we leave this place," TB states, taking my hands in his and looking up at me with those haunting black eyes. "I need my family to be safe."

Fear of losing a child resonates in TB's gaze and I feel that pain deep in my soul. I think of my darling Lillye, whom we miss with all our hearts, and the twins about to enter this world. What will it take to keep us safe?

"And I need to give up this ghost talent for good," I add. "I'm done with being a SCANC and having this danger constantly so close at hand."

He stands and pulls me forward, arms wrapped tight around my shoulders despite the two children between us. Thank God for this man, I think as I smell the heavenly scent about him.

"Just for the record," I mumble into his shirt. "You smell better."

His head tilts against mine and I close my eyes, wish the world would disappear and leave us standing like this forever. Preferably on our darling houseboat in Emma's Cove.

But a harsh knock on the door makes up jump. Literally.

"What are you two doing in there?" Maribelle barks. "We need you out here."

TB and I return to the living room to find things looking

more like the newsroom. Morgan carries a notebook in one hand, reading information to Nellie while she types furiously on my laptop. I hear Tennessee's Best mentioned and Nellie announcing, "Wow, that's good!" Carol looks over both their shoulders and points out a dangling modifier. Portia's still on the phone, discussing the recent fire, and Sebastian's on his cell talking to an insurance agent.

"Community meeting in thirty," Maribelle tells us.

"What?" I ask.

"Everyone's gathering at the diner to discuss what happened and what to do going forward. Clayton and some of his men will be there too."

TB and I share a look. Now it's Maribelle's turn to ask "What?" and mine to inquire, "Do you trust him?"

Maribelle's been promoting that line of thinking since we arrived. How did I miss Clayton being a suspect?

But, she surprises me.

"Of course, I don't trust him, he wants to put me away. Plus, I think he's a lousy FBI agent, especially after the events of the past two days."

She rubs a nervous hand across her forehead like Lillye used to do when we quizzed her on the alphabet.

"Don't get me wrong, I wish the man would go away and leave me alone. But, I don't think he's working against us, if that's what you mean."

"I guess we'll find out tonight," TB utters quietly.

Nellie leans back in her chair, arms outstretched in triumph. "Story filed! My editor said they will post straight to the website so the TV stations will pick it up for the ten o'clock news."

"Awesome." Morgan slaps her hand in a high five.

Nellie glances at Maribelle. "Tennessee's Best is not going to like me announcing to the world they're in league with a possible arsonist and a man suspected of murder."

Maribelle straightens. "Wait, what?"

"We couldn't find much on Dwayne Garrett," Carol interjects, "but last night a man matching his build with a scar down his cheek was seen outside the chemistry building on campus, hovering around TB's car. The witness, according to police, said she remembered him because of the scar. He was acting strange around TB's pickup and she thought he might be trying to steal it."

My spirits pick up for the first time this week. "Awesome, that means the police have cause to arrest him."

"Well, dang," Portia says. "They have plenty of cause."

"If we can find him," Nellie adds. "He's disappeared."

"He hasn't gone far," Sebastian says. "If he was brave enough to show up at the fire he's likely to show up again."

"Your brother, on the other hand…." Nellie glances at Maribelle as if she's afraid to say more.

"Go on," Maribelle says.

"My source at the police department, who won't go on record for this so it won't be in the paper tomorrow, said the FBI suspects him for two murders."

"My parents."

Nellie shakes her head. "No, two separate murders."

Gunner killed Jack? I search my brain trying to think of a motive.

"That's impossible," Maribelle says. "I would have known if Gunner had been in the area around the time of Jack's murder. He wouldn't have missed the opportunity to…."

Her lightbulb extinguishes.

"Clayton confirmed it today," Nellie says quietly, as if she climbed inside Maribelle's painful memory and had seen its ugly history. "Gunner is wanted for questioning in both your parents' murders and your husband's."

Maribelle stands in the center of the room shaking her head. I wonder if she's shocked at the news or frustrated that it took the FBI this long to turn the microscope on Gunner and away from her.

We're all so wrapped up in the revelations that we fail to notice the front door opening. When a gust of night air rushes in, still charged with the rainstorm outside, we all turn to the giant standing in my doorway.

I can't doubt this man, not for a second. For cradled in Clayton's arm is my beloved cat, nestled there like a baby.

CHAPTER 15

$\mathcal{I}$'m standing in the diner with a host of town residents waiting to hear from Clayton and his men, while talking to Aunt Mimi who's stuck in Branson because of severe thunderstorms.

"The radar's showing the bad stuff heading your way," she tells me.

I peer outside the diner's giant window overlooking the lake and view the lightning display in the distance, but nothing too threatening yet.

"Wouldn't surprise me. It's been an insane two days."

"I'd be there if I could."

Sebastian called her after I left for the newspaper that morning and she attempted to fly into Chattanooga but the storm front derailed her.

"You really don't need to be here, Aunt Mimi. In fact, it's best you stay away. There's some bad stuff hitting the fan." And I don't use the word stuff.

I hear a strong huff on the other end. "Those are reasons why I need to be there. Sebastian told me what's going on. Y'all need all the help you can get."

I gaze around at the room filled with FBI agents, journalists, Emma's Cove residents, and my family, all waiting to brief us. Outside, half of Lightning Bug's finest are scoping the area. I'm starting to rally but am still determined to leave this place, give up the ghost.

"You can't leave," my aunt says quietly.

I shake my head because I'm convinced the woman can read minds. Is this a witch thing? If that's the case, I failed to nab that gene.

"And no, I'm not reading your mind, just know how you think."

I can't help but laugh.

"Seriously, Vi." My hippie aunt turns solemn. "The world needs you and your talents. Don't give up on the people who rely on you."

"My twins need me, too."

"And what kind of world will you give them if you let evil win?"

"A world in which they're alive?"

I can hear her sigh on the other end, hear announcements being broadcast on the airport intercom.

"Yep, my flight's cancelled. And I'm not sure I can get out in the morning. This storm may be hitting you tomorrow."

The meeting shouldn't take long, I'm thinking, and Clayton has insisted that we hunker down afterward with several agents guarding the houseboat.

"I'll be fine, Mimi. Please don't fly here on my account. Plus, TB and I are planning to go to his parents' house as soon as we can."

I hear her humming on the other end and can't make out if it's a tune or an incantation.

"I don't know, something doesn't feel right."

"Exactly why I'm heading to Florida as soon as the sun rises."

Mimi keeps humming and it's unnerving.

"Mimi?"

She begins so quietly I almost don't hear her. "We live in a world that's out of balance, Sweetpea. If we're not in harmony with the natural realm, we are out of balance with the divine."

Not what I'm expecting.

"It's so easy to turn people against each other, to raise fear that our neighbors are out to harm us in some way. That way those in power can do what they will, keep us out of balance, smother our magic."

She sounds like she's channeling someone, her voice distinct and plain.

"Mimi," I ask, "are you okay?"

Her voice turns normal again, that old Southern accent hailing from Alabama returning.

"Oh darling, something's coming and your running away to Florida won't help."

Now, she's scaring me.

"Don't let fear take over. Stand your ground and face it. You're not alone."

I close my eyes and look heavenward. Finding balance in nature, believing that God is within and you can face anything is all so easy to understand but oh so hard to implement. Like *The Secret*, that book and movie everyone's talking about these days. I want to believe that everything I need is coming my way but when I try to imagine it already here, I can't stop asking how that will happen and doubt creeps back in.

"I don't know how to do that, Mimi. Plus, I'm rotund and that doesn't help with the balancing part."

"Sweetheart, everything we need is within and all around us. There is no part of Mother Earth that is not a part of us. Put yourself in the presence of the divine and you'll find the divine within you."

I've heard this all before from Mimi, how witches were healers, herbalists and midwives who saw nature as integral to life, used nature's best to heal others, connect to God or the Goddess and the divine or whomever they saw as a higher power. The word *witch* dates back hundreds of years to England, meaning "wise one, healer, shaman." Men worried and jealous of their power corrupted the word and in the process of burning hundreds at the stake moved society further away from nature. Since then, witches took on the hag image, their pots of healing herb power became evil cauldrons, brooms used to maintain hearth and home something to ride in the night, innocent cats their familiars.

Okay, maybe the cat part is correct.

But, creating magic, Mimi always told me, comes from within and through the power of connecting with nature.

"Women don't realize how much power they have," she once told me. "Magic happens when we tap into that power."

Right now, I don't feel powerful. My back aches, the twins are kicking, and I have to pee.

"Spirits and guides are here to help us," Mimi tells me now. "Don't be afraid to call on them."

I'll be calling the bus lines for two tickets out of here, I think, but I say nothing, assure Mimi I will do what's best.

"Please do. And call me in the morning."

I flip my cell phone closed as Maribelle calls the meeting to order. TB, my siblings, and journalism buddies have been huddling around the coffee and donuts but they head my way.

"I'm going to ask Agent Sheridan explain what's going on first," Maribelle tells everyone.

Sheridan approaches the group but already I feel the tension rise. The women are not pleased that trouble has come to Emma's Cove, nor are they happy with the FBI's response.

"First, we have someone break into our community center and now this?" Kelly shouts out.

"Where have y'all been?" asks another resident. "You've been lingering around since the break-in and you let this guy torch a building?"

The crowd buzzes with people voicing their disapproval, some blurting out concerns. Sheridan waits patiently for a few moments, hoping the noise will die down, but when the agitation remains, waves his hands and shouts out like an aggravated father.

"Come on now, let's try and do this in a logical, non-emotional way."

"Oh no," says Portia at my side. Not what women want to hear.

The noise level increases and some women start shouting. Clayton places a hand on Sheridan's shoulder and whispers in his ear. The young agent slouches off and Clayton stands before the unruly group. He holds up a hand and waits for the shouting to stop. Finally, the crowd grows silent.

"What my young agent meant is let's discuss this in an *orderly* way. If you don't mind, I'll explain what happened tonight and what the FBI knows so far. Then we can open it up to questions."

Clayton details how Dwayne attacked me in Natchez, and most of the women turn my way. He mentions the scar delivered by my cat and, as if on cue, Stinky lets out a meow and stretches.

And yes, my cat's in the room. I tried keeping Stinky at home but he kicked and clawed whenever I picked him up, rushed out the door the minute we opened it. We caught him twice and twice he escaped our clutches. Finally, we gave up and he followed us all the way to the diner, made himself at home once inside, garnering love from pretty much every person there. That and a can of tuna from Patrice.

Next, Clayton tells the group how they chased Dwayne around the South, knew he might show up here after I spotted him in the Atlanta airport.

"We almost had him outside Atlanta, but he keeps running one step ahead," Clayton admits. "And then Viola had a run-in with him in Lightning Bug. After that, as you know, he broke into the community center."

"And you've been here ever since," says Patrice. "So, why haven't you caught him."

"He's not what you think," I say, dodging a worried look from my husband.

Clayton sends me a "don't go there" look too, but he adds, "He's capable of a lot more than you realize."

"Like what?" says the woman to my right.

I'm not sure what to say, now that I alluded to Dwayne's powers. But, then I think of Gunner and how some people lack morals, born to display licentious behavior.

"Dwayne Garrett is the kind of man who doesn't care about anything except what he wants," I explain. "He wants to get back at me and he'll do whatever he can to make that happen."

"But again, why can't you find him and stop him?" Patrice asks Clayton.

"Some men are cunning," Portia adds. "Some men are smart enough to evade police and the FBI, even fool their own families. How many times have you seen mass killings and the neighbors are interviewed saying, 'He seemed like such a nice guy.'"

"They get caught eventually," Clayton says. "Think of serial killers, most of whom are smart and cunning as our illustrious lawyer here mentioned."

"Portia represents abused women," I throw out there.

"These men were eventually caught but how many people did they kill before they were?"

The crowd titters again and Clayton holds up his hand. "That's not going to happen here. Not on my watch."

Patrice huffs and several women cross their arms across their chests.

"What about Maribelle?" Kelly asks. "What plan do you have for her?"

Maribelle stands fearless like a sentinel off to the side.

"We have a suspect in the murder of Jack Greene, but he's been eluding us as well," Clayton explains.

"You've got to be kidding," a woman in the back yells.

Clayton sends Maribelle an uneasy look. "These things take time, I'm afraid. You can't force justice or it will backfire in your face. Unfortunately, what we have against Gunner Bronagh right now is mostly circumstantial."

This does not sit well with the crowd but Maribelle's countenance never falters.

"Let me get this straight," Patrice says, standing. "The man terrorizing our community is still out there and you can't catch him, and the man responsible for Maribelle's husband's death is running around town because you don't have enough evidence on him."

This sets the crowd abuzz once more and Clayton runs a nervous hand through his hair, knows he's losing both control and the trust of the group. If he ever had their trust.

Maribelle holds up her hands. "Friends, you can't rush into things or the courts will throw the case out. I'm sure Agent Clayton knows what he's doing and likely I'm still a suspect until further notice."

I gaze at Maribelle who's watching the action without emotion. I think of how different she appears now than when we first arrived, when she hardly gave me the time of day and distrusted our reasons for moving to the cove. And now, when she's convinced the town has been infiltrated by an epidemic of paranoia, she appears calm and collected.

I slip to her side.

"What do you know that no one else does?" I whisper.

She nods to the room that has dissolved into chaos, women

arguing with each other, Kelly exclaiming that their homes are in danger, Clayton attempting to regain control.

"Fear does this to people."

I think back to earlier tonight when TB and I had resolved to leave town, right after Dwayne set fire to Sebastian's restaurant and threatened my life. Again.

"We have a lot to be fearful of."

Maribelle shakes her head. "Then they win."

"But our lives are at risk."

When she finally looks my way, her eyes are filled with sadness, as if her months-long teachings have been for naught.

"So, what do we do, Vi? Give up Emma's Cove to development? Leave our homes in this idyllic place because some men are jealous of what we have?"

"I think Dwayne is more about revenge."

"Whatever." Now, her dander is up and I regret my impulsive comment. "It never stops. There's always someone out there who means us harm, wants what we have, out to get revenge, especially toward women. We have to stand up to the onslaught or we will always be the ones burned at the stake."

In my peripheral vision, I catch a small slice of lightning over a distant mountain. I think of Caroline Montclair, standing up to the drunk men of Lightning Bug on that dark, horrible night, refusing to give in to their demands and that she return to an abusive husband. Emma Harrington re-imagined her in fabric, a courageous woman who stood her ground with love, not fear.

I think of the hundreds of women who also perished in fire over the centuries, accused, like Caroline, of something sinister and evil.

Suddenly, I'm ashamed of wanting to run from this place, this remarkable oasis where women thrived despite the violence that constantly threatened. How do I turn my back on their stories and struggles, especially when it's been me who brought the enemy here?

"Magic happens when we tap into that power."

Like that lightning bolt cascading down from the heavens, a strike of energy flows through me. And I realize, too, what changed about Maribelle over the past few months. I gaze at my husband standing quietly at the side of the action, with two black eyes and possibly a headache from hell, but watching his neighbors with concern. I touch my core and feel two innocent young lives moving within. My sister's animatedly speaking with my journalism friends, assuring them the law will be on our side, while Sebastian sends Maribelle a loving smile.

Can love give us strength, fight off the evils of the world?

It happened once. I was hired to help rid a town of ghosts in central Louisiana and found more than I bargained for, mainly a company dumping toxic waste into a spring, polluting the town's water system. I had read about Masaru Emoto, a Japanese scientist who studied water crystals and found that energy, either positive or negative, had a profound impact on the water's makeup. Positive thoughts and words created beautiful water crystals while negative thoughts and words produced distorted ones. He believed that words and thoughts were vibrations called "Hado," which means wave. If the energy of a place was negative, people would say that its Hado was low. If a place emitted good vibes, people believed it had a powerful Hado.

"These vibrational waves of thought, words and consciousness can change things, even at the atomic level," I had told the Louisiana townspeople before rallying them to action. "If all energy is vibrating, then we can change anything by shifting the vibration."

And we did. Together, with our hearts filled with love, we asked the departed roaming the town to return to their resting places. Then we blessed the waters, our hands connected, and what resulted was powerful.

"I know what to do."

Without so much of a word between us, Maribelle smiles, nods her head. She's with me. And the energy that suddenly appears between us flows outward, creating waves throughout the room like a pebble thrown into the cove. One by one people stop arguing and look our way, until the room becomes silent and all that's heard is the sound of distant thunder.

"Patrice," Maribelle calls out to the diner's owner, "get the salt. The rest of you follow us to the Village Green."

The crowd begins to murmur now that something concrete is called for, and some begin to question our actions.

"We'll explain when we get there," I say, and we all head toward the door.

Maribelle, however, pauses at the threshold, turns toward Clayton and Sheridan.

"If you don't mind, I'd rather the FBI stay out of this."

Sheridan looks insulted. "Don't be silly, you can't go down there alone."

"And like you're going to keep us safe?" someone from the back shouts out.

Clayton ponders this scenario and finally looks at Sheridan, nodding toward the door. Sheridan appears surprised to be dismissed but he follows orders and heads out to the parking lot where the Lightning Bug police are still milling about.

Maribelle smiles smugly at Clayton. "Uh, that means you, too, Agent."

Clayton leans toward both of us. "I can help."

This makes Maribelle laugh. "I can't speak for the rest of the group, but you've help me enough, thank you very much."

Clayton straightens, glances over to TB who's been following me to the door. Clayton leans in to speak to Maribelle and me but he's looking straight at my husband.

"You need to trust me because we can help."

TB shoots me a worried look and I shake my head. I want to explain that Clayton knows of his predilection but I wasn't the one who spilled the beans, but saying as much will only bring the secret out.

"We?" Maribelle asks, following Clayton's gaze, finally landing on mine.

I suddenly realize everyone's staring at me and I honestly don't have the answer. I have no idea what Clayton is made of, nor what he's capable of doing. But he's been on my side since I met him in Galveston, seems to understand the mysterious nature of life.

I shrug and give in, hoping this "supe" of a man won't kill us all.

"We could use all the help we can get," I say, hoping for the best.

Maribelle sighs. "I hope you know what you're doing."

I hope so, too, I think, as she heads out the door with Emma's Cove residents, my family, and three journalists following behind. Stinky trots alongside.

TB grabs my elbow and pulls me aside.

"I never said a word," I tell him.

"But how does he know?"

I raise my shoulders, then fall back in line, heading down to the brown patch in the center of the Village Green that skirts the shore of our cove. When we arrive to the place where nothing grows, enveloped by darkness due to the continuing storm and lack of moonlight, everyone pauses and looks to Maribelle for guidance.

"Make a circle," she commands. "Hold hands."

Most of the women move to encircle the brown patch while Patrice pours salt around the exterior and Maribelle begins chanting a protection mantra. I pull my six protection stones from my pocket, which I carry with me always, and place them in the circle's center.

Stinky never leaves my side, watches me carefully. Even though I know he hates oppressive affection, I pick him up and give him a tight squeeze, planting a kiss on the top of his head. Surprisingly, he lets me.

"Love you, cat."

"What do I do?" Portia asks me, looking out of place, but Sebastian reaches over and leads her to the circle, grasping hands with the rest of the residents.

Morgan and Nellie hang back, naturally acting as reporters and not participants, but Carol heads to the circle and joins in.

"Y'all aren't coming?" she asks them.

I think to explain how reporters never participate—it's their job to be on the outside of the action—but Clayton places his hands on their shoulders and pushes them forward and the two fall into place.

Clayton, however, remains outside the activity, not taking a hand from one of the women when it's offered. When I look for my husband, he's lingering on the periphery as well, speaking quietly to Clayton. I'm not the only one noticing their odd behavior. Kelly drops her hands from the women on either side.

"What's going on?" she asks nervously.

Maribelle pauses and all eyes turn toward the two men and a quietness descends upon the group. Off in the distance, I hear a peal of thunder so faint you'd think it was a truck on the northbound highway on the other side of the lake. Even the trees are quiet tonight, motionless as if they, too, are waiting for Clayton and TB to explain. TB looks at me with widened eyes, as if silently asking me what to do.

"You have to trust us," Clayton says softly.

The crowd begins to murmur and Kelly crosses her arms across her chest. "Trust you? Are you kidding?"

I feel a combination of paranoia, anger, and fear rise from this place, the same darkness I felt months ago when TB, Sebastian, and I paused here. The rancid energy snakes up from the ground, slithering around our legs to pull us under. My skin crawls with the sensation, my heart races.

"No!" I shout, as much to stop the evil rising as to take back control of the group. "We have to stop this."

"But, not with him," Kelly begins, pointing at Clayton.

"He's not the enemy." I point to the dark ground that's been lying in the heart of Emma's Cove for decades. "We are. Poisoned by whatever past lingers here. It's time we move on and we can't do that fighting among ourselves and using that energy against each other."

"But, he's not one of us," a woman states.

I turn toward the massive man, recall both the moment he entered my houseboat for the first time, being welcomed by my feline, and then earlier this evening, holding my precious cat like a baby. I look down at Stinky who winks.

"Of course, he is," I tell them softly.

"I don't know," Kelly says, shaking her head.

"I do," I say with more confidence than I really have. "I say we do whatever Clayton asks of us."

Reluctantly, everyone resumes holding hands and we create a large circle that surrounds the dark patch of land. I let Stinky down and he enters the circle's center where he joins Maribelle facing east toward my houseboat and her motel, her arms outstretched. She calls upon God and the Goddess for protection and a couple of the women release a hand to make the sign of the cross.

"I consecrate this circle of power, asking for assistance from those with us here tonight and those who have passed before," Maribelle begins. "To our Mother, who gives us life, may you purify your land of the trouble lingering here."

A breeze stirs the woods around us and the tree tops rustle. Maribelle turns clockwise to the south.

"Give us the courage, oh sacred ones, to face the challenges before us, to meet evil head-on and defeat its wicked warriors who mean us harm."

Something tepid and ominous leaks up from the ground. I'm not the only one who senses this, for several women twitch in discomfort. Maribelle turns to the west.

"I call upon the spirits of our ancestors, the sprites of the forest, to God and the Goddess. Help us rid this place of all evil. Let us forgive those who mean us harm. Help heal the horrors that have occurred here and leave only love in its place."

The darkness intensifies and there's an angry energy swirling about, moving counterclockwise within the circle. I look at Maribelle who's struggling to remain upright and unfaltering as she turns her attention to the north. Stinky has sunk his claws into the earth, his back fur standing straight up. He's howling for all the world.

"To our cove and the waters that sustain all life," Maribelle yells over the noise toward the lake. "Keeper of dreams and love, please cleanse this sacred space and make it whole again so that whatever life bursts forth will be sustained."

Finally, Maribelle returns to facing east, but the energy is now at its apex. I can barely make out my neighbor in the darkness flowing around me.

"As we return east, to the coming of the dawn, may fresh life spring forth from this troubled spot and may the sun rise on our blessed cove free of all evil that resided here."

She struggles to remain standing, shouting out, "May we be grateful for all healing established here tonight. We thank you. Blessed be."

We barely make out Maribelle in the commotion but most of us glimpse her arms waving for us to repeat her last words. Several women recant the final blessing, others cry out "Amen," but the dark energy only intensifies and I know I'm not the only one thinking this may not have worked, that whatever festers on this lone piece of earth is stronger than we imagined.

But I'm not ready to give up. I look at TB and he nods.

"Close your eyes," Clayton shouts out.

"What?" says the woman to my right.

"Close your eyes," I tell her.

"I don't understand." She's scared and not trusting so I squeeze her hand and lean close so we can see eye to eye. "Please. We can do this."

She's frightened to the core, but she nods. I yell to the others to do the same and one by one the women close their eyes.

"Do not open them until I say so," Clayton says. "Please, you must trust me."

The darkness swirls around me so hard now my head aches from the clamour. Stinky continues to howl and Maribelle's still chanting in the center but the energy's angry and mean, seeping into our pores as if to unravel us all. The woman to my left squeezes my hand so hard I feel my bones may break and my other neighbor whimpers quietly.

"It'll be okay," I tell her, hoping I'm right.

Suddenly, the storm arrives. The trees release a burst of activity, waving as though possessed as the wind hits our circle like a hurricane. Great, I think, now it's going to pour on us, but the rain doesn't come. I hear Clayton murmuring something incomprehensible behind me but I keep my eyes closed. The wind picks up speed and the trees respond and that angry vibration in the center of the circle cries out like a battered animal. Whatever Clayton's doing is working its magic for the energy struggles to remain, rising up angry and aggressive, but falling back with less force. Each time, the vibration becomes weaker and weaker.

Finally, the darkness rises one final time, pushing upward, emitting a sound that turns our blood cold. It's stronger now than ever, feeling like it's reaching into our souls and stealing pieces.

"No," shrieks a woman in the crowd.

"This is too much," yells another.

"Keep your eyes closed," Maribelle warns them. "Don't let it move you. Come from a place of love."

I think of my precious angelic husband, whose role in life is to rescue those in danger and make the world a better place. I remember my darling Lillye, whose smile and laughter could change the worst day to the finest, even when she was gasping for her last breaths. I savor the precious children inside me, my family, my friends, the circle of which I'm a part. I'm surrounded by love.

And in that moment when I'm certain my ear drum will explode, I spot through my eyelids a white light encompassing the area. Its loving force warm and comforting wraps around us like a giant hug, slips beneath our feet and thrusts the evil force into oblivion. As quickly as the light appeared, the darkness resumes.

In its place falls sudden silence.

We all stagger from the impact, open our eyes and gaze at each other in amazement. Maribelle's gasping in the circle's center, looking from one person to the next to make sure we're all right. Whatever darkness resided inside the circle has disappeared, the trees silent and unmoving, even the sky shows signs of stars.

"What just happened?" the woman on my left utters.

Does it matter? I think. The air turns cool and inviting, the frogs call out to one another along the shore—even the trees appear happier, as if the removal of evil makes their branches lighter. Patrice laughs and others join in.

"Well, that was fun," breathes the woman to my right, wiping away tears.

"But what happened?" asks a middle-aged woman whose name is Verity, I learn from the other.

Maribelle walks over and takes Verity's hand. "Better not to ask questions but to be grateful that it's done," she tells her.

Verity isn't moved. "Really, what was that all about?" But she doesn't receive an answer.

The circle breaks and we head up the hill, some to return to the diner, some home, me and my tribe to the houseboat. My heart is full thinking of how we stood up to hatred, how love ruled this night. I'll never doubt Maribelle or my Aunt Mimi again, I vow, taking TB's elbow and hugging him close.

"You were amazing," he whispers to me.

"That light show was pretty frickin' awesome, too."

"What light show?"

I don't have to look up to know he's smiling.

"When we get home you're going to tell me what Clayton was doing."

He kisses the top of my head. "Sorry sweetheart, not going to happen."

I pull away, trying to meet his eyes in the darkness, despite the moon peeping through the clouds. "TB…."

But my husband's focus turns to Stinky, picking up the cat and carrying him on to the deck. He reaches for my hand and I allow him to pull me up—no easy feat considering my current weight—but when I ask again, he shakes his head. Before I can inquire further, Portia, Sebastian and Maribelle arrive, talking non-stop. We all head inside, Sebastian insisting that Maribelle spend the night and Portia none too pleased to be relegated to the couch. TB closes the door behind us and heads to the kitchen with drink orders. Gazing around the room I'm amazed that everyone acts as if nothing weird has taken place, that we didn't cast out demons from Emma's Cove with the assistance of a witch, a tree man and an angel.

Maybe Maribelle's right, it's best not to ask question, be grateful we have at least enjoyed one victory tonight.

As I move to the front door to turn off the outside light, however, I spot Jack in the woods near my home.

He's shaking his head, acting as if I'm the greatest fool there is.

CHAPTER 16

We're all riding high after the evening's exorcism, then Morgan and Carol show up asking a million questions. Naturally, everyone wants to know about the dark energy, the sudden wind that appeared out of nowhere, and the white light that capped off the scene. I keep glancing at TB but he's not saying a word. At one point when he catches me staring, he shakes his head. I won't find out, either.

I keep thinking about Clayton and the Ents in J.R.R. Tolkien's *Lord of the Rings*, tree-like people who were guardians of the woods who almost turned into trees themselves when the woods became dark and silent. Or the mythical Green Man who appears in ancient cultures. But maybe I need to take TB's advice and let it go.

Yeah, I'm a journalist, like that's going to happen.

What's bothering me more than the supernatural events of the night is Jack's reaction after we cleared the bad juju from town. I can't get his expression out of my mind, thinking I'm totally missing something.

"What's the matter?" Maribelle asks me once she nabs a glass of wine from TB's hands.

I grab her sleeve and pull her toward the back bedroom. Once inside, I close the door.

"I have no idea what Clayton and your husband did," she says. "My eyes were closed like the rest of you."

"It's not that." I make sure no one's in the bedroom or master bath. "It's about your husband, Jack."

"What about him?"

Sebastian opens the door and pokes his head in. "We never finished my brilliant pasta so we're thinking of ordering pizza."

"Good idea." I move to close the door.

He attempts to get his head farther inside the room. "What are y'all doing?"

"Talking pregnancy," Maribelle says.

"Okay then." Sebastian closes the door.

I turn the lock so we won't be bothered again.

"What about Jack? Did you see something?" Maribelle asks.

I explain how he appeared a few moments ago, shaking his head.

"That's odd."

"I know." I sit on the edge of the bed, rub my swollen ankles. "I'm pretty sure he was letting me know there's still a mystery to solve."

"Clayton suspects my brother."

"Do you think he did it?"

Maribelle sighs and joins me on the bed. "Likely. Although if you knew my brother he would likely find some way to let me know, to gloat about it. He sent me cryptic postcards after mom and dad's death."

"Dang, Maribelle, did you tell the FBI?"

She smirks. "Of course, I did."

I surmise Clayton may have guessed Gunner murdered Jack all along, but kept it quiet because, as he told us in the diner, Maribelle never stopped being a suspect.

"Was Gunner mad at your parents for kicking him out of the will?" I ask.

"I don't know, Vi. He was an enigma. I'll never understand why my brother did the things he did. He always seemed so normal to the rest of the world."

"Most psychopaths do."

I stand because the lack of back support causes my nerves to pinch.

"You need to get off your feet," Maribelle tells me. "I'm worried about you."

"Funny," I say, stretching my lower back with the palms of my hands. "I was thinking the same thing about you."

"Gunner's not going to kill me. I'm the only family he has in the world."

I shake my head wondering how someone so courageous, so wise could miss the fact she may be next on her brother's list.

"Maribelle." I pull up a chair we have next to the bed, one with a back and a pillow, thank goodness. "Have you ever thought it might be about the money?"

"My inheritance? Yes, of course, but why would Gunner kill my husband? Jack had no money."

"Yeah, but you did. And you weren't divorced from Jack yet."

"So?"

"So," I repeat, "if you died and Jack was still alive, Gunner wouldn't inherit anything. Jack would. If Jack was out of the picture, wouldn't everything you own immediately pass on to your brother upon your death? He would be next of kin."

She offers up a sad smile. "Unless I have a will."

"Do you?"

Maribelle looks to the ceiling and winces. "No, been meaning to. Kinda got sick of lawyers after the last fight with the law."

"Good thing I know a good lawyer. And she happens to be in the living room."

Maribelle's not convinced. "I still don't think he would kill me. Not for an old motel in the middle of Tennessee. His tastes run more toward living the good life in New York City."

Follow the money. That's what we learned in journalism school when studying Watergate, one of the greatest investigative stories ever conducted. The Washington Post discovered that the break-in of the Democratic headquarters at the Watergate Hotel led all the way to the office of the president and they knew this by following the money trail.

"I still think Gunner's after your money. If he owned this land, he could sell it to Tennessee's Best Resorts."

This has Maribelle thinking, but I sense the doubt lingering inside that head. She doesn't want to imagine her brother, no matter how horrible he might have been growing up, killing her parents or her husband and now on the hunt to take her life.

I decide to change course. I relate all the things Jack has told me either verbally or through sign language since I met the ghost in Wisconsin last February.

"He kept telling me to ask MB," I say. "Then Caroline Montclair said the same thing."

"Ask me what?"

Good question and one I would have easily answered standing on the Village Green only moments before. Over the past few months Maribelle, or MB, taught me the ways of the Craft, the laws of the universe, the use of protection and purification elements, and how to face my fears. Somehow, that wasn't enough and I have no idea why.

I think back on the few times I spotted Jack in the woods. I scour my brain remembering how he was dressed, his mannerisms, anything that might be a clue.

"He kept pulling on his earring," I mutter, wondering if that meant something.

Maribelle straightens. "What?"

"He had this earring," I continue. "On one ear. Three fish dangling in a row."

The knowledge hits me like a lightning bolt. I know what this means.

"Touché!" I shout out.

Maribelle looks confused, no doubt wondering if I'm speaking of the infamous doctor or exclaiming that I made a clever point at her expense.

"He has this taxidermy on his wall, three fish in a row. Apparently, he's super proud of it."

Maribelle's face turns numb as if she's contemplating something horrible.

"What?" I ask.

"That was Jack's favorite. He always wore it in his left ear."

"It was found on the dock that night, according to Clayton."

The blood drains from her face so fast I worry she might faint.

"Maribelle?"

"That earring showed up on the hotel counter one day. I had no idea where it came from, assumed a visitor had left it behind. I asked the maid about it but she swore she hadn't found it. I kept it for a week or two but Jack took a liking to it so I let him have it."

"Do you think it might have been…?"

She rises and this time grabs my sleeve. "We have a visit to make."

We exit the bedroom and slip through the crowded living room smelling of pizza. A small group huddles around Carol reading the newspaper's website and what I hear is prime. Nellie has reported in her story the connection between Tennessee's Best Resorts and two men on the lam for possible murder and arson charges. She included their hefty contributions to city council members' re-election campaigns and a giant sum paid to the mayor that surprises everyone.

"Holy Moly," Portia says.

Maribelle and I silently slip out the front door with no one the wiser, except for Stinky, who gives me a look my mother used to inflict upon me when I came in after curfew.

"That cat is definitely strange," Maribelle says as we head down the dock. "But I like him."

Clayton's talking to Sheridan while sitting on the hood of his car. He appears exhausted, as if he carried two hobbits on his shoulders and rallied trees to take over Isengard. I shake that image from *The Two Towers* out of my head as we approach and he pulls on his jacket. He does it slowly, however, as if he's just worked out and every muscle aches.

"Can I help you, Vi, Maribelle?"

There's no amiable greeting and I can't help but wonder if he's worried we'll demand to know what he did on the Village Green.

"Feel like a drive?" I ask him.

We stand for several moments staring at one another, the two of us confident that we know what we're after and Clayton slowly realizing that letting us take the lead might get him somewhere.

"Okay," he answers without question. "Get in."

We pile into the car, me in the front seat and Maribelle in back. But she doesn't close the door until she insists I help her test the locks.

"Glad this isn't one of those police cars where you lock people in the back seat," she mumbles.

"I can fix it that way, if you like," Clayton offers.

Maribelle sends him the evil eye.

We take off, drive silently through the darkness toward Lightning Bug, a sprinkle of rain dotting the windshield. After a few moments, Clayton speaks.

"You want to tell me what's going on? Or maybe where I'm going?"

But I know he knows because he's following the highway taking us straight downtown.

I explain about the three fish in Touché's office and how the ghost of Jack Greene kept showing me the earring. Maribelle pipes in about how the earring was found at the hotel, conveniently placed on the counter.

"Jack loved anything with a fish on it."

"And you think that was a sign from your brother?" Clayton asks.

"It's something Gunner would have done because he never committed a crime without letting someone know. It would have been like creating a painting and hanging it in a closet. He always had to have an audience. When he killed my cat he left a picture of Garfield on my bed, cut into pieces."

I gasp.

"Couldn't imagine he would kill Jack. I just never put two and two together."

Clayton ponders this information, never asks why we're going to Touché's office, making me wonder if Touché has been on his radar all this time. For the final stretch, Maribelle relates horrific tales of Gunner when they were growing up, and how every time he left messages for Maribelle, showing proof of his actions and announcing that she may be next.

"I should have seen this coming," she says quietly.

"We have a hard time believing our loved ones do horrible things," Clayton says with so much pain in voice I wonder if he's speaking from experience.

"Plus, you've been distracted," I tell Maribelle. "You had the Po-Po on your tail. And then you met my handsome brother. Who looks amazingly like his twin, I might add."

My comment gives Maribelle a perk but Clayton looks at me as if I've lost my mind. "How can you joke at a time like this?"

How indeed? An hour ago, I was so frightened of my situation I was contemplating death by in-laws. But, then I kicked some nasty old energy into the ether.

"Someone taught me to be fearless tonight. And no, Treebeard, it wasn't you."

Clayton shakes his head but I can tell, even in the darkness of the car, that he's smiling.

We pull up to Touché's office in the heart of downtown and the street appears deserted except for a Lexus in front of the office and an old VW across the way.

"That's Linsey's, from the coffee shop," Maribelle says, nodding in the VW's direction. "She works late cooking up scones for the morning."

Main Street feels so empty and forlorn I'm waiting for a tumbleweed to come rolling by. Likewise, Touché's office appears vacant, only the under-cabinet lights illuminating the nurse station of the waiting room. I'm beginning to assume that the Lexus belongs to someone else, until a light comes on in a back room.

"You both stay here," Clayton says.

"As if," I say, opening the door and sliding out, stomach first.

Clayton is already out of the car and he looks at me over the hood like a forbidding father. "No way."

I lean over the car and whisper. "Way. Or maybe the FBI would like to know there's a 'supe' in their midst."

His eyes narrow and I'm worried I've gone too far, have absolutely no plans to out him. I look around to see if there are trees ready to attack but the small crabapple sapling in front of Touché's office is hardly threatening. In fact, it's listing fifteen degrees to the left and my ADHD brain thinks to bring this poor tree to Clayton's attention once we finish here. Maribelle pulls my attention back to center, emerging from the back seat and reaching Clayton's side. He exhales in defeat.

"Both of you stay behind me," he barks. "And do what I say."

"Yes, sir," I say with a salute.

"Damn it, Vi. I mean it. Whoever is in there could be dangerous."

Clayton pulls his gun and stomps off toward the alley alongside the building, me following behind. Maribelle grabs my elbow, pushes me behind her.

"Behave," she says sternly.

Okay, so maybe I'm taking the fearlessness a bit far.

There's a mechanical whining sound coming from inside as we reach the back door. Clayton peers through the window and from my perch nearby I spot Touché busily shredding papers. Clayton throws a foot against the back door, breaking it open with a bang, then Clayton straddles his feet, gun raised, and shouts at Touché. It all happens in seconds. I'm so startled by the action I bite the inside of my cheek to keep from peeing on myself.

"Back away from the shredder," Clayton shouts at the good doctor.

"It's not what you think," Touché answers, looking as if he might wet himself too. "It wasn't me."

"Back away!"

Maribelle and I watch from the window as Clayton shoves Touché up against the wall with one hand, the other still pointing the gun. He then calls for backup.

"He made me do it," Touché says, looking as if he's about to cry. "I only wanted to see my investment flourish."

I can't stand it anymore, slip inside the door. "Who?"

"Damn it, Vi," Clayton says, seriously exasperated with me. "Stay out of this."

But, I'm hell bent on knowing. "Who made you do what?"

Suddenly, a muffled noise comes from the front office, followed by feet shuffling. Clayton keeps a hand on Touché's chest but his attention has shifted.

"Stay here," he commands Touché and slips into the interior of the office.

The good doctor and I remain, staring at each other across the room.

"Who made you do what?" I repeat.

Touché doesn't recognize me, stares frightened in my direction, his face devoid of blood.

"I had nothing to do with burning the restaurant. Garrett is your man. I just wanted a piece of the action. I poured a lot of money into that project, practically everything I owned."

He shakes his head as if to juggle the gray matter back in place, then heads toward the shredder like a zombie. I reach for a nearby letter opener—with a three-fish design, weird—and step in between.

"I don't think so."

Maribelle's patience reaches its conclusion and she slips inside. When Touché spots her, his deferential attitude turns ugly.

"What are you doing here?" he barks, attempting to move forward but I wave the fish letter opener and he backs up.

"Watching you go down," she answers.

Touché has nothing but contempt for Maribelle. It shows in every inch of his body language.

"Your brother was right. You're bad news. You take and you take and leave nothing for the rest of us."

"Are you kidding me?" I start. "She owns a motel in another town, how does that affect you?"

Maribelle holds up a hand. "Vi, it's okay."

"No, it's not." I feel my blood pressure rising. "This man has everything—reputation, money, a strong following in his field— hell, a Lexus! But he has to take your business away?"

"I know what you women are doing up there," Touché adds.

"What are we women doing up there?"

Now, my head starts to pound and I'm thinking my blood pressure's spiking again.

He points to Maribelle. "Her little coven's sitting on a gold mine, always has been. We have this reputable company wanting to come into our community and bring us prosperity and she won't let them in. She wants it all to herself."

"Gold mine?" I exclaim.

I know I'm getting too excited but I want to argue his ridiculous claims. Maribelle sends me a stern look so I keep quiet. Maybe she's right, how do you refute arguments from a person who's lost all logical thought?

We hear noise coming from the front office, sounds like chairs being turned over and men grunting. Suddenly Clayton bursts into the back room, holding a thirty-something man in front, his arm held tightly behind his back next to Clayton's pistol. The tall lean man resembles Maribelle only slightly, his face marred by acne scars from previous years, his hair stringy and long, hanging down over one eye.

"Gunner," Maribelle whispers as I watch my steady friend retreat into a small child.

Gunner, on the hand, greets us smugly, as if being held by an FBI agent happens every day.

"Dear Maribelle," he says with a smile as the words come out cold and menacing. A shiver runs through me and the three fish in my hand vibrate.

Tears threaten but Maribelle pulls it together. "How could you?"

"Could what, dear Belle? Tell Mom and Dad lies about you, like you did me? Make them cut you out of their will?"

Maribelle huffs and I can tell she's rallying. "I pity you. You're sick."

Not what a psychopath wants to hear. Gunner struggles in Clayton's grip and lurches forward a few inches while Maribelle steps back. The fear he causes in her makes him laugh. Now, he's rebounding.

"I don't know this man," Touché throws in. "I have nothing to do with him and what he did."

"Shut up, Touché," Gunner says quietly but with a glare that causes Touché to step back and not say another word.

"I'd suggest you both take that advice," Clayton says. "You'll be hearing your rights as soon as my agents arrive to arrest you."

"Arrest me?" Touché is freaking out now. "I'm a prominent member of the community. I did nothing wrong. It was his idea to put pressure on his sister to sell. I had no idea he was going to kill that poor man."

"I said, shut up Touché," Gunner says menacingly.

"And that Garrett fella, he came up with the plan to burn the building."

Gunner struggles to face the good doctor, his countenance turning into anger and frustration. "You're an idiot, you know that?"

"And you're a murderer." This time, it's Maribelle speaking, tears streaking down her cheeks.

"You took what's mine, bitch." His face contorts into something sinister and I back up, wish to get as far from this evil man as I can. "You lied and then they cut me off. But then they always loved you more."

That steel of a spine returns and Maribelle marches forward, gets right in her brother's face.

"I never asked for anything from them except to believe me. I had to marry Jack to get away from you and even then they wouldn't see the truth. I have no idea what you did to make Mom and Dad come around but they finally saw you for what you are."

Gunner's creepy Hannibal Lecter smile returns. "You have no idea what I am."

I hear sirens in the distance, know the police will be here soon. This time, I notice Touché's hands shaking he's so scared of what's coming.

"I didn't do anything," he whispers like a frightened child.

Gunner huffs. "Just a little tax fraud, money laundering, bribing elected officials and accessory to murder and arson."

Touché's eyes enlarge so much I fear for the blood vessels in his brain.

"I had nothing to do with that man's murder," Touché insists again.

"I know," Gunner says with that creepy smile, a long string of hair falling further over his eye. "You never had the smarts to pull that one off."

Gunner looks toward Maribelle, the smile still plastered on his pock-marked face. "And you! I'm surprised you finally figured it out. You were never very bright, were you, Belle?"

Maribelle doesn't react, stands stiff and confident but the tears don't get the message, continue to slip down her cheeks.

"What I want to know," I start, waving the letter opener, "is did you mean for us to know it was you with the three-fish earring? Did you leave it on the dock that night as a message? Or did you want us to turn our attention to Touché and pin the murder on him?"

I didn't think Touché could become more agitated but he's now about to have a stroke.

"What did you pin on me? I did nothing," he shouts.

Gunner's face never changes, he's as confident as ever, ignoring me and glaring back at his sister with that knowing smile. "Relax. They have nothing."

"I wouldn't say that," Clayton pipes in. "You got a little sloppy."

I notice Gunner's cheek twitch but his smile never wavers. "What are you talking about."

"Your DNA was on the earring."

Finally, that smile disappears and Gunner turns into a frightened animal, starts cussing and shouting about everyone who wronged him. He spits at Maribelle, struggles to break out of Clayton's hold, and yells through the reading of the

Miranda Rights when Sheridan and the other agents arrive. Once Clayton hands him over, it takes Sheridan and two local policemen to drag his guilty butt to the car. Two more follow holding Touché, but he's crying too much to make a fuss.

Clayton pushes us into the alley, away from the chaos and to protect the crime scene. When we're finally far enough away, he bends forward, hands on his knees.

"You okay?" I ask, feeling a bit faint myself.

"Long night," he mutters to the ground.

I practice a healing technique Maribelle taught me, rubbing my palms together to produce a nice heat, then applying that to Clayton's back.

"Thank you, that feels nice," he whispers.

Maribelle, on the other hand, is too busy pacing.

"So, you've been on his trail for a while now?" she asks Clayton.

Our tree man straightens and rolls his neck to release the tension there. "We've been on his trail from the start, but like I said in the diner, you were still a suspect."

"But his DNA!" Now, she's shouting.

Clayton appears exhausted, from the night's brutal activities and this conversation.

"Guys, that DNA crap you see on TV, it's not real life. We don't get the results back in an afternoon. It takes a long time. We only found the earring a few months ago."

"Still...," Maribelle insists.

"And then we had to find Gunner. We knew he was working with Touché and we figured Garrett would show up eventually. This resort idea? Not a new one. Been in the works for a long time. And Touché has had a heavy financial interest in it. The Mayor has too."

Maribelle shakes her head, mouth open. "A long time?"

The two begin arguing, Maribelle heatedly and Clayton too

tired to get into it with her. What I keep pondering are the words Gunner shouted at the end.

"Don't y'all even care about what Gunner said back there when they were reading him his rights?" I ask them.

Maribelle finally pauses in her tirade and now it's her turn to place hands on her knees and study the cement. While Sheridan handicapped Gunner to take him away, years of pain poured from his lips, starting with him being abused at an early age. He shouted at Maribelle, revealing all kinds of horrors inflicted on him by a friend of the family.

"I had no idea those things happened to him," Maribelle says when she finally rises. "I know my parents couldn't have known he was abused by their best friend. There's just no way they would have let that continue as long as it did."

"Certainly explains a few things," I say quietly.

"Yes, it does."

The night seems darker now, eerie and devoid of sound except for the police scanners in the distance.

Finally, Maribelle breaks the silence. "I can see why he would have resented me all those years but that doesn't excuse what he did to me, Jack, or my parents."

Clayton does the unthinkable, places a hand on Maribelle's shoulder and squeezes, waits to see if she repels him. When she doesn't, leans slightly in his direction, he pulls her into his broad shoulders and holds her while she sobs.

I slip away, giving them both privacy, and head out to the parking lot where Sheridan relays information to someone on his cell.

"Crap," I say to myself. "I forgot to call TB."

I pull my phone out of my purse and there's a thousand missed calls and several voice messages. I don't bother listening to any, call my husband straight away.

"Where are you?" he yells.

"Hello to you, too."

"Jesus, Vi, where are you?"

I explain how Maribelle and I had a hunch about Touché and asked Clayton to check it out, discovered not only Touché in the act of destroying evidence but Gunner Bronagh in the other room. This all comes out after I apologize several times.

"Apparently, Gunner tried to escape out the front door but it was locked by the fancy alarm system."

I hear him exhale for all the world.

"I'm sorry, sweetheart," I tell him one more time.

"We were worried sick. You could have been hurt."

"I'm with Clayton and Maribelle and surrounded right now by FBI agents. Two people have been arrested. I'm fine."

"No, you're not," TB whispers. "He's still out there."

"I'm in good hands and I'm on my way home."

"You don't understand, Vi." I hear a door being shut and his voice gets quieter. "My senses are slowly returning, must have been the cleansing we did tonight. They're not fully restored but...."

Maribelle was right, that bad mojo in the Village Green has been distorting everyone's good sense. Dwayne likely stirred it up, driving the residents of Lightning Bug against us, causing Emma's Cove women to become paranoid.

"The tide's finally turning," I tell him.

TB doesn't share in my excitement, turns silent.

"TB?"

"It's not that great, Vi. Dwayne's still out there. And I feel like he's getting close."

CHAPTER 17

fter I give TB details on the events of the past hour—leaving out the part about me threatening Touché with a letter opener and Clayton having to pull his gun—I assure him I will take all precautions and come straight home with Clayton as protector.

I hang up the same time Clayton and Maribelle emerge, Clayton's arm around her shoulders like a father's. At least one person goes home tonight with closure.

We drive back to the cove in silence, traveling through the thick woods that separate the two towns, me in the back this time reveling the intense darkness and quiet so I can keep company with my varied thoughts. We've won one battle but another looms and where does that place me? Jack may have transitioned on his own, but he may be waiting for me in the woods. Sometimes ghosts, especially new ones like Jack who lack a connection with our world, need to be informed that their mystery is solved. If that's the case, what do I do then?

TB had me convinced we should move to Florida to live within the safety of the Boudreaux angels but my heels are dug in now. Staying put allows him to graduate on time, which was our goal in moving here in the first place, but it will be a tough argument getting him to see my side. He's determined to keep me and the kids safe, reiterated that on the phone. On the other hand, I'm resolved more than ever to see Dwayne locked up and out of my life. Otherwise, as Emma Harrington said decades before, I'll be looking over my shoulder the rest of my days.

Clayton pulls up outside the houseboat and accompanies us like a good date. TB throws open the door and greets us the moment our feet hit the deck. He envelopes me into a tight hug —as tight as he can, considering the acreage between us.

"I'm fine," I mumble once more into his chest. "Love you, too."

In the meantime, Maribelle slips inside and I hear her own homecoming with Sebastian, a thousand questions from my sister.

When I finally come up for air, I turn toward my protector. Clayton appears as if he could sleep for an entire weekend.

"I'll be right outside," he says, then heads to his car.

We thank his back and he sends us a wave without turning around.

"He's exhausted," I say.

"Tough night."

And that's all I'm getting out of TB because when I send him a curious gaze he shakes his head.

"One day," I threaten his back as we enter the house.

Now, it's my turn to endure a thousand questions from Portia as Maribelle and Sebastian head to their room. My journalism friends have gone home and TB's struggling to keep his eyes open.

"Tomorrow," I finally say when she starts interrogating me about Gunner. "Let's do all this in the morning."

"Fine." Portia rises. "But I'm not doing the sofa. Maribelle gave me a key to her apartment and I'm heading that way."

"But don't you worry about...?"

As soon as those words are spoken, I think of how my sister doesn't fear anything or anyone. She's one tough lawyer.

"He doesn't care about me," she says with a shrug. "I'll be fine. Besides, that cute Agent Sheridan's walking me to the door."

TB clears his throat and sits up and it's then I realize he had fallen into a deep sleep while we were talking.

"I'll get your bags," he says, blinking.

"Go to bed," Portia commands. "Sheridan will take my bags to the motel."

Poor Sheridan, I think.

TB doesn't argue, rises from the chair and heads straight for the back bedroom. "Good night then."

"Big day," I tell Portia.

"And how."

She doesn't mention the light, or question TB's abilities, has suspected something strange about TB since our road trip through Texas, when my husband thwarted a robbery in a convenience store with a flash of light and a gallon of Blue Bell ice cream. She was curious at the time of the incident but I sense she's come to the conclusion she's better off not knowing.

Sheridan arrives and his smile disappears when he sees the giant luggage, but he grabs her bags and the two head out. I lock the door behind her, but I'm too wound up to go to bed so I put the kettle on and grab some of Maribelle's magical tea. I feel a softness at my ankles and find Stinky rubbing up against my legs.

"Hey baby. I'd reach down to give you proper loving but there are two people in between."

Once I pour my cup of goodness, add lots of local Tennessee honey, I head back to the couch, throw off my shoes and get comfortable. I'm going to enjoy the view, even if the impending storm has blanketed the sky, making it almost impossible to see the water. No matter, the lightning occurring across the cove provides for exciting entertainment. I sip my tea and watch the streaks illuminate the sky, while thunder from the west breaks the silence.

Stinky howls by the door, starts scratching at its base.

"You're crazy if you think you're going out tonight," I tell my cat. "Use the litter box."

I lean to look down the hallway, make sure our bedroom door is open so he has access to his box in the master bathroom. It's closed, so I place my tea on to the coffee table and slowly rise. And I mean slowly. I do it in phases, lean my shoulders back against the couch, slip my butt forward while my stomach protrudes and give my knees the workout of the year as I swing my arms to accelerate my upper body. I rise in a curve, my shoulders the last to go upright. It's comical, actually. TB and Sebastian once took bets on how long it would take for me to rise from the easy chair, which believe me, wasn't easy. Sebastian won. TB was too kind to bet on the longer time.

I pause once I'm standing, stretching my lower back with my hands, enjoying the feel of a few vertebrae falling into place. Meanwhile, Stinky's still fighting with the door.

"I'll open the bedroom door," I tell my cat. "Give me a moment."

But once I look in Stinky's direction, I see him. Outside the door's window.

"Shit."

I've been working hard to curtail my use of profanity, something that comes easily in a newsroom but should not be done around children about to be born. But, I can't help myself tonight. For there in the woods outside my home stands Jack Greene, his eyes pleading.

Stinky howls again and I move closer to the window, notice a shadow next to my ghost in the intense darkness of this stormy night. In that moment, I surmise what's happening.

Dwayne lurks nearby, waiting for Jack to transition so he can steal his soul and regain his spirit, continue his immortality.

I have two options here and Dwayne knows it. Tell Jack his murder's been solved so he can transition or let him ascend into heaven on his own after Dwayne relays the information. If I let Dwayne do the honors, Jack's soul is toast. If I walk into those woods and tell Jack myself while defending him from Dwayne, my life may be the one in the toaster.

Naturally, I consider enlisting help but there's little time and everyone's asleep. I'm riding high from conquering my fears earlier tonight and feel up for the challenge, although I'm not so stupid to think I will win. Still, deep down inside I know this is my fight, an obstacle I must face.

Don't I?

Trust your instinct, Aunt Mimi always told me. Your gut is always right. Right now my gut is home to two human beings who have no say in the matter.

I look down at Stinky who pauses in his clawing at the door, looks up at me and howls. Gunner's not around and my cat saved me once, should we risk this again.

"What do I do?" I ask my feline.

He looks at me as to say, "What are we waiting for?" So, I close my eyes and groan, open the door and step outside, Stinky rushing ahead into the woods. I follow the deck to the shore, pass Clayton sleeping inside his car, and step into the dark night, immediately enveloped by the woods and the cool mud squishing between my toes. The oncoming storm electrifies the air and I feel my curls rising. I grab the three-fish letter opener still in my pocket and hold it tight as I make my way toward where I first spotted Jack.

It doesn't take me long to reach my long-suffering ghost. I feel the familiar softness against my bare feet so I whisper, "It's done. Go."

It's a beautiful thing, watching ghosts transition. You witness the peace in their eyes, the knowing of their voyage to come, the warm white light pouring down from the heavens that's filled with God's love. Jack smiles as the light appears and his eyes send me a gleam of gratitude. It only takes seconds and within a heartbeat, Jack's gone.

I don't do this without precaution, however. I hold the letter opener in front of me and circle my ghost, my back to Jack, until Jack safely disappears. Stinky remains at my feet, his claws firmly entrenched in the ground, waiting for someone or something to interfere.

But no one does.

I exhale the breath I've been holding and drop my arm. Maybe I was wrong about Dwayne being here. Maybe my nemesis got spooked by the FBI raid and left town.

I look down at Stinky but he's not convinced. He's sniffing the air and glancing around, growling low in his throat.

"What is it, Stink?"

The words aren't out my mouth when something strong and invisible kicks my cat—and hard. Stinky cries out and goes flying into the woods. I hear him land against a tree but then nothing.

I'm so angry I turn toward Dwayne and thrust my knife in his direction. But it's not the metal weapon in my hand that causes him to fall backwards, it's the force of my emotions.

"Nice one," he says, picking himself back up, shaking the leaves off his pants. "You're finally learning how to use your powers."

"How dare you hurt my cat?" I shout out, but my anger's quickly turning to fear and hurt.

"Funny how it leaves you, doesn't it?" he asks, walking closer. There's hardly any light this far from my houseboat and the street, but as his face becomes clearer I make out that horrible scar Stinky inflicted.

"What does?" I ask, my knife pointing in his direction.

"Anger. Such a powerful emotion, gives you so much strength, but then it slips away as fast as it arrives. Really only hurts the originator."

He's right. Fear now grips my heart and my strength subsides. I took a gamble with Jack and now I've put myself and my two children at risk.

"What do you want?" I ask, offering more bravado than I really have. "Jack's gone, so you gain nothing from me."

Dwayne laughs and the sound chills my heart. I realize how alike he and Gunner are, both methodical in their evil with cold water in their veins. But Gunner's actions resulted from inner pain and suffering while Dwayne simply has no concern for anyone but himself. There's no fear or hurt behind his desires, simply a disregard for human life. How do I fight this?

"I don't want Jack," Dwayne says with a sinister smile. "I never did, really."

I swallow hard, not wanting to know the answer to what I'm about to ask. "What do you want, then?"

He examines a nail. "Oh Vi, such power bestowed on a simpleton. What was the universe thinking?"

He inches closer and I wave the letter opener.

"There's a good example. Like that's going to save you."

I glance toward the parking lot, wondering if Clayton will hear me scream, but the thunder has moved closer and his car seems so far away.

"He won't hear anything. And I doubt your hubbie will either. Doesn't matter what you witches did tonight, it will be a while before your husband gets up to speed."

He moves closer and now I spot the dark centers of his brilliant blue eyes, orbs that once entranced me with their beauty.

"You're sick," I say, remembering how Maribelle said the same thing to her brother only hours before. But, it doesn't hold the same power over Dwayne.

"No, sweetheart, just anxious to get this over with."

He's closer now and I wave the letter opener again. "You're not going to hurt me."

My weapon flies from my hands and disappears into the darkness of the woods.

"Really?" he asks sarcastically.

He's so close I can smell that sickly sweet cologne he wears. I step back, my heart racing, feel my chest tighten up and my head begin to pound, know my blood pressure's frighteningly high. Oh, why didn't I stay put in the safety of the houseboat?

"You're so amazing, Viola. Did just what I expected you to do. I mean, did you really think I wanted Jack when I could have three souls with you?"

My children. He doesn't want just me, he wants my children. My precious twins who have yet to see the world.

For a moment, the buzzing in my head disappears, I'm able to breathe, and my eyesight becomes crystal clear. The darkness fades as lightning cracks around me and thunder shakes the ground. I look straight at Dwayne and view him for what he is, a descendant able to offer so much to humanity but inside choosing to be an abomination walking the earth.

I'm no longer scared of this man. I feel an intense power brewing deep inside my womb and flowing outward through my body until the electrons pour from my fingertips. I'm fearless. I'm a mother!

I step forward and Dwayne senses the change, begins walking backward.

"You will never harm me or my children," I begin, pulling forth an energy originating in love that a mother has for her children, one so strong she will face the evils of hell to protect them.

Dwayne attempts a laugh but it comes out hollow. He's doubting himself.

"You can't win, Vi. Not against me."

Now, it's my turn to smile. "Sorry, Dwayne. Guess your mother never told you that moms are always right."

His confidence disappears and anger overtakes his features. "Bitch, you owe me."

"I owe you nothing," I say slowly and succinctly, still moving forward, Dwayne backing up toward the Cove.

He shakes his head. "You're mine."

Dwayne was right about one thing. Anger does give you power but it leaks away as fast as it comes. He bobbles unsteadily as his feet hit the water, closer than he realized in the intense darkness. Still, he attempts a counterattack, raising his arms to destroy me, his eyes flashing with hatred.

But I come from a place of love. It's as clear as the water's surface waiting for the rains to arrive. I raise my own arms and shield myself and those I love from this hateful man. When he sends a force my way, I send one back, knocking him off his feet, him landing fully in the waters of Emma's Cove.

And that's when the lightning hits.

I watch in horror as Dwayne Garrett twitches with the electricity pouring through his body.

"Help me," he whispers.

I reach for him, but lightning crackles around me, illuminating the water that will kill me just as easily if I step forward. When the impact ceases, Dwayne's eyes appear lifeless and he falls back into the water.

I think to run to Clayton and get help, but the blood drains from my head fast and the chest pain returns. I gasp for air as the world spins around me. I'm hyperventilating and worry I'm having a heart attack. I fall to the ground, praying that my kids are all right.

Before I lose consciousness, I hear footsteps approaching, hear TB calling my name and feel two giant arms scooping me up and carrying me away. When I come to again, I'm in an ambulance wearing an oxygen mask and an EMT inserting an

IV. TB's holding my hand, calling my name, tears pouring down his face.

"Stinky?" I ask.

"He's fine," TB tells me, petting my hair. "We've got him."

I smile but it hurts to do so. I want to tell him I've met the enemy and defeated him, that everything will be okay, but my exertion causes a sharp pain to pierce my chest and darkness returns.

At first, the gloom frightens me, but then my pain disappears. I'm back in the light, in the ambulance looking down on everyone, at the top of TB's head, the EMT struggling to find a vein. I realize I'm also gazing down on my lifeless form while the heart monitor beats threateningly. The EMT calls out to the person driving the ambulance and TB starts crying harder. I reach to place a hand on TB's shoulder, to let him know I'm right here, but I float away.

Now, I'm surrounded by a light reminiscent of the ones ghosts experience when they transition. There's no pain anymore, no frightened love ones, no scary medical equipment. Just an intense feeling of love and peace. I close my eyes and relish the emotion, so pure and divine.

"Hello Viola," a voice calls out.

I open my eyes to discover Grandma Willow, a woman I never met but know from the many photos my mom and Aunt Mimi have shown me. She's short and stout with wiry hair like mine, except hers is brushed with streaks of gray. Her face denotes kindness and love and I realize I take after this psychic woman who attracted followers from miles around. She holds out her arms and I rush into her embrace, savor the comfort her arms offer.

It's then I realize that there's nothing between us. Look down and find myself thin.

"It's different here," my grandmother whispers. "We return

to our most authentic selves. Plus, your babies are still very much alive in the other world."

I should think about what happened and where my twins are now but I'm surrounded by such peacefulness, like soaking in a salt-water hot tub where all you want to do is float unhindered.

"Where am I?" I ask.

Grandma Willow releases me, steps aside, and it's then that I spot my baby. Lillye stands in front of me looking the picture of health, appearing as if leukemia never wrecked her body and stole her life away.

I fall to my knees and open my arms and my precious angel fills them up. I hug her so hard I'm afraid I might hurt her damaged body but realize she's fine, that we're where nothing bad happens. I pull away and study her intensely, pull my fingers through her fine hair, gaze into those sweet brown eyes she inherited from her father and smell her sweet scent. I kiss every inch of her face. If this isn't heaven, then I don't want to end up there.

"I'm fine, Momma," she says through all the affection. "Grandma Willow takes good care of me."

I look up at my grandmother with gratitude.

"She's an angel."

"Like her dad," I say and we all laugh.

"You beat the bad man," Lillye tells me proudly. "You're invincible."

"Yeah, Mommy beat the bad man."

I don't remember what happened with Dwayne, don't even care I'm so focused on seeing my baby. I sit down and pull Lillye in my lap but she appears concerned.

"What is it, sweetheart."

"Are you supposed to be here?"

"I'm not going anywhere." And I mean it.

I feel Grandma Willow's hand on my shoulder. "Honey, you're not supposed to be here."

I rub Lillye's arms, relish her precious smile, hug her close. "I missed you so much."

She leans her head against mine. "I missed you, too, Mommy."

"We're together now," I say, enjoying the sensation of her cheek against mine.

Grandma Willow squeezes my shoulder. "Darling, you can't stay."

I'm not going anywhere, not leaving my beloved child.

She squeezes again. "Viola. Sweetheart."

I close my eyes, sensing a pain deep in my chest. "No, I'm not leaving."

This time, it's a tiny hand on my chin. "Mommy?"

I can't resist my baby so I open my eyes and smile. "Yes, my angel."

"Michael and Gaia need you."

"Who?"

"And Daddy, he needs you too."

I take her face in my palms. "But I need you."

She was so young when death took my child, but wise beyond her years, always caring about everyone else.

"I know, Mommy, but I'm always with you."

It's what everyone has told me since Lillye passed away, a wisdom I believed but could never feel or accept. That pain in my chest intensifies.

"But this is what I want," I tell her. "To hold you, see you, hear your sweet voice."

She shakes her head to move the hair that's fallen over her eyes, the way she used to and it warms my heart.

"If you listen hard, Mommy, you can always hear me."

I know that, too, have been convinced the longer I deal with the paranormal that those on the other side assist me as much as I do them. Still, it's not like holding your daughter close.

I shake my head. "No, I'm staying here."

Now, Lillye looks worried, glances over my shoulder. "What about Daddy?"

"Daddy will be fine."

In the background, I hear a beeping, but I try to push it from my mind.

"What about my brother and sister?"

The twins. My children. I lean backward, start to falter thinking of my other precious angels.

"You have to go back," Grandma Willow states firmly.

I look back at Lillye, wanting to hold on to her forever.

She nods. "It's okay, Mommy. I'm in a beautiful place."

"But I miss you so much."

Grandma Willow sends me an empathic smile. "But they will miss you. And there is so much left for you to do."

I hear TB call my name as a jolt of energy pulsates through me.

Lillye appears really concerned now. "Don't let Daddy do this alone." She rushes into my arms and holds me tight, then gently lets me go and turns me around. I see TB standing in the corner of what looks like an emergency room, hands over his mouth in horror as they apply defibrillators on my chest.

I don't even know how it happens, but the next second I'm back inside my body, excruciating pain filling my chest. I suck in a breath with a dramatic gulp.

"She's back," I hear someone say.

Another person warns TB to stay back but my husband's at my side, grabbing my hand, calling my name. I look over into those loving brown eyes.

"I'm fine," I whisper.

"You left me," he whispers back.

I think about where I went, who I saw. I squeeze his hand. "I saw her. I saw our baby. And she's really good."

I don't have to explain because TB knows exactly who I'm talking about, leans forward and cries quietly into my shoulder. I reach a hand, the free one without the IV, and stroke his hair.

"She's so happy. And she's with my Grandma Willow."

He leans up and nods, attempts a smile.

I feel a hand on my shoulder and expect to see said grandmother at my side. Instead, it's Doctor Mahoney.

"You went into maternal cardiac arrest so it's imperative that we do a C-section immediately," she tells me.

"Of course," I respond. "Whatever you need to do."

TB's looking frightened again. "Will she have another heart attack?"

Mahoney glances at the heart monitor by the side of the bed. "Her numbers came way down. Right now, her blood pressure's normal, she's doing great."

"Then let's go," I say, convinced there are people on the other side watching over me.

It all happens so fast. They wheel me into the operating room, TB never releasing my hand, even when a nurse dresses him in a gown; he does it one arm at a time. I receive an epidural, then a nurse drapes my bottom half. Doctor Mahoney literally has run to get scrubbed and re-emerges with a collection of nurses who gather around.

And then the fun starts. Not like I feel any of it, but it sounds intense. I look at my husband who I'm convinced has no blood left in his face.

"They're going to be fine," I whisper. "Breathe."

The first cry I hear sounds healthy and strong. In fact, this child screams for all the world.

"Here she is," Mahoney announces. "Your baby girl."

"Gaia," I say.

TB frowns and tilts his head. "What?"

But I don't have time to explain because Michael emerges. He's quieter, utters a soft weeping.

"And you have a healthy son as well."

TB and I start crying like the babies we just produced. In that divine moment, we forget all about FBI agents, arsonists, murderers, and a Lucifer descendant who may be lying in our Cove's waters. All is well and we're parents again.

And Lillye's looking down upon us all.

When the babies have been examined and Doctor Mahoney announces they each have ten toes and ten fingers, the nurses bring us our children.

"They came almost a month early but they're six pounds each and very healthy," Mahoney said. "After what happened and your heart attack, you're a lucky woman."

I gaze into the tiny faces of my adorable twins, back at my husband with tears lingering on his lashes. I think back on the five years I shared with another sweet angel.

"Yes, I am," I state proudly.

The nurses finish cleaning me up—thank goodness I can't see any of that mess–while TB and I fuss over our babies. It's then I notice something odd about Gaia.

"Is it me, or does she have a green aura?" I ask TB.

"You can see that?" he asks.

I look around the room but no one else's bodily energy is visible to me. Maybe I can spot my daughter's aura because we once shared cells.

Suddenly, Michael lets out the tiniest sneeze. It's adorable, of course, and we all smile but the lights flicker in response.

"What was that?" a nurse asks.

"We need to check on that," another says anxiously, and leaves the room.

I look at TB who returns my concerned gaze. Did we just birth a witch and a descendant? On command, we both break into laughter.

· · ·

Because of my heart attack and the C-section, I remained in the hospital for several days. Fine with me because after the week I had I needed the rest. Not to mention that my life from here on out means two babies to care for—at the same time!

My parents arrived, my mom promising to assist until college resumes after Labor Day; she has a full schedule ahead at Tulane. Portia agreed to help out as well, in between representing Sebastian with his insurance claims and helping some of the town's residents with lawsuits involving abusive spouses.

Clayton showed up the morning after the twins were born, explained how Stinky appeared at his car, howling like a hound from hell.

"I hadn't meant to fall asleep, Vi. I'm so sorry."

I took his hand and assured him I had it all under control. I laughed at the thought which failed to relieve Clayton's guilt.

"I'm glad that you arrived in the nick of time," I said and gave him a big hug. "Glad that Stinky's okay."

Turns out Stinky suffered from the impact with that tree but ran for help. After he woke Clayton from his dreams, he headed for the window outside of our bedroom. TB had sensed that Dwayne was afoot, had woken up, and was already halfway out the door by the time Stinky arrived. The lot of them could have showed up earlier, I'm thinking, but then I wouldn't have found my inner strength, wouldn't have experienced what Maribelle had taught me all those months.

Speaking of my neighbor, Maribelle's not the same, appears in a dark place despite the two babies she consistently insists upon holding. She arrives today with a potted herb and a present, but no smiles.

"You okay?"

She shrugs a shoulder. "There's a lot to process. I'll be all right in time."

"Sebastian will get the buildings back in shape," I say, trying to lighten the mood. "Things will turn around."

She nods, deep in thought.

"Dwayne's in a high-security facility. Not too far from your brother, in fact."

My nemesis didn't die after all, which makes me happy. As much as my actions were in self-defense and no one would have blamed me for pushing Dwayne into Emma's Cove that night filled with lightning, I didn't want murder on my rap sheet.

"He's not going anywhere," I add.

"I'm not thinking about Dwayne."

"Then what is it?"

She hesitates, finally answers so quietly I almost don't hear her.

"That gold mine Touché mentioned. The one he said we were sitting on."

"Yeah?"

She fiddles with the blanket draped over my feet, appears contrite. "He was right."

"What?"

I don't have time to inquire more because the family arrives, everyone pouring into the hospital room, talking at once. Who should be bringing up the rear but my Aunt Mimi, arms full of stuffed animals, flowers, and a book on what to expect raising twins. Wait until my aunt discovers my children carry their parent's weird DNA.

Maribelle gets absorbed by the crowd, starts heading toward the door, mentions how a group of Emma's Cove's best are meeting to discuss turning the brown patch into a children's park and she's late. I stretch my head trying to make eye contact, find out what she meant about the gold mine, but she's already out the door. I catch up with family and Aunt Mimi, still pondering Maribelle's cryptic message. And I can't help recalling the emphatic words of Jack and Caroline: "Ask MB!"

"What's the present?" My mom brings me back.

I look down and realize I never opened Maribelle's gift. I

tear off the paper and find a wooden plaque with a quote by Marianne Williamson written on top of a photograph. The image is Emma's Cove at sunset. It's gorgeous.

" 'Our deepest fear is not that we are inadequate,'" I read. " 'Our deepest fear is that we are powerful beyond measure.'"

I smile because right now, I'm invincible.

AUTHOR'S NOTE

South Louisiana summers suck the life out of the hardiest among us. During a particularly hot summer writing this book I decided to live vicariously through my supernatural couple and set the story in the mountains of southern Tennessee. Emma's Cove, however, doesn't exist. Neither does a town called Lightning Bug and Smoky Mountain University. All were born from my imagination hungry for cooler weather. Emma Harrington never existed either and her quilt doesn't hang inside the Hunter Museum of American Art in Chattanooga, although some wonderful artwork does and I highly recommend a visit.

ACKNOWLEDGMENTS

In addition to raising children, it takes a village to produce a book. Thanks go out to my amazing editors who save me from embarrassment. Pamela Keene you're a wizard with a red pen and Danon Dastugue, you balance my boat. Thanks, too, to my wonderful partner in crime Bruce Coen and the amazing Joshua Coen for his dreamy covers.

ABOUT THE AUTHOR

Cherie Claire is a native of New Orleans who like so many other Gulf Coast residents was heartbroken after Hurricane Katrina. She works as a travel and food writer and extensively covers the Deep South, including its colorful ghost stories. To learn more about her novels and her non-fiction books, upcoming events and to sign up for her newsletter, visit her website www.CherieClaire.net.

ALSO BY CHERIE CLAIRE

Viola Valentine Mystery Series

A Ghost of a Chance

Ghost Town

Trace of a Ghost

Ghost Trippin'

Give Up the Ghost

The Ghost is Clear

Ghost Fever

Ghost Lights

The Cajun Embassy

Ticket to Paradise

Damn Yankees

Gone Pecan

The Cajun Series

Emilie

Rose

Gabrielle

Delphine

A Cajun Dream

The Letter

Carnival Confessions: A Mardi Gras Novella

Under the name Cheré Dastugue Coen:

Exploring Cajun Country: A Historic Guide to Acadiana

Forest Hill, Louisiana: A Bloom Town History

Haunted Lafayette, Louisiana

Magic's in the Bag: Creating Spellbinding Gris Gris Bags and Sachets
with Jude Bradley

A SNEAK PEEK INTO CHERIE'S NEXT NOVELLA

THE GHOST IS CLEAR - CHAPTER ONE

Bliss is steaming hot coffee in a bathrobe with the sea breeze in your hair.

And no kids.

I wince because no matter how I spin this glorious morning looking out on to the emerald green waters of the Atlantic Ocean from my resort balcony, cradling the coffee and chicory concoction I've been addicted to since my New Orleans youth, guilt assaults me. I remind myself this luxury hotel room on the Georgia coast is part of my job and Michael and Gaia are having fun on a school field trip we paid handsomely for, thanks to my placing a story with Traveling High magazine—no judgments!—and making my first big-bucks check.

But, still….

I try to shake off those maternal feelings of separation and enjoy my coffee, savor the relatively warm coastal temperatures considering its February, and think about how far I've come since Hurricane Katrina took everything away fifteen years ago.

After the storm broke the city's levees in 2005 and flooded our home, I retreated to a mother-in-law unit in Lafayette, two hours west of New Orleans, and decided that losing my newspaper job to that bitch of a storm was ironically the best thing to happen to me. That's when I dedicated myself to travel writing, my dream job, which has carried me forth to this day. The storm also helped me reconnect with my eccentric husband, and our circuitous path to reconciliation gave us two adorable children, twins that are now almost ten years old.

They say there are blessings from Katrina. As I gaze out over the Atlantic, watching brown pelicans glide by in a formation, I thank the waters for uprooting my life and sending me on this new path.

Speak of the devil—or angel, if you will. I feel two hands rest upon my shoulders before lips appear at my neck. I lean to allow TB ample space and he applies kisses from my shoulder blade to my ear lobes. I shiver with pleasure.

"Breakfast?" he asks in a sultry voice.

I'm starving. I have a right to be, after what we just did.

"Quick shower and I'll be ready."

My husband straightens and his tall, lean form casts a shadow in the morning light. "I'm going for a quick walk on the beach. I promised Gaia I would find some shells. Be back in ten, fifteen."

I smile at my adorable husband with the weird name, glad I didn't let my grief and anger from those days long ago cloud my thinking about staying with this man. But then, leaving TB after the storm forced him to grow and follow *his* dream, so Katrina offered lots of blessings, if you look at it that way.

TB squeezes my shoulder and turns to leave. "Your phone buzzed. Think you have a missed call."

I shrug because it happens all the time. Between my endless traveling, article writing, and working on call at the *Chronicle* newspaper where we live in Tennessee, someone's always looking for me. I relentlessly finished deadlines and photo edits and turned them in to my editors before leaving on this trip, with notes that insisted those with questions contact me before or after my traipse along the Georgia coast. Editors are notorious for demanding early deadlines of writers, only to wait until the last minute for changes, usually when I'm chin deep in another story, or like today, on another trip.

But I'm determined that won't happen this week. Since my children's school back in Tennessee offered the field trip during their winter break, I pitched the idea to a couple of magazines and got a bite. Writing for a *high* audience leans outside my expertise, but as I tell most people who ask what publications I write for, it's "Anyone with a checkbook." It's an easy piece to tackle, interviewing a local man working to change marijuana laws in Georgia along with a bong shop owner. The rest of the trip on St. Simons Island is relaxation and collecting fodder for the regular travel magazines I write for. And with Valentine's Day at trip's end, I'm going to enjoy endless sex with my husband if it kills me. Editing questions will have to wait.

TB leaves whistling a seventies tune and I head to the shower, relishing in the resort's endless hot water that won't be interrupted by little voices asking for everything under the sun. I hope my twins are enjoying their field trip on neighboring Jekyll Island, but can't help thinking and worrying about my tykes. But oh, this shower feels so delicious.

After a good ten minutes, I exit the shower a new woman, ready for a day exploring St. Simons at the southeastern point of the Georgia coast. I pull out my professional clothes but think twice, reliving in my mind the pot heads I knew at LSU who were never well dressed. My interviewee insisted on meeting us at the World War II Museum so I wonder if he's a veteran. I keep the jeans but throw on a nice shirt.

I hear the hotel door open and discover two arms at my waist as I'm buttoning up the blouse. They snake around me, pulling me back against a sweaty but sweet-smelling chest. Those familiar lips find their way to my neck again.

"Are you sure you want breakfast?" I ask with a grin.

"You're the one with the schedule," TB mutters into my neck.

I pull away and look at my phone, the light blinking announcing several missed calls, no doubt the man or museum calling to confirm. "We need to be at the museum in twenty minutes."

TB grabs my purse and camera, hands both to me. I forgo nice shoes and slip on my favorite Converse sneakers and we take off for the lobby, asking the kind maître'd outside Echo restaurant if we could have two muffins to go. TB's driving so I pull the paper off both muffins, hand him one, and devour the other. They both disappear just as we pull into the parking lot of the World War II Home Front Museum and TB and I shake the crumbs from our chest.

"Two minutes to spare," I tell TB.

We're close to the beach so I look longingly at the ocean, wishing I could pull off my shoes and sink my toes into that inviting sand. I love my job and travel to places I never could afford normally, but boy, sometimes I wish I could spend more time relaxing and less time working at these fabulous destinations. I shake my head and go into travel writer mode, head inside the museum located in the historic 1936 Coast Guard Station that's been lovingly restored. Calibre Fogarty hasn't arrived yet but a museum docent named Wendy tells us a brief history of the station, how in 1942 Coast Guard crew members rescued survivors of an American ship torpedoed off the coast by a German U-boat.

"There were German submarines off our coast?" TB asks with amazement, gazing around at the exhibits.

"Most people don't realize that," Wendy says. "Hundreds of ships were sunk by the Germans, with numerous casualties off the Atlantic Coast. Gulf of Mexico as well."

Wendy's a talking machine, most docents and historians are. She discusses the German's close presence and the men and women who helped patrol and spot the submarines. The museum includes oral histories and interactive displays that explain what life was like on the home front, including the massive shipyards in nearby Brunswick and the "Rosies," the local women who helped build the ships that saved us all, ones made famous by the "Rosie the Riveter" posters back in the day. I nod and try to absorb the historic information, but my eyes keep finding that beach.

I spot a man in a tweed coat and jeans rushing up the path, and can't help noticing how meticulously he's dressed. It's been a long time since I've spotted men wearing deep blue jeans with a crease. His buttoned-down plaid shirt has been ironed too I notice as he enters the building and removes his coat.

"Hey there, Wendy," he says to the docent, who immediately blushes.

It's then I spot incredibly blue eyes behind a pair of stylish tortoiseshell glasses. Did GQ just walk in the door?

"Cal," Wendy announces, "this is Viola Valentine, the reporter."

Wendy pronounces my name Vee-o-la like the instrument and not Vie-o-la, like the character from Shakespeare's *Twelfth Night*. Usually I let it pass but not with this fine specimen of a man. Did I mention his eyes are gorgeous?

"Viola," I tell him correctly, holding out my hand, which he accepts with a strong handshake. Wendy apologizes to my back and I usually put people at ease but right now nothing's taking my gaze off those azure eyes.

TB clears his throat.

"Uh, sorry," I say, finally releasing his hand. "This is my husband, Thibault Boudreaux."

I don't know why I use his full name. TB never does, prefers his silly abbreviation.

"Tee-bo?" Cal says with a frown.

"It's Cajun."

TB launches into how it's a family name but he prefers TB.

He waits for Cal to ask of the nickname's origins but Cal only politely nods and smiles. I don't know if it's because I'm impatient and want to get the interview done or that I'm weary of hearing my husband's story, but I interrupt.

"We call juniors in Louisiana T this and T that," I tell Cal. "Thibault is a junior and his family called him T-boy to differentiate him from his father. He shortened it to TB."

Why, I'll never know, but I love my goofy husband.

Cal's smile brightens with the knowledge. "I get it. Comes from the French. Petite-boy. And y'all shortened it to T-boy."

"Exactly." TB's smile mirrors Mr. GQ and the two begin chatting in French. As in whole conversations. I'm shocked, speechless. I've never seen my husband say more than a Cajun expression or two.

I gaze at Wendy who appears equally puzzled. Finally, the two men laugh at something and Cal turns my way. "We should get started."

Wendy leads us to a meeting room down a long hall.

"What was that about?" I whisper to TB, but he just shrugs.

We make ourselves comfortable in the room lined with World War II photos, including one of a Rosie the Riveter wearing a head scarf and holding her elbow up in strength with the words, "We Can Do It!" I pull out my recorder and start asking Mr. GQ questions. Cal discusses how lawmakers allowed medical marijuana to be legal in Georgia but insisted it remain illegal to grow the plant, sell it, or move it across state lines, which means those wanting to access medical marijuana or doctors hoping to prescribe it to their patients had no product.

"What's the use of a law like that?" he asks.

Cal's biggest push is for CBD oil. He lists the many reasons certain elements of hemp, such as CBD oil, have been shown to have medicinal properties.

"CBD, made from hemp, contains only minute traces of THC so it doesn't make you high," Cal adds. "It's non-intoxicating but has incredible benefits. If anything needs to get to market, it's CBD, but marijuana has its medical uses, too."

After about thirty minutes of questioning, I thank my subject and he shakes my hand, insisting I call him anytime day or night if I need more information. I blush at the contact and feel TB's stare. Hey, I can't help but admire a beautiful man.

We all stand to leave but as I do the world begins to tilt, as if I've been inhaling something illegal. I grab the back of my chair to steady myself, think it's the sudden rise that's making me dizzy, but the room continues to spin.

"Are you all right?" I hear Cal ask and feel his hand on my elbow.

"Yeah," I mutter, but my knees give way and I fall backwards. I sense TB catching my descent but I know I'm on the floor when my last thought before all turns to black is that Berber carpet is rough on the face.

When I come to, I rise on my elbows and gaze around, but the meeting room has disappeared. The world feels ethereal, as if I've been dropped into an alternate universe like Eleven in *Stranger Things*. Within seconds, however, the darkness fades and I feel a lovely breeze. I'm sitting in grass, eavesdropping on a couple flirting on a park bench overlooking a marsh. The sun burns warm on my face and I imagine it's summer.

"What do you do at the shipyard," I hear the man ask.

The woman, who appears about eighteen, her hair tied up in a handkerchief and dressed in shirt and pants that resembles those of factory employees, shrugs. A lunch box lies in her lap, her sandwich untouched on waxed paper. "You know, the usual."

The man leans in closer. "No, what?"

His closeness makes her giggle. I suspect she's not had male attention like this before.

"I work on the ships, like everyone else."

The man very gently begins toying with her fine brown hair

that could use a better haircut. It's too short and jagged, as if her mom did the cutting or it's been too long between haircuts.

"Well, so do I, Gabriella, but we all have special jobs," the man says.

"Gabby," she corrects him, shivering at his touch, but it's clear she's enjoying the flirtation. "No one calls me Gabriella."

He smiles seductively. "But I'd like to, Gabriella. Such a beautiful name."

Gabby's blush floods her cheeks.

"I'm not on the warehouse floor," the man says. "I'm in parts but I'll be working on the new project soon."

"Me too," she responds enthusiastically, turning on the bench to face him. "My boss said I have potential so they're putting me on the *James Wayne* next week."

The man straightens somewhat. "Oh, so they're starting the Liberty Ships that soon?"

"Don't you know?"

His smile never falters. "Yes, but I'm still in the back warehouse so I don't get the scuttlebutt."

Gabby looks around to see if anyone's listening. "I'm not supposed to discuss any of this outside of work but since you're going to be working on them too, they're talking about starting next Tuesday."

" 'Loose lips sink ships,' " the man says, nodding. "Doesn't count if it's just another shipyard worker."

I hear someone call out and turn to find a lanky man who couldn't be more than twenty approach the couple.

"Hey Peter," Gabby says, finally taking a bite of her sandwich.

Close up, I spot Peter's acne-poked face and hair that could also use a good cut, its curls kissing the top of his collar. With his worn pants and a flannel shirt with a hole at the elbow, he's no match for the well-dressed man on the bench who so far has appeared suave and sophisticated. Peter's saving grace is his concerned gaze emitting love for the woman on the bench. I feel empathy for this Peter, because I sense he's carrying a torch for Gabby and he's not liking what he's seeing here, a stranger encroaching on his territory.

I'm right because he asks tersely, "Who's this?"

Gabby appears uncomfortable as well. "Peter, this is my new friend, Mason."

Mason extends his hand but Peter hesitates. Finally, he shakes Mason's hand but it's clear he's wary of the man.

"Peter," Gabby admonishes him.

Mason laughs it off. "Are all the folks in Brunswick this friendly?"

"We have reason to be suspicious," Peter says. "After what happened last week."

"Seriously?" Mason asks. "You think I'm a German?"

"Really, Peter, that's ridiculous," Gabby says. "He's American as apple pie."

Peter deflates, no doubt wondering if his jealousy has taken hold of his rational thinking.

"Everyone says we have to be cautious," he answers defensively. "I don't know anything about you."

Mason turns on the charm, holds out his hand again. "Mason Fry. From Indianapolis. Came to the Georgia coast to build ships so we can win the war against the Nazis."

When Peter accepts his hand again, Mason pulls him in close so only Peter can hear. "I'm a dedicated warrior against tyranny. And I won't let anyone stop me."

A violent chill runs through me and I wake up with three pairs of eyes studying me intently, one of which looks so familiar. When I rise to a sitting position, hearing TB ask a million questions, I can't help staring at Cal's brilliant blue gaze. Since I'm a medium, I've channeled people before, and many times in this way. But why these people and why here? And does this have anything to do with the gorgeous man leaning over me now?

"We should get you to a doctor," Cal tells me, clearly concerned.

"Maybe it was all the pot I smoked on the way over."

The joke falls flat.

"Just kidding," I add.

Wendy pulls out her phone, but I place a hand over hers and look to TB for assistance. He's used to my blackouts when ghosts come calling.

"She'll be fine," he says. "This happens on occasion."

"Low blood sugar?" Wendy asks. "I have that problem."

"Exactly," I say with enthusiasm. "I skipped breakfast."

Cal isn't convinced. He's studying me with skepticism. I rise and shake off the vision, show him that I'm perfectly healthy. TB hands me my purse and notebook while Wendy mentions orange juice and rushes off.

"I'll be fine," I reiterate.

Cal shakes his head. "You were perfectly normal one moment and the next on the floor. You need to see a doctor."

A doctor might put me in the loony bin.

I've been seeing dead people since my youth but I repressed the talent because of people's reactions, not to mention said ghosts would never leave me alone. When Hurricane Katrina barreled through New Orleans that psychic door blew wide open again and now I see ghosts who have died by water. I'm called a SCANC, an annoying acronym that means "specific communication with apparitions, non-entities and the comatose" and believe me, I've experienced all three. But because of my hurricane trauma, the ghosts all revolve around water. Only water. I wonder who of the three people I just witnessed met such a fate.

"It's fine," I tell Cal again with a smile, trying not to remember how I traveled to the 1940s and ended up next to a marsh. "Seriously, it happens sometimes and I'm fine once I get some sugar."

When Wendy returns with the orange juice I gulp it down to prove my point, then smile as if I'm the healthiest person on the planet.

Cal finally accepts my argument. "Since you're new to town and you need nourishment, let me take you both to dinner tonight."

"Will there be a brownie for dessert?" I ask with a smile.

He returns a grin and an adorable dimple emerges. Sheesh, could this man get any cuter? TB looks at me with slanted eyes.

"May I bring my fiancé?" Cal asks, which makes TB straighten and grin.

"Of course," I say with enthusiasm, ignoring my husband. "When's the lucky day?"

He beams. Simply beams. "Valentine's Day."

Cal writes down the name of the restaurant address on the back of his business card and hands it to TB. "Shall we say seven?"

"Sounds perfect." TB shakes his hand.

We all do small talk leaving the meeting room, although Wendy asks if we want to tour the museum.

"Another time," I tell her, glancing at the ocean yards away outside the picture window. If I can type up my notes and make a few phone calls, I should be able to squeeze beach time in today.

"Please do." Wendy hands us both free passes. "And ask for me if you want a personal tour."

We say our goodbyes and TB and I jump into our Toyota.

"Beach?" he asks me, but I catch a sly glint in his eyes.

"Or a stop in the hotel room?"

The most adolescent smiles emerge on our faces and we giggle. Kids are great but they sure do interrupt adult fun.

As if my kids know what we're about to do, my phone vibrates.

"Better check that," TB tells me. "My phone died so if the school needs us, they'd be calling you."

I pull the phone out of my purse that bouncing on the car's floorboards. "More than likely an editor asking me to add an Oxford comma somewhere."

"What's an Oxford comma?"

"Jeff, a semicolon, and an Oxford comma go into a bar," I reply, saying "comma" at the appropriate places so he knows what I'm talking about. "They both had a great time."

TB looks at me as if I've lost my mind.

"Sorry, writing joke. You use the Oxford comma before 'and' in a series. The joke here is that it's three things going into the bar but it sounds like Jeff is a semicolon so only two people visit the bar."

Again, no one's home.

"A comma can change the meaning of a sentence. How about 'Let's eat grandpa' but with the comma, 'Let's eat, Grandpa.'"

Nothing.

I sigh. "It's a grammar thing magazines and newspapers do differently. I cut my teeth in newspapers so I don't use them and the magazine people I work for get all anal about it."

I've totally lost him so I look at the phone and realize there are numerous missed calls.

"Shit."

TB looks at me concerned. "What?"

I open my phone app and find several messages from the kids' teacher. Plus, there are a few from Clayton, the twin's godfather who's also an FBI agent.

"Shit."

TB's about to wreck the car because he knows I don't cuss unless it's really bad. At least, not around family. "What?"

I don't bother listening to the messages, call Lana Davis immediately.

The twins' teacher answers on the first ring. "Where are you?"

"What's happening?"

"How soon can you get here?"

I look at TB and he's sweating. "What's wrong?"

"Can you get here now?" she asks again.

"Tell me what happened?"

There's a major pause on the other end and I swear I can hear my heart beating.

"It's Michael," she finally says. "He disappeared."